WYRMEWEALD
THE BONE TRAIL

THE BONE TRAIL

PAUL STEWART AND CHRIS RIDDELL

INTEGRATED MEDIA
NEW YORK

ISBN 978-1-4804-1611-6

Published in 2013 by Open Road Integrated Media, Inc.
345 Hudson Street
New York, NY 10014
www.openroadmedia.com

P.S. – For Anna and Joseph
C.R. – For Rick

WYRMEWEALD
THE BONE TRAIL

Kith – those who hunt and trap wyrmes

Kin – those who bond with wyrmes

Keld – those who dwell underground

The Six Seasons of the Weald

The Dry Season

The Rain Season

Halfwinter

Fullwinter

Halfsummer

Fullsummer

One

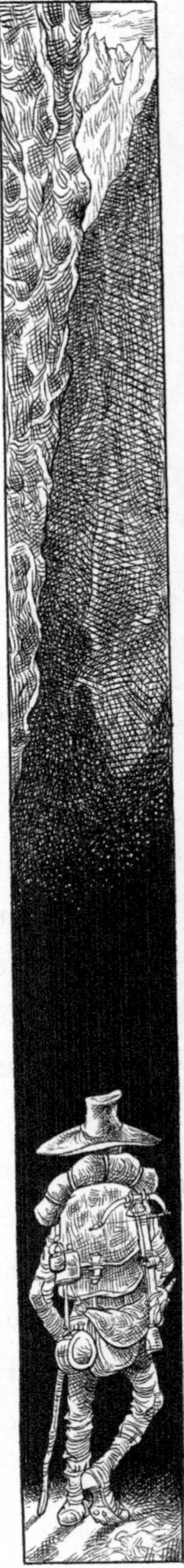

Eli Halfwinter surveyed the mountains that rose up out of the mist ahead. Fullwinter's grip had relaxed. The snow and ice had mostly gone. The green shoots of halfsummer were sprouting.

Eli's eyes narrowed.

The summit was a good day's climb by his reckoning, and the way looked perilous steep. The high sun cast long shadows down the ochre-brown rockface that were like stains. Eli glanced north along the range, then south. The mountains seemed to stretch off into the distance for ever, and he was loath to set out on such a detour.

Looking up, the cragclimber saw dozens of wyrmes flitting round the cragtops and upper ledges. Striped orange manderwyrmes. Spikebacks. Metallic bluewings. He heard their squeaks and chitterings echo off the wall of rock as they pitched and dived in search of insects.

He looked down again, scouring the lower reaches of the mountains. His gaze fell upon a jagged black crevice away to the south. It was a cleft through the rock, large enough for wyrmes to pass through. The scree at the entrance looked trampled, and it was spattered with wyrmedung.

This was what he'd been looking for. A wyrme trail. One of the migration routes that linked winter hideout to half-summer pastures.

As Eli approached, he found that the crack in the rock was narrower than he'd thought – just wide enough for the great lumbering greywyrmes to pass through in single file. He stepped into it.

The sun was snuffed out like a candle flame and the air felt chill. High above his head was a thin slit of blue sky. The rock was sheer and dark at his sides, and at the most constricted points of the trail had been chafed and grazed by the flanks of the migrating herds. The shadowed track doglegged sharply to the left, then right again, then opened up.

Eli found himself on a small stretch of flat sand. It was enclosed by vertical rockfaces that rose up around him, curved and ridged like giant hands. Behind him was the narrow opening he'd entered. In front of him, blocking the way ahead, was a great pitted boulder.

Except it wasn't a boulder. It was a greywyrme. Massive. Recumbent. And dead.

The corpse was lying on its side, the back bowed and turned away, the long neck and thick tail curved round towards him, and between them the four limbs, outstretched, claw-stiff. The head of the creature was draped over a slab of rock, its great maw gaping open to reveal rows of yellowpearl teeth. Deep empty black eyesockets stared back blindly at him.

It was a bull male, seventy summers old by the looks of it, perhaps even older than that. Eli rested a hand on the hard cracked skin of the greywyrme's flanks. It hung loose over the framework of jutting bones beneath.

The creature must have died just before the start of full-winter, and its body been covered with thick snow that had protected it from carrionwyrmes and other scavengers, and frozen it solid. With the thaw, the wind whistling through the ravine had dried the body out, mummifying the remains and rendering its skin and flesh too brittle and desiccated to be of use.

But the teeth and claws, now they were a different matter . . .

Eli straightened up. He pulled his rucksack from his back and set it on the ground. He loosened the ties. He pulled out a small hammer, a pair of pliers, then unsheathed the knife at his belt.

The claws of the greywyrme's hindfeet were brown and nubbed, but beneath the pitted surface Eli knew they would be fine-grained and make for excellent carving. They would bring high rewards at a scrimshaw den. He set to work.

The knack was to slide the point of the knife in at the back of the toe, where the curve of the claw left a small gap between the knuckle and the scaly skin, and twist. Eli jerked the handle round and the blade sliced through the tendons like they were yarns of wool. Then, keeping the knife in place, he gripped the claw with the pliers and wrenched it back hard, twisting as he did so.

There was a dull cracking sound and the claw came away from the foot. He turned it over in his hand appraisingly, then set it down on the sand.

Eli removed all twelve of the claws from the hindfeet. Then he moved on to those at the front.

These were longer, sharper. Paler. They would make a fine set of pickspikes. Eli took a swig of water from the watergourd at his side, mopped his brow, then set to work again.

He started humming. It was a plodding tuneless rendition of something he'd once heard. He wasn't even aware of doing it.

When the last of the front claws had been extracted, Eli pushed back his hat and turned his attention to the teeth. He peered into the dark yawning hole of the creature's maw, then reached inside. He ran his fingertips over the spike of an eye-tooth, the chisel-edge of an incisor.

Using his knife, Eli drove the blade down between the teeth, one after the other, and sawed into the gums. He worked swiftly and efficiently. When the final cut had been made, Eli straightened up. The teeth were loose now. Setting the knife aside, he seized a front tooth with the pliers, then *tap-tap-tapped* at the gum with the hammer. Slowly. Gently. Taking care not to crack the enamel. Until, with something almost like a sigh, the gum finally gave up its grip on the roots and the tooth came free.

Eli turned it over in his hand, then laid it down next to the claws. It was a fine specimen, and he would have liked to point out its qualities to the boy – the fact that its size alone would furnish a dozen knife handles, and that its grain, even finer than the greywyrme's claws, would make for flawless carving.

But Micah was not there. He was off on the high bluffs to the west with the girl, Cara.

They needed time on their own, the youngsters. Eli accepted that. Especially Micah, after everything he'd been through that fullwinter past – not to mention the couple of seasons before that with the kingirl, Thrace. It had been a tough year, and that was a fact. But they had survived. Him and the boy. And now Micah had Cara to look out for . . .

Eli smiled. Young love. There was no accounting for it.

Eli Halfwinter on the other hand was a loner. He'd learned the hard way that most kith could not be trusted. They would cheat and rob you as soon as look at you. They would kill you over a small nothing. No, so far as Eli was concerned, he was better off steering clear of other folks.

He glanced back down at the tooth. Though he sure did miss Micah to talk to.

Returning to the gaping jaw of the greywyrme, Eli removed the rest of the teeth in rapid succession. He stood back, wiping the sweat from his forehead, and surveyed the haul. Then, swallowing drily, he unhitched the gourd from his belt and took a long slug of water.

It was hard work. Despite the chill, he was sweating.

He took another swig from the gourd and was fixing it back to his belt when he saw it.

The broken shaft of a harpoon. It was sticking out from the base of the greywyrme's neck.

Eli had assumed that, given its age, the wyrme had died of natural causes. Certainly he hadn't been looking for evidence of injury. Yet there it was. A harpoon. A *kith* harpoon; the backslant barbs at its base bore testimony to that.

The harpoon was of a type fired from a kind of upright crossbow, favoured by those kith who went hunting for big game. The tip of the blade had penetrated the soft underskin of the greywyrme between the adamantine creases, and punctured its lungs. The ancient creature must have died instantly and, despite himself, Eli was impressed with the cleanness of the kill.

But why bring down so magnificent a creature, then fail to butcher it for meat and strip it of the valuable bone and ivory to barter with in a scrimshaw den? he wondered. It surely made no sense.

Eli shrugged, and was about to stow the claws and teeth in his pack when he noticed the small wound at the base of the creature's throat.

The flameoil sac had been removed.

Eli frowned. His mouth grew taut with rising anger. The

kith hunters hadn't been interested in food or ivory, just the tiny gland in the greywyrme's throat.

Returner's wealth.

Small, easy to carry and highly prized. Apothecarists down on the plains would pay handsomely for greywyrme flameoil and its supposedly miracle properties. Anyone returning from the high country with a full pack of the stuff would have their fortune made – never mind that they were responsible for the slaughter of countless wyrmes.

Eli hawked and spat. The thought of it turned his stomach.

He wrapped the teeth up in an old blanket along with the claws, and stuffed the whole lot inside his rucksack before hoisting it onto his back. The pack was heavy, but at least he had honoured the magnificent greywyrme by using what it had to offer.

When it came to moving on, Eli found that the curved back of the greywyrme was pressed against the crevice, stopping up the gap in the rock like a cork. He had no option but to climb over it if he was to continue his journey. Reaching up, Eli gripped the folds of the wyrme's vestigial wings, then clambered onto the creature's back. He was about to climb down the other side – but then stopped.

His jaw dropped. The trail ahead was blocked.

Before him, like a rockfall of huge grey boulders, were hundreds and hundreds of greywyrmes. They were crammed into the narrow ravine, their throats cut and flameoil sacs removed.

Eli swallowed numbly. These kith hunters had been clever, he could see that now. They must have tracked the herd across the pastures on their long migration to their full-winter hide in these mountains, and as the old bull wyrme had led them through the ravine the hunters had struck. They had shown no mercy. They had slaughtered the entire herd. Male and female, young and old alike, sparing not a single one.

And for what? For an ointment that supposedly reduced the signs of ageing . . .

Eli's face had turned a dark raw red. His lips trembled and his pale-blue eyes glistened. He was going to have to be late meeting up with Micah and Cara at the stickle falls. He would turn back, find another way through the mountains. He could not face clambering over all these bodies; all that needless death.

'Oh, Micah,' he whispered, 'I'm glad you're not here to see this.'

Two

Micah pulled his canteen from his belt and took a swig of water. It was warm, but better than nothing. He wiped his mouth on the back of his sleeve. High above him something screeched, and Micah looked up, his hand shielding his eyes from the glare of the high sun, to see a dozen or so carrionwyrmes circling far above his head on those tattered black wings of theirs.

He smiled grimly. If they'd been fixing on having him for their next meal they were going to be sore disappointed. But then, unless he missed his guess, it wasn't him they had their eyes on . . .

Micah pulled off his hat and scratched his scalp, easing the heatprickle. Then, with a single motion, he jammed the hat back on his head and jumped down lightly from the bluntedge rock he'd been standing on. He kept on up the steep screescritch slope, head lowered. The shadows of the carrionwyrmes orbited his hunched body like dark stars, while his own shadow pooled around his feet, black as pitch.

It was good to be back on the trail after the long months of fullwinter spent cooped up underground. The warm half-summer air tasted good. His limbs felt strong. He climbed the screescritch effortlessly, silently, his fresh-greased boots picking out the best way through the jagged stones like they had a mind of their own. As the ground levelled out, Micah passed clusters of tall mottled rapierspikes that were just coming into flower. And there was new-grown chafegrass and rockvetch and feathermilt underfoot, and a brace of tall mountain oaks over to one side, their stubby branches hazed with green from half-opened buds.

There came a sound.

Micah's hand shot to the handle of his hackdagger.

The sound came again. Scritching and scratching. Micah peered into the shadows beneath the mountain oaks, and relaxed. A small squat squabwyrme was rubbing its rump lazily up and down the rough bark, sloughing off ribbons of old skin.

Micah turned away and continued over the flat rock and up the next slope. A couple of basking scratwyrmes, the size of his hand, scurried over the jumble of rocks before disappearing into crevices between them. As he approached the top of the slope, Micah slowed down, stooped forward and headed for a tall angular rock that lay precariously close to the edge. He crouched down behind it.

Slowly, breath held, he peered round the side of the rock.

The land fell away on the other side into a flat-bottomed dip. And there, at one end of the depression, was a youth.

He was hunkered down on his heels, his back turned but his face in half-profile. He was thin, fair-haired, with high cheekbones. Downy hair above his top lip suggested he was close to his first shave. He was wearing the clothes of a steerhand or a ploughboy from the plains; a collarless shirt, a homespun jacket, buckskin boots and breeches, all of them frayed and scuffed. His pack lay a little way off, propped up against a flat rock, the burnished copper cookpot strapped to it glinting in the sunlight.

It was this dazzle Micah had spotted from the trail. It had also drawn the keen eyes of the carrionwyrmes that continued to circle overhead.

There was a knife raised in the youth's hand. And as he shifted awkwardly round, Micah saw that he had trapped a wyrme in the longnet that lay at his feet. The long-limbed brown wyrme was thrashing about furiously, screeching, squealing. One of its hindlegs and both forepaws stuck out through the oversized holes of the net, claws slashing at its captor's shaking hand.

It was a splaywyrme by the look of it, Micah thought. Dullwitted creatures. Easy to catch but difficult to kill, on account of the heavy carapace that covered their wide bodies from neck to tail. Down on the ground, his chin resting on his clasped hands, he watched the youth grip the knife with both hands and stab down stiffly through the net.

'Not that way,' Micah murmured.

The knife bounced harmlessly off the splaywyrme's shell. Spitting and snarling, the wyrme lunged back at its attacker, its vicious snout thrusting at the rope mesh so hard that its head burst out through the net. Its neck swivelled round and its fangs slammed together. The youth pulled sharply back and jumped to his feet. He kicked at the squirming net, but half-heartedly.

The wyrme bucked and writhed, and screeched all the louder. The youth looked close to tears.

He was obviously a greenhorn, out on the trail. On his own. He reminded Micah of himself, all that time ago, when he had first entered the weald. Lonely. Frightened.

Micah climbed to his feet.

Below him, the youth continued his strange ungainly dance, hopping about, dodging the snapping jaws of the trapped wyrme as he attempted to land a fatal blow. Micah pulled the hackdagger from his belt.

'Need some help?' he called down.

The youth spun round, fear in his eyes as his gaze fell upon the glinting blade in Micah's hand. Micah smiled and raised his hands defensively.

'S'all right, friend, I don't mean no harm,' he said. 'But I can show you how to deal with that there splaywyrme.' He started down the slope towards the youth. 'Trick is to flip 'em over and aim for the base of the neck . . .'

The blow to his arm seemed to come out of nowhere. It

struck him with a dull crack just below the elbow, making him cry out with pain and surprise and sending his hackdagger scuttering over the dusty gravel. A hefty arm wrapped itself round his neck, squeezing tight and pulling him backwards, and he felt the sharp tip of a knife at his shoulder blades.

'Keep still,' hissed a voice in his ear. 'Y'understand?'

Micah struggled, cursing his stupidity. The knife jabbed harder. Micah fell still. He smelled the sour tang of hunger on his attacker's warm breath.

'One more move and it'll be your last.'

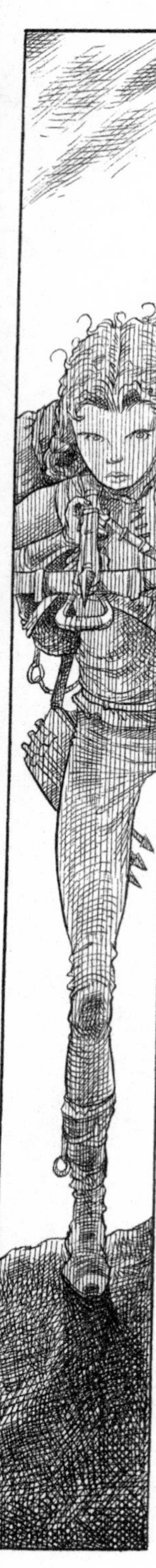

Three

'Drop the knife.'

The arm around Micah's neck tightened, and he heard the quickening of his attacker's breath.

'I said, drop the knife.' The words were quieter and more measured than before, but hard.

Micah squinted into the setting sun. There at the top of the slope, her slim body silhouetted against the pale sky, was Cara. Her legs were braced, and the primed spitbolt in her hands was pointing over Micah's right shoulder at his assailant.

'I'll kill him.' The voice was close by Micah's ear.

Cara's face registered no emotion, though Micah recognized a grim determination in her eyes. When he'd gone ahead to scout the trail, Micah had told her to follow at a distance, and keep him covered. This green-eyed kithgirl of his had done exactly that. She had handled herself well, just like she always did. And Micah was proud of her.

They had met in the settlement of Deephome two short months earlier in the depths of fullwinter. Bone-chilled and half-starved and nursing a broken heart, Micah had been in a bad way. Cara had looked after him. And he had fallen in love with her. She was gentle and loyal and caring – and surprisingly tough when she had to be.

'You kill him and I'll kill you,' she said evenly. 'And then I'll kill your kid brother. Got another one of these loaded and braced at my side.'

Cara's eyes flicked over to the fair-haired kith who stood frozen over the netted splaywyrme, which continued to snap and struggle at his feet. The youth had already seen the second spitbolt, and so had Micah's assailant, for Micah felt the grip round his neck get tighter still. Cara's finger whitened on the trigger.

'For pity's sake,' the fair-haired youth blurted out. 'Do as she says!' He raised his hands towards Cara imploringly, his brow furrowed and eyes wide. 'He was just looking out for me, is all. We surely meant you no harm—'

'Hush up!' the voice by Micah's ear snarled fiercely, and at his back Micah felt a sharp jabbing pain as the tip of the blade pressed hard against his skin.

Then, abruptly, the pressure round his neck relaxed and he was shoved roughly in the back. He stumbled forward and landed heavily on his knees, grazing his hands. Behind him, he heard the knife landing on the rock, and the sound of it being kicked across the dust. He looked round.

His attacker stood glaring back at him.

He was about the same height as the fair-haired youth, but older and far more powerfully built, with broad shoulders and a thick neck. He had dark hair hacked down close to the scalp, and blueblack stubble on his jaw that put the other's wispy moustache to shame.

'They don't look much like brothers to me,' Micah observed.

'It's their eyes,' Cara said, striding down the slope, the spitbolt gripped in her hands.

Micah climbed to his feet. 'Their eyes?' he said.

'They're the same,' said Cara. 'Same shape. Same shade of green.'

Micah looked. 'Happen you might be right,' he said. He reached down and picked up the dark-haired one's knife, then, spotting his hackdagger, crossed the gravel to retrieve it. 'You two got names?' he asked as Cara unhooked the spitbolt at her belt – *his* spitbolt – and handed it to him.

The weapon was too cumbersome when you were out scouting. But it sure felt reassuringly weighty in his hand now.

The two brothers shuffled towards one another. The fair-haired youth's thin arms dangled at his side, his fingers plucking at the frayed cuffs of his sleeves. His older brother folded his arms. His fists were clenched. They were both bone-thin and dressed in tattered plains' clothes that spoke to Micah of an arduous journey up here to the high country, recently made.

'I'm Ethan, and this here is Cody,' said the fair-haired youth. 'We are indeed brothers. The young lady was right on that score . . .' He glanced over at Cara. 'We're fresh to the weald and we're not looking for no trouble. Leastways, not this early on in our new careers.' He attempted a smile.

Beside him, his heavy-set brother continued to glare at Micah.

Micah smiled back. 'We ain't either,' he said quietly. 'Name's Micah. And this is Cara.' He frowned, then added, 'When did you two last eat?'

'A week since,' said Ethan. He nodded back at the splaywyrme, now lying still inside the longnet. He shrugged, his arms before him, palms up. 'I was hoping this wyrme might make us a good meal, but the damn thing sure is hard to despatch . . .'

'Like I said, they can be,' Micah said. 'Unless you know the knack to it.'

He smiled to himself, realizing how he must sound to these two greenhorns. The voice of experience. He bent down and flipped the splaywyrme onto its back with the tip of his boot, then, with his hackdagger, swiftly slit the creature's neck. The wyrme convulsed for a couple of moments, then lay still. When Micah spoke again, there was a certain drawl to his words.

'Got to do it quick, y'understand, and with a sharp blade, so the creature doesn't suffer any more than it needs to. Respect wyrmekind and use what they have to offer to the full and you'll prosper in the weald.' He paused. 'A friend taught me that.'

He dragged the dead wyrme out of the net by its hindlegs and held it up.

'Either of you boys know how to skin a wyrme?'

Ethan nodded vigorously. 'I reckon I can handle it,' he said. 'I used to skin jackrabbits and squirrels back on the farm.'

'Well, get down to it,' Micah said, 'while we get a fire going.'

He glanced over his shoulder. The circling carrionwyrmes had come in to land a little way off and stood peering back at them, their yellow eyes glinting with hunger and stubby barbels quivering at the corners of their fang-fringed mouths.

'There's brushwood down there a piece,' he said, pointing back the way he and Cara had come. 'Want to help us gather it, Cody?'

Cody was looking at Cara.

'Cody?' said Micah. 'The brushwood?'

'Uh-huh,' Cody grunted.

An hour later, as the sun set and the carrionwyrmes skittered and snarled in the distance, the four of them sat crosslegged around a small fire, feasting on the splaywyrme meat and tossing the picked bones into the flames. Micah noted the relish in the two brothers' eyes as they chewed and swallowed.

'You sure it's only been a week since you last ate?' he asked. 'I swear them carrionwyrmes couldn't have done a better job than you two at stripping the bones.'

Cody shrugged, and Ethan laughed good-naturedly. 'Might as well make the most of it,' he said. 'Don't know when we might eat again.'

The younger brother was open and friendly, quick to laugh and eager to talk. The older was silent and brooding, and had hardly spoken the whole time they'd been sitting there.

'We'll manage,' he told Ethan gruffly. 'Somehow . . .'

Micah and Cara exchanged looks in the flickering firelight.

'So how long have you been in the weald?' Cara asked.

'It's been nigh on two moons now,' Ethan said, throwing a leg bone that he'd picked clean into the fire. 'There was still snow upon the ground when we got up here. Ain't that right, Cody?'

Cody grunted, but added nothing.

'I swear I ain't never been so cold in my life,' Ethan went on. 'It was springtime down on the plains, and we thought it would be the same up here,' he explained. 'We were soon disabused of *that* notion.'

Micah nodded grimly. He knew all about the bite of full-winter.

'And what do you plan to do, now you're up here?' Cara persisted.

No one spoke. There was the sound of windsough. Carrion-wyrme chatter. The cracking of the fire.

Micah drew his legs up and hugged them tight to his chest. He looked across at the brothers. Their clothes were threadbare, their boots near worn out, and as for their kit – it was nothing more than an old saddlebag and a couple of rolled blankets for a pack, and the net the splaywyrme had been caught in. The two of them had been lucky so far, that much was clear, but the chances of them surviving much longer were slim at best.

Ethan looked at Cody, who shrugged again.

'Travel on, I guess,' said Ethan. 'Further into the weald. Seek our fame and fortune,' he added with a desperate grin. 'Ain't that right, Cody?'

Cody sighed. 'Bit of fortune would be welcome enough,' he conceded. 'I ain't bothered about the fame.'

The two brothers suddenly looked forlorn and grim in the firelight.

Micah unclasped his hands and reached out for a greenwood stick that lay beside the fire. He poked the embers absent-mindedly, sending clouds of orange sparks billowing up into the air. He glanced at Cara, who seemed to have read his thoughts with those blue-green eyes of hers. She nodded encouragingly at him, and Micah saw Cody read her look in turn.

Cody's face coloured and he stared down at his battered boots.

'If you had a mind to,' said Micah at length, looking at Ethan, 'happen the four of us could always travel together.'

Ethan's face lit up with relief and expectation, and he was about to speak when a cough from his brother stilled him. Ethan turned to Cody, his eyes filled with hope. Cody kept his gaze fixed to the dusty ground before him, his brow creased like he was thinking things through. Ethan looked at Micah and Cara, then back at his brother.

Finally Cody looked up. He nodded. 'Happen we could,' he said.

Four

The cave was round and black like a yawning mouth. It was set into the mountainside above a fall of scree and moss-covered rubble, and seemed to be the only shelter from the wind that was cutting through the shallow gulley. Micah looked away. He slipped the backpack from his shoulders and pointed to the base of the screeslope.

'Reckon this is as good a place as any to rest up,' he said, and scanned the darkening sky. 'Besides, the light's going and I don't want to lose our trail.'

Cara nodded. The weald was wild, daunting, especially by night. But she felt safe with Micah.

Keeping to the north-west, he had followed a trail that Eli had taught him. He'd pointed out to her the landmarks that he was tracking. Some, like the speckled stacks and boulder ridge, were obvious enough. Most of them, however, Cara would not have spotted if Micah hadn't shown her.

The dust skillet. Bear mount. Strutting rooster

rock. Hangman's crag . . . Now they were heading for the stickle falls – where Eli would be waiting for them.

Cara smiled to herself. It was as if, in urging them to set off on their own for a few days, the cragclimber had been setting them a test. And despite her initial trepidation, Cara felt that they had done well. Though what Eli would make of their new travelling companions, Maker only knew . . .

She let her pack fall to the ground and crouched down next to Micah, who was sitting in the lee of a boulder, half-sheltered from the icy wind. The two brothers, Cody and Ethan, approached heavy-footed through the dusk.

'There's a cave up yonder,' said Ethan, pulling his collar up. 'I for one would not mind sheltering from this wind. It is painful bitter.' He shivered expansively.

Micah shook his head. 'Caves need careful scouting,' he said. 'Ain't no telling what or who might be lurking in them. Most times it's best to leave 'em be.'

Cody hefted the pack from his shoulders and slumped down next to Cara and Micah, but Ethan remained standing, glancing up at the black mouth of the cave and shivering.

'Get what sleep you can,' said Micah, as Cara scooched up beneath the folds of his bedding blanket. 'We'll head off at first light.'

Despite the caustic wind, with its last taint of fullwinter, fatigue and the warmth of Cara's body pressed close to him lulled Micah into dreamless sleep. High overhead, the slice of moon came and went. Gnarled trees bent over stiffly as the cold wind gusted, subsided, then gusted again. Dryleaf scrub whispered. Rocks softly whined . . .

The scream broke through the lulling nighthush like something being shattered. Micah sat bolt upright. Cara's eyes snapped open.

It was almost dawn. Thin silver-threaded strands of cloud were scudding across the dark sky, but there was a glow on the horizon. Cody was already up and on his feet.

'It's Ethan,' he said urgently, and nodded down at the empty space beside him where his brother's bedroll had been.

There was another scream, followed by a coarse hissing sound.

Cody started up the scree towards the cave. Micah jumped to his feet, grabbed his spitbolt and scrambled after him as fast as the shifting rocks would allow.

'Cara, bring the torch,' he called over his shoulder as he reached the cave entrance.

Cody had already disappeared into the darkness. Micah went in after him. The pitted walls at the mouth of the cave suddenly flickered with golden light. Cara was behind him, a flaming dip-torch gripped in her hands. She raised the torch higher and followed Micah inside.

The cave was large, its narrow entrance opening out into a cavern forested with stalactites and flow columns that glistened and shimmered in the torchlight. Micah spotted Cody first. He was frozen in an attitude of terror, his back against a limestone outcrop and eyes unblinking. Micah followed his gaze.

Ethan was curled up in a defensive ball on a bed of moss at the centre of the cave. Clustered round him were dark brown pebbles that Micah recognized as wyves. Wyrme eggs. Above, clinging to the ceiling with outstretched claw-tipped wings, was a mottled stormwyrme, the size of a plains eagle, its muscular neck curled back and its nostrils flared. The flameoil sac at the base of its throat pulsated.

The wyrme was poised to engulf the cowering youth in a jet of flame. Only the proximity of its precious eggs was preventing it from turning Ethan into a human torch.

'Don't move,' Micah said.

'I ain't fixing to,' Ethan whimpered. 'Found me a soft bed, only to wake and find *that* looming over me . . .' He stifled a sob.

The stormwyrme swivelled its head and glared at Micah. Its jaws opened and the sac at its throat swelled. There were no eggs protecting Micah, Cody and Cara.

Micah raised the spitbolt and fired.

The stormwyrme recoiled with a hissing screech and tumbled from the cave ceiling, Micah's bolt embedded in one yellow eye. Its lifeless body fell limp and heavy upon Ethan below.

'Help,' he moaned. 'Get it off me.'

Cody leaped forward and tore the dead wyrme off his brother.

Ethan looked up at him, his eyes wide with fear. 'I thought I was a goner, Cody. I thought—'

The blow from Cody's clenched fist struck Ethan's jaw

with a sharp crack. His head went back, his mouth opened and he stared at his brother.

Cody stared back furiously. 'You stupid damn fool . . .' he began, then fell on him, hugging him, his arms wrapped tightly round Ethan's quaking body. He rested his chin on his shoulder and rubbed a hand over his brother's tousled head. 'You gotta stay close, Ethan, or else how can I look out for you . . . ?'

'Come on,' said Micah softly, resting a hand on Cody and Ethan's shoulders. 'Gather up them wyves while I see to the wyrme.' He fixed Ethan with a look. 'And if you won't heed my advice, then at least listen to your brother, greenhorn.'

Micah picked up the mottled stormwyrme by the wing and strode out of the cave. Gathering up the eggs, four in number, Cody followed. He didn't look at his brother.

Ethan climbed slowly to his feet, picking bits of the mossy nest off his bed blanket. He swallowed hard, a sob catching at the back of his throat.

'They're right,' he murmured. 'I'm nothing but a stupid greenhorn, and this here wyrmeweald's going to be the death of me . . .'

'Hush now, Ethan,' came a soft voice. It was Cara. She reached across to him, took a hold of his hand. 'Everyone makes mistakes,' she said. 'It's what we learn from them that counts.'

Five

The sun had risen to its zenith when the line of jagged mountaintops came into view. They jutted up from the fine mist that hung in the valley below, and looked like a line of sharp teeth set in milky gums.

Micah glanced at Cara, who had kept pace with him on the steep trail, then looked back at Ethan and Cody. The pair of them were struggling to keep up.

'That's the stickle falls up yonder,' he called to them.

Ethan paused and wiped the sweat from his forehead on his sleeve. His face was bright red, which made his fair hair appear fairer than it was, and there was uncertainty in his eyes.

'How can you tell, Micah?' he asked, trying but failing not to pant. He frowned, scratched his scalp. 'It don't look too different to any number of other jagged mountaintops we've passed.'

'If he says them there's the stickle falls,' said Cody, pausing in turn, 'then I for one take him at his word.'

The older brother not only carried what passed for their kit – the old saddlebag and rolled blanket – but also both their watergourds, which were slung from his broad shoulders. In contrast to Ethan's chatter, he had not said a word since daybreak when they'd set out on the trail. Now the day was at its hottest, with the air above the rocks shimmering in the midday sun.

'You two all right?' asked Cara

Ethan grinned back at her. Despite the heat and the exertion of the climb, he was still determinedly cheerful.

'Ain't the mountain been Maker-fashioned that Cody and I could not scale,' he said. 'Eh, Cody?'

Cody looked up and surveyed the surrounding rockscape. His eyes narrowed against the dazzle of the sun. They were high up, and the ridges and canyons lay round about them like folds of sacking.

'Happen not,' he drawled. 'Though a bit of down would not come amiss.'

Micah nodded along the line of glittering spikes of rock. 'We crest that ridge up ahead,' he said, 'and it's downhill from thereon in.'

Sure enough, as they rounded the first of the tall pinnacles, the valley beyond opened up below them. It was broad and flat-bottomed, the tree-clad sides rising up vertical. Ethan let out a long low whistle.

There were splashes of colour in among the shades of green, where blooms and blossoms were on gaudy display. And streaks of silver and gold and metallic blue as, far below them, burnished-winged wyrmes wheeled and swooped through the misty air. They called out to one another constantly, yet their screeches and squawks were barely audible above the sound of rushing water.

With Micah leading the way, the four of them continued along the line of jagged columns of rock that fringed the ridge, until the majestic stickle falls came back into view. Cool spray blew into their faces as a frothing torrent of water flowed out of a chasm in the rock between the last two stickles and tumbled down into the valley in a vast tremulous pillar.

Beside the falls was a track. Trodden down by silvertails and billywyrmes, and widened by rainwash, the rocky trail zig-zagged its way down the far side of the mountain range. Below, at the foot of the waterfall, was a lake. The sun was in their eyes as they set off towards it, an easterly breeze plucking at their sweat-drenched clothes.

'One step at a time,' Micah called back, his voice indistinct against the roar of the waterfall as they began their descent. 'And watch your footing.'

Soon they were walking at the same level as the wyrmes they had seen flying so far below. There were garish purple-crested fisherwyrmes, and pitchwyrmes, their drab cousins; and pale-blue mistwyrmes that were large and ungainly in flight, calling out their characteristic *whoop-whoop-whoop*.

Ethan stumbled and almost fell as a pitchwyrme suddenly emerged from the waterfall, a great speckled rocksalmon clamped between its jaws. It circled overhead for a moment, then flapped off into the mistblur trees that lined the slopes around them. Cody steadied his brother with a hand on the shoulder, and they continued down the winding track.

As they neared the valley bottom, it levelled out some, and the roar of the waterfall grew louder still as they approached the broad lake at its base. They stopped at the water's edge, hot, tired, footsore, and gazed at their reflections in the rippling surface.

'Better set up camp,' said Micah. 'Forage for firewood, catch some fish maybe . . .'

'First things first,' said Ethan, sitting down. He pulled off one boot, then the other, then climbed to his feet and removed his jacket, his shirt, his trousers and tossed them behind him. He was about to pull off his underwear when Cody – who had unshouldered the pack and pulled off his own jacket and shirt – stayed him with a furious nudge in the ribs. He nodded at Cara.

'There's a lady present,' he said.

Ethan stopped. A smile tugged at his mouth. 'My apologies, Miss Cara,' he said. 'I was not thinking.'

She looked back at him, and then at Cody, and was embarrassed to realize that her face was flushed. Cody was looking straight at her. She could not hold his gaze. Ethan turned back to the water, his eyes gleaming with amusement. He waded into the lake five, six steps, then threw his body forward and began swimming. Cody jumped in after him, and the pair of them swam towards the middle of the lake, out of their depth, where they stopped and twisted round and trod water.

'Come on!' Ethan shouted out to Cara and Micah, beckoning wildly. 'It sure is refreshing!'

Cara and Micah exchanged looks.

'There's no sign of Eli yet,' Micah ventured. 'And that water does look inviting . . .'

He dropped his own pack to the ground and pulled off his jacket and shirt, then his breeches, before plunging into the lake. Cara watched him for a moment, then, with a single fluid movement shrugged off her rucksack and cape, and wriggled out of her wyrmehide breeches. She ran to the water's edge, kicking off her boots as she went and, to the encouraging whoops and cheers of the others, plunged into the cool clear water of the lake in her underslip. She swam underwater for a few strokes before surfacing.

'That is refreshing!' she exclaimed, and she splashed Micah, who splashed her back, and she dived back down under the water.

Cody laughed, and lunging forwards, placed his hands on Micah's head and pushed him under. Then he turned to Ethan, but his brother was nowhere to be seen.

He swivelled round, his arms paddling at his side, keeping himself afloat – then cried out as someone grabbed at his ankles. He kicked out wildly, but the grip was too firm, and the next moment he was yanked down under the water, his laughter turning to gurgles.

Micah resurfaced, then Ethan, and the two of them wrestled with one another, each one trying to push the other one down. Cody swam beneath them, seized both of them by a foot and pulled them under.

Cara watched it all, laughing and splashing each of them in turn. Then, turning away, she set off for the shore, pushing the water behind her with long steady strokes. Her toes touched the gravel of the lakebed. She crawled the last few yards on her hands and knees and was about to climb to her feet when her gaze fell upon a pair of dusty boots directly before her.

'Eli!' she cried, looking up.

The cragclimber smiled down at her, helped her to her feet, then nodded out into the lake, where Micah, Cody and Ethan were still splashing and diving and dunking one another, unaware of his presence.

'Seems like you've made some new friends,' he commented.

Six

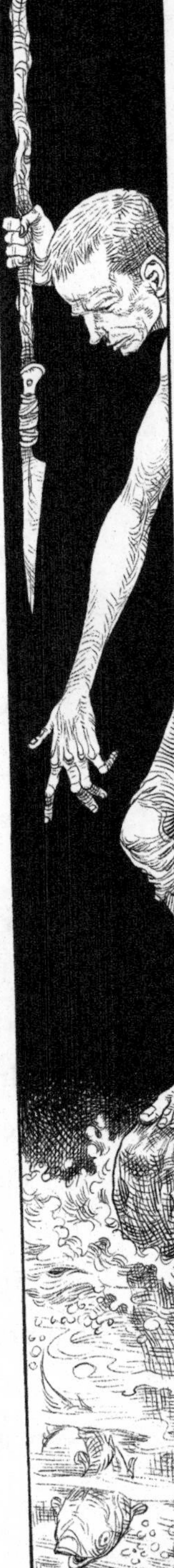

'Got to know just when to strike . . .'

Eli froze. He was standing on a broad rock at the bottom of the falls. The water foamed around him in the depths, tugging at the cottonweed and churning up bubbles. His legs were spread and braced; his knife, strapped to the end of his walking staff, was raised in his hand. He stared unblinking into the water.

Below him, in the swirling eddy, a stunned tunny rose to the surface. And, in the split second before it could recover itself and dart away, Eli struck. The sharp point of the makeshift spear skewered the fish and Eli raised it above his head.

'That's another,' he muttered. 'Two more to go.'

On the adjacent rock, Micah held out the net. Eli reached across and deposited the fish next to the other two with a flick of his wrist.

'You make it look easy,' said Micah.

'It's how I started out,' said Eli. 'Fishing the

falls when I first got to the weald. I'm sure I told you that before.'

Micah nodded. 'You did,' he said. 'But I had no notion of what a skill it was.'

'Trick's to get them just after they land,' he said, looking up at the torrent of water.

Micah followed his gaze, and saw the wyrmes still wheeling round in the air and diving through the falls after the tumbling streaks of silver.

'*They* make it look easy too,' he said.

Eli had resumed his stance on the rock, legs braced, spear poised. When he spoke his voice was low and steady.

'Nothing is easy in the high country, Micah. You of all people should know that. You have to be vigilant at all times . . .' The cragclimber's blue eyes were fixed on the bubbling water. 'Search for food, spot the best place to rest up, cover your tracks on the trail . . .'

He thrust down into the water with the spear, pulling it out a moment later with a fourth fish wriggling at the end. He dropped it into Micah's net, then glanced across the lake at the camp.

Cody was tending the fire, while Ethan was making Cara laugh with some animated story or other.

'It's hard enough as it is in the weald,' he said, 'without acquiring extra mouths to feed.'

Micah was about to reply, to explain that Cody and Ethan were all right, just a little green was all – just like he had been when Eli had found him; and that if he and Cara hadn't teamed up with them, they would most likely be starving by now, or worse . . . But he was cut short by Eli's grunt as he thrust the spear into the water once more. A moment later, the fifth and final fish was flopping about inside the net with the rest.

'I'm gonna have to have a word with them,' said Eli evenly.

The cragclimber stepped off the rock and into the foaming water, which rose to chest height as he began picking his way across the uneven gravel of the lakebed, taking care to avoid the dark shadows of the depths. Micah watched him go, then followed slowly after. On the bank, Ethan and Cody looked up as the pair of them approached, and the sight of their eager smiling faces made Micah knot up inside when he thought of what Eli was about to tell them.

'Did you catch anything, sir?' Ethan was asking him. 'I was just telling Miss Cara about the time Cody and me was fixing to catch us some supper, only I lost my footing and—'

'Five,' Eli interrupted him. 'Big fellers too.'

Micah held out the net and tried to smile, but the sick feeling in the pit of his stomach only grew.

'If you'll allow me, I'll gut and clean 'em ready to cook,' said Ethan eagerly. 'My brother here's got a mighty fine fire going, ain't you, Cody?'

'I have,' said Cody, colouring. Unlike his younger brother, he seemed to have noticed the cragclimber's unwavering stare and taciturn manner.

Eli nodded. 'Best get on with it then,' he said quietly.

Ethan gutted the fish, and Cara skewered them on sharpened greentwigs and set them over the hot embers.

'Sure does smell good,' Ethan said as the fish began to brown on one side. He shifted across to the fire on his knees and turned them over, one at a time.

When the fish were done, Cara handed out the greentwig skewers. They ate in an awkward silence, as if Eli's reticence had infected the others and cast a solemn shadow over them all. Overhead, in the deepening dusk, the wyrmes dived and swooped, dark shadows against the ochre sky as they called to each other and headed off to their roosts in the wooded valley slopes.

Ethan and Cody finished their fish, and Ethan thanked Eli profusely while Cody stared disconsolately into the fire. The cragclimber said nothing. He tossed his skewer into the flames and watched it burn, the firelight playing on his weather-beaten features.

Finally Micah could stand it no longer. 'Tell them,' he said grimly, his gaze fixed on Eli. 'This . . . this just ain't fair. Tell them once and for all, Eli, for pity's sake, and get it over with.'

He fell still, his face burning.

Everyone was staring at at him. Ethan seemed bewildered; Cody looked dejected as if he guessed what was coming. Cara appeared to have understood too, for she reached over and took Micah's hand and squeezed it. There were tears glistening in her green eyes. Micah kept his gaze fixed on Eli, as the cragclimber stared impassively into the flames.

Eli took a deep breath. He pushed his hair back from his forehead, which creased up thoughtfully. He looked up at Ethan, and then at Cody. He observed their threadbare clothes, their meagre kit and their faces – one pathetically eager and full of hope, the other shy but strong – and Micah could tell that he was noting the exact same things that he and Cara had noticed on *their* first meeting with these greenhorns.

Micah's stomach gave another lurch. High above them, a mistwyrme gave a whooping call into the night.

Eli glanced over at Micah, then back at the Ethan and Cody. 'Micah and I had words earlier,' he said. 'And since then I done a deal of thinking . . .'

Micah swallowed.

'Life in the weald is harsh. To survive, you need to organize your year wisely. Gather as much you can during the seasons of plenty to see you through the privations of fullwinter. Then find a den to store it in. Away from prying eyes . . .'

He paused. Ethan glanced at Cody, then back at the crag-climber.

'Fact is,' Eli continued, 'I've a notion to head out to the west into valley country as yet little travelled. Find a winter den there. It'll be a hard trail, but there's rich pickings to be had where others ain't trod before.' Eli's eyes were fixed back on the fire now, and his voice was so low he seemed almost to be talking to himself. 'And we'll need rich pickings. It might only be halfsummer now, but already time is short. If we're to survive next fullwinter we got us a whole lot of work to do . . .'

Micah watched Eli closely, hope suddenly thudding in his chest. The cragclimber smiled.

'Happen we could do with extra hands in this endeavour.' He paused. 'Would you two boys care to join us?'

For a moment, there was absolute silence. Micah was overwhelmed with a mixture of relief and gratitude. It seemed the cragclimber simply hadn't had the heart to cut these greenhorns loose. Then Ethan broke the silence with a whooped cheer, and Cody reached forward and shook Eli's hand.

'It would be an honour, sir,' he mumbled.

'And we won't let you down, no sir,' Ethan babbled. 'We'll work hard and earn our keep and . . .'

Cara climbed to her feet and crossed to the brothers. She clasped their hands, one after the other, smiling broadly. Eli looked across at Micah.

'And you, lad?' he said. 'Anything more you want to say on the matter?'

Micah swallowed and shook his head. Then he smiled. 'Out to the west,' he murmured. 'Where the great whitewyrmes come from . . .'

Seven

They set out at first light, Eli scouting the trail ahead, with Ethan tripping along at his heels like an eager puppydog. Cody followed, carrying both his and his brother's kit, while Micah and Cara hung back a ways, allowing a distance to build up between them and the rest of the party.

The roar of the stickle falls diminished as they crested and then descended the first of the jagged ridges that lay beyond to the west. Scrubthorns and thistle sprouted from between the grey-green rocks, and small clumps of dwarfoak tufted the hill crests around them. A watery sun shone dimly through the early morning sky, and the air smelled of rain.

'The west,' Eli had said as they'd sat watching the dying embers of the campfire the night before. 'Into the heart of the valley country, where the great whitewyrmes dwell and kith have yet to venture . . .' His blue eyes had taken on a faraway look and his face appeared suddenly careworn and grim. 'Not even the kith gangs with their harpoons could slaughter all the wyrmes that live there. But it'll be a hard trail,' he'd added.

The cragclimber had been right. The ridges to the west stretched to the far horizon, a seemingly impenetrable barrier of deep ravines, stormgulleys and scree-scattered slopes. It would take all Eli Halfwinter's experience and ingenuity to find a route through them, Micah realized.

He reached out and took Cara's hand. It was soft and warm. The callouses and scars of life on the trail had yet to leave their mark.

As they picked their way carefully between thorn-fringed boulders, Micah glanced round at Cara. Her auburn hair was tied back with sky-blue twine. She wore a scarf of Deephome red at her neck and a tooled leather belt at her waist. These were the only touches of decoration to her person. The tan wyrmehide breeches and heavy greywyrmeskin cloak, creased and worn in, and the battered broadbrim hat that hung at her back, were the unadorned apparel of a weald traveller. But with the simple addition of scarf and belt, Cara had made it look stylish, becoming. Even the heavy boots, cross-laced and toecapped, seemed to flatter her, emphasizing the length and the shapeliness of her legs.

Cara caught Micah's glance and smiled, her green eyes crinkling at the corners. Her skin was freckled and honey-coloured from the sun, and her lips glistened with the mintroot salve that she applied every morning, and made Micah want to kiss them. He tightened his grip on her hand and pulled her towards him, but she laughed and pushed him away.

'Not now, Micah,' she said, and flashed him a mischievous smile. 'There'll be time enough for foolishness when we make camp tonight – and I reckon we've a deal of ridges to scale before that happy outcome.'

Micah laughed in turn and let go of Cara's hand. She was a beauty, this kithgirl of his, and tough and resolute to boot. And she loved him. And Micah blessed the Maker to have found her.

'Sure is hot,' said Ethan, pushing his hat back and making a show of wiping his sleeve across his forehead.

Eli did not reply, his eyes fixed on the uneven cleft-ridden rock ahead as he walked.

'Don't think I've ever known it so hot,' Ethan added, and was rewarded with a soft grunt for his perseverance.

Three days they'd been on the trail – three gruelling days – yet Eli had to concede, the youth was bearing up better than he'd feared. This ridge country was rugged, the constant climbing and descending taking a toll on muscles and kit alike. He pulled his water bottle from his belt, took a swig, then held it out.

'Thank you,' said Ethan, taking a mouthful and wiping his mouth on the back of his wrist. 'I appreciate it.'

Eli grunted again, then added, 'Reckon you should be carrying your own water.' He looked over his shoulder at

Micah and Cara, and at Cody, who was carrying Ethan's kit and watergourd as well as his own. 'Ain't right to leave everything to Cody.'

Ethan blushed. Carrying their stuff was just something his brother did – all part of the way he looked out for him, but Eli's words had stung nonetheless. His skin prickled and burned at his scalp, at the tips of his ears, at the nape of his neck. He restoppered the water bottle and handed it back, and they kept walking, with Ethan repeatedly checking to see whether Eli looked as angry as he had sounded. But he could not read the cragclimber's impassive expression.

Ethan swallowed. Perhaps it would be better to drop back and walk with the others, but he wasn't sure how to take his leave of the cragclimber without seeming offended or petulant. Anyway, he didn't want to drop back. He liked walking ahead with Eli. It made him feel safe in the great threatening expanse of the high country to have this calm experienced weald traveller at his side, and he was loath to give that up.

Eli paused, dropped to his haunches and examined the ground at his feet.

Ethan stopped next to him. 'Looks like a footprint,' he commented. He crouched down and ran his fingers round the splayed clawmarks. 'It's big.'

'Blackwing,' said Eli. 'Size of a packmule full-grown. They have an orange crest that runs down their backs,' he continued. 'And angular black wings that they hold aloft to shadow their bodies.'

Eli rose and resumed walking, and Ethan trotted along beside him in the hope that Eli would talk some more. He liked to listen to the cragclimber's voice. It was warm and dark and reassuring and wise.

'So this blackwingwyrme,' Ethan said, 'it's heading westwards?'

Eli nodded. 'In search of food,' he told him.

'There's food to be had to the west?' said Ethan. He looked around at the ridged landscape of pleats and crevices. 'Coz there ain't a whole lot to be found around here.'

'Grasslands, most like,' said Eli. 'Blackwings are grazing creatures.'

Ethan nodded. 'So you reckon there's grasslands out to the west?'

Eli sighed. The youth never gave up.

'If we track this wyrme, follow the signs it leaves us, most likely it'll lead us through these here ridges, and then we'll find out.'

'*Signs*,' said Ethan. 'You mean, like the footprint?'

'Footprints. Dung. Bruised scrub. Cropped sagegrass,' said Eli, his voice deliberately patient.

'Sagegrass?' Ethan persisted.

Eli tipped his walking staff towards a bushy tussock, half its seedheads bitten off.

'I see,' said Ethan. He shook his head in awe. 'Seems like there ain't nothing you don't know about the weald.'

Eli made no reply but continued walking, staring down at

the ground, and Ethan felt foolish for having spoken at all. He was nothing but an over-talkative greenhorn, trying too hard to ingratiate himself with this seasoned weald traveller.

'I talk too much,' he confessed. 'It's what my brother's always telling me. Says I like the sound of my own voice. Says it gets on folks' nerves.' He paused. 'I've been trying not to. Leastways, not so much.'

'Your brother's right,' Eli said drily. 'Happen you should try harder.'

And Ethan did try harder. For the next couple of hours, he kept his mouth resolutely shut. They continued over one ridge after another, some steep and barren, sunk in deep shadow; others shallow and verdant with scrub and thorn bushes. As the sun sank, they crested a ridge to find a sheer drop on the far side with a narrow series of ledges leading down into shadowy depths.

'Wait for the others,' Eli instructed, 'while I scout for a way down.' The cragclimber turned away and was about to begin his descent when a raucous screech echoed in the canyon.

The wyrme appeared out of nowhere, a flash of red and green and gaping fang-studded jaws. Ethan saw it coming straight at him; saw the dripping fangs, the outstretched claws . . .

He stumbled backwards. His boot skidded on the ridge-top, and he slipped. His knee gave way. Rock cracked and crumbled and fell away in a shower of stones and, with the screeching wyrme spiralling up into the sky overhead, Ethan teetered on the edge. Eli shot out a hand towards him, only for Ethan to shrink back from the cragclimber, his shoulders hunched and twisted and arms raised about his head, as if he thought Eli was going to strike him.

Then he fell.

Eli snatched at the back of the youth's jacket and held on tight to it, stopping his fall. Then, with a grunt of effort he hauled Ethan back onto the top of the ridge. He released his grip on the jacket and Ethan dropped to his knees, trembling, panting.

'That was a redwing,' the cragclimber told him. 'Happen there's a nest close by.'

He held out a hand to Ethan to help him to his feet, but again the youth flinched and shrank back. He was white-faced and quaking.

'The wyrme spooked you that bad?' Eli said. He frowned. 'We startled it, is all. It wasn't attacking, just warning us off.'

Ethan shook his head. 'It's not that,' he began. His face crumpled up and he began to shake as sobs convulsed his body. 'My father,' he wailed. 'Back on the plains . . .' He gulped for breath. 'Used to beat me pretty bad . . . The last time, nigh on killed me. Till Cody put a stop to it . . .'

Tears were streaming down his face.

'Permanent.'

Eli watched him thoughtfully.

'It's why we came up here to the high country,' said Ethan, struggling to regain some semblance of composure. 'For they'd have hanged Cody for sure had we not.'

He fell still, his body shuddering as if gripped by a bitter chill. Behind them, coming up the ridge, were the voices of the others. Ethan looked over his shoulder, sniffed and wiped his eyes on his sleeve.

'Don't want them to see I've been blubbering,' he muttered. 'I'm only sorry *you* had to witness it.'

Eli reached out and laid a hand on the youth's shoulder, and this time Ethan did not flinch.

'There's one thing I do know about the weald,' Eli said, his pale-blue eyes fixed on Ethan.

'What's that?' said Ethan, looking up and meeting the cragclimber's gaze. Eli smiled.

'It's a good place for leaving the past behind,' he said.

'You think he does it on purpose?' said Cody. 'Setting us these tasks of his?'

'Of course,' said Cara. 'There isn't anything he does that is without intent or design.'

Cody grunted. 'So he's learning us deliberate,' he observed, and nodded. 'I suspected as much.'

It was the sixth day on their westward trail. They had finally made it over the ridges and were now crossing a barren plain of rock that was dry and honeycombed and awkward to walk upon.

The night before they'd eaten meat from the carcass of a blackwing that had missed its footing, and that Eli had discovered dead at the base of a wedge-shaped rock. Eli had set

Ethan the task of stripping the wyrme, and Cody the task of cooking it. Later, Cody had mended his net, using wyrmegut and a needle that Eli had fashioned for him from a splinter of bone, while Ethan worked on a rucksack made from the pelt of the stormwyrme under the cragclimber's watchful eye.

Cara looked up along the trail. Far ahead were Micah and Eli, the pair of them scanning the horizon with their spy-glasses. The landscape ahead was beginning to look more favourable; level and thick with long blue-green grass that swirled like water in the cool high air. Some way behind them was Ethan, shambling along, pausing now and again to strike loose rocks and pebbles with the walking staff Eli had lent him. He had his rucksack on his back and a watergourd slung over one shoulder.

'He's carrying his own kit,' Cara said, and smiled at the older brother, who blushed under her gaze.

This journey of theirs seemed to be agreeing with him, Cara observed, for Cody had lost the pallor in his complexion and now looked tanned and healthy. He smiled back at her shyly. His teeth were white and strong.

'It's another of Eli's lessons,' he said. 'Told Ethan that everyone should shoulder their own burden. That's why he got him started making that rucksack out of the wyrmehide.' He nodded. 'I ain't seen Ethan so proud of something since . . .'

He fell silent and looked off towards the distant grassland. For a moment, the only sound was the crunching of their boots on the honeycombed rock.

'Since?' Cara said quietly, glancing at Cody.

The muscles in his jaw twitched like he was battling with something going on inside.

'. . . since we left the plains.'

He watched his younger brother in the distance. Ethan had almost caught up with Micah and Eli, and had adopted the purposeful stride the cragclimber had taught him.

'Before we hitched up with you,' Cody went on, 'he would cry himself to sleep every night. Said the wyrmeweald would be the death of him, and never stopped talking about returning to the plains . . .' He paused. 'But he seems happy now though, specially under Eli's guidance.'

'And you, Cody?' said Cara softly. 'Would you like to return to the plains.'

Cody turned to her, and he held her gaze with an intensity that made Cara tremble inside. 'No, Cara,' he said. 'Ain't no place I'd rather be than right here. With you.'

Micah and Eli stopped at the top of a low hill and surveyed the landscape. To their right, the grasslands stretched into the distance, where tall purple mountains lined the horizon. To their left, the ground fell away into undulating folds, before rising up into a distant range of pale peaks.

A short way ahead was a thin stream, like a piece of string, twisting through a dried riverbed. The meltwater floods were over and by the end of halfsummer the water would dry up completely. A stunted tree grew some way up the bank on the near side of the stream, dense with dust-green leaves and clusters of purple fruit. Some branches were broken and hung limp, their splintered breaks glowing white in the late sun; some had been snapped off and lay below on the ground.

'Blackgages,' said Micah, and glanced round.

Cody, Cara and Ethan were further back down the trail, Ethan walking beside the other two, waving his arms about as he talked animatedly in that way he had. Micah smiled, looked back.

'Reckon them'll make good eating,' he said, and headed down the soft sandy bank towards the tree.

The cragclimber continued to scan their surroundings with his spyglass.

'Do you think anyone's ever been this far into the valley country before?' Micah asked, reaching up and picking a ripe fruit.

'It's doubtful,' said Eli, looking around. 'That's a rugged trail we've trod. Most kith go for easier pickings back east.'

Micah's face broke into a smile. 'Which means that I am the first person ever to have plucked a blackgage from this here tree.' He bit off half of the fruit, spat away the stone, then pushed the rest into his mouth. Yellow syrup trickled over his chin.

'The unripe ones'll give you the gripes,' Eli observed, then returned his attention to the magnified view through his spyglass.

Micah stood back and eyed the tree. The ripest fruit was out of reach. He edged slowly round to the back of the tree, which is when he saw it.

A skull, white against the dark rocks. It was human.

Micah approached the bleached skull gingerly, hoping against hope that it might be an isolate; a skull that some wyrme or other – maybe a redwing; they were fierce enough and strong enough – had carried and dropped here far away from the peopled parts of the weald.

But there were other bones. Ribs and femurs. And the tattered remnants of clothes. Backpacks. And a tent frame. A circle of charred rocks . . .

'Eli!' Micah shouted. 'Eli! Eli, come look!'

Eli turned. He slip-slid down the bank, ran round the back of the tree. He saw Micah hunkered down, and saw what he was hunkered down over.

The cragclimber groaned. 'I guess I was wrong,' he said grimly.

Micah climbed to his feet. 'Looks like there were three of them,' he said.

'More,' said Eli. He nodded at the quantity of strewn belongings. He prodded at a length of yellowed shawl with the toe of his boot. 'And they had an infant with them.'

Micah saw something glint, reached down and plucked something of bronze and glass from the dust. He wiped it on the front of his hacketon coat, then looked up at Eli, who nodded gravely.

'If kith were responsible for this slaughter, they would not have left equipment like this behind,' he said.

Micah stared dumbly at the compass. 'Kin?' he said.

Eli shook his head. 'See how their bones are smashed up,' he said, his brow deepfurrow thoughtful. 'They have been dropped. And that ain't kin way.'

Micah swallowed. 'Wyrmes, then.'

Eli did not reply, and Micah watched the cragclimber crouch down. He picked up something dark and opalescent and blew the dust from it. Micah crouched down beside him.

He was holding two huge claws, with dried tendons knotting them together and blueblack scales clinging to the skin. The cut at the end was clean, like it had been made with a knife. The kith had clearly fought back against the wyrme that attacked him.

'It's wyrmes all right,' said Eli grimly. 'But not like any I've encountered before. These claws are more than twice the size of a great whitewyrme's – and they're the biggest wyrmes in the weald.' Eli turned to Micah. 'Or so I thought till now.'

Cara and the two brothers were sore disappointed that they were not to be resting up for the night at the place with the stream and the blackgage tree and the tall boulders that offered relief from the chill wind. But Eli was adamant that they should continue, and Micah seemed happy to go along with the cragclimber's demands.

They followed the stream into the night. It twisted and

meandered, and from the position of the stars, Micah was able to show Cara they were now heading north-west. Cody walked close behind them, his breath coming short and his feet dragging. Ethan was beside him. Like the others, he was weary and footsore. Like them, he did not question the decision to keep going, but concentrated on not stumbling as he trudged on after the cragclimber. It was past midnight when Eli finally stopped.

'We'll rest up here,' he said gruffly. 'Get us some sleep.'

The following day broke misty and cold. A heavy dew had fallen that had soaked into their clothes and that turned to a glistening spray of droplets as Micah shook the wyrmeskin out that he and Cara had been curled up upon.

Ethan and Cody stirred, pulled on their boots and, unbidden, started packing up. Eli was back uptop a ridge, his spyglass raised, staring at something in the far distance to the north. Micah joined him.

'Anything interesting?' he said.

Without saying a word, Eli passed Micah the spyglass. He put it to his eye and focused the lens.

Something appeared before him, far off across the patchgrass plateau, where the plains hit the mountains. It rose out of the swirl of mist – a great cliff-face of pale sandstone, but eroded and weathered in an extraordinary way, unlike anything Micah had seen before in the weald.

'What is it?' Micah asked, his voice little more than a whisper.

'Wyrme galleries,' said Eli simply. 'Biggest, most magnificent I've ever seen.' He frowned. 'And there's only one creature I know of capable of fashioning a roost out of a cliff-face like that . . .'

'You mean?' Micah began.

Eli nodded. 'The great whitewyrme.'

Eight

Zar jolted awake.

There were sounds coming from outside – soft almost imperceptible sounds that mingled with the low whisper of the breeze through the fluted columns of the wyrme galleries. Zar listened. And there they were again. The windwhirr of wingbeats, the sigh of wyrmebreath . . .

Asa had heard them too. He uncoiled himself from the spiral pillar next to her and flexed his wings.

Picking up her kinlance, Zar rose to her feet and looked into her wyrme's pale yellow eyes. He nodded.

They had visitors.

Zar and Asa had discovered the deserted wyrme galleries by chance two months earlier in the savage blast of fullwinter, and taken shelter there. They had explored the vast chambers with their winding pillars and niches, their alcoves and perch-ledges, all carved out of the rock over countless ages by the curved talons of the great whitewyrmes who had once lived there. And they had marvelled at their magnificence.

Later, the kinboy, Kesh, had arrived with his wyrme, Azura. They were wild and savage and smelled of sulphur and blood, and Zar and Asa had been afraid. But then Thrace and Aseel had appeared, and Zar and Asa had felt safe again.

Thrace had explained everything. How the great whitewyrmes who once lived here had shunned those of their kind who kinned with humans, as Aseel had kinned with her and Asa had kinned with Zar. But the colony had abandoned the galleries to search for new lands far from the taint of man, rather than fight the way Thrace and Aseel, and other wyrme-kin, did.

During those bitter days of fullwinter, the older kingirl had taught Zar and Asa how to wield a lance and how to swoop down in attack, shooting deadly jets of flame. This ancient place rising above the rolling grasslands would now be a fortress for kin, Thrace had told her. And Aseel had sent out the call, in deep and resonant wyrmetongue, like the rumbling of a distant storm – a call to other kinned wyrmes to gather here at the wyrme galleries and resist the tide of humans approaching from the east; to stand and fight together in a great host, rather than spread out across the weald, each defending their own territory, as had been the kin way before.

And as Zar had listened she had been aware of Kesh also listening, from the shadows just beyond the fire, crouched at the feet of his wyrme, Azura. She had heard the mounting excitement in his voice as the two of them had whispered together of the war to come.

And she had trembled . . .

Zar crossed the sandstone floor of the chamber soundlessly, the early halflight playing on the smooth white contours of the soulskin she wore. She shrank back into the shadows of a pillar and felt Asa's warm smoky breath at her back. Her heart was beating rapidly in her chest and she tightened her grip on the black tooth-grooved wood of the kinlance to steady herself, before peering out into the chamber beyond.

It was bigger than the chamber Zar and Asa had been sleeping in and, at the far end, opened out onto a ledge. The golden light of dawn was colouring the sky, with pink-flecked clouds streaking the far horizon.

As Zar looked out, the sound of wingbeats grew louder and four great whitewyrmes swooped down out of the sky and landed on the ledge, silently but for the faint *click-scritch* of their claws on the smooth stone. They were large ancient females, their scales crisscrossed with scars and pitted with age. They exhaled great clouds of breath from their horned muzzles as their riders slipped from their backs, lances in hand.

Suddenly, from behind her, Zar heard a growl rise in Asa's throat and felt a hand grip her shoulder and push her violently forward. She stumbled, fell. Her kinlance clattered to the floor just out of reach. She looked over her shoulder to see the kinboy, Kesh, his own lance in his hands, grinning down at her. Behind him, his wyrme Azura, another scarred and ancient female, had her claws poised at Asa's throat, and Zar could see the helpless anger in his glowing amber eyes.

Kesh sniggered unpleasantly. '*So you heard them too,*' he said. He spoke in the language of the great whitewyrmes, but his voice was guttural, challenging. '*Allow me to introduce my kin. Finn, Baal, Timon, Ramilles,*' he said, gesturing to each of the four riders in turn. '*This,*' he announced to them, '*is Hep-zi-bar.*' He broke up her name like he always did, like it was something derisory. '*Or Zar for short.*'

Behind him, Kesh's wyrme Azura greeted the other wyrmes in the soft clicking sighs of wyrmetongue, so much more resonant in the mouths of the great whitewyrmes than their riders.

'*Avaar, Amir, Aakhen, Aluris . . .*'

The ancient females bowed their sinuous necks in turn, their eyes glowing a deep yellow.

Zar climbed slowly to her feet. The wyrmes suited the scale of the cavernous chamber, while she felt horribly small and vulnerable before them. And her face coloured as she looked at the wyrmekin in their yellow-tinged soulskin, who were staring back at her. At the one called Finn, with his dull hooded eyes and sticking-out ears. And at Baal, with his shock of black hair. At Timon, who had thin lips and small dark eyes that were impossible to read. And the one called Ramilles, who was bigger than the others, taller, brawnier, but whose face was hidden inside his yellow-stained soulskin hood.

She glanced back at Kesh. The gathering light gleamed on his jawline, his cheekbones, his greasy red hair.

He stepped forward and shoved Zar hard in the chest. Off balance, she staggered backwards, onto the upraised palms of Baal, who shoved her again. She tottered forwards, and this time it was Finn who pushed her away, shoving her at Timon. Like a bean in a hot skillet she bounced backwards, forwards, sideways, to and fro across the circle, hands pushing her away whenever she came close.

She felt dizzy. Weightless. Each time she was shoved, it jolted. But Hepzibar did not cry out. She would not give them the satisfaction. She clamped her lips together and kept her head held high, which only seemed to encourage Kesh and his friends in this rough game of theirs.

As she was thrown against Kesh, she looked up and smiled. '*Coward*,' she whispered.

With an animal snarl, Kesh pushed her viciously away from him. She hurtled across the floor and struck Ramilles with such force that he was knocked backwards, breaking the circle. His hood fell back, and for a moment Hepzibar stared into his face. Blush-red cheeks. Curly black hair. Blue eyes – blue eyes that stared back at her with a curious mixture of pity and guilt, and admiration for her refusal to be provoked.

Ramilles did not shove her away. Instead he held her steady for a moment, then bent down and picked up her kinlance, which lay at his feet. He handed it to her and glanced over at Kesh for a moment, then back at her.

'*Any friend of Kesh,*' he said, his wyrmetongue softer and more lilting than Kesh's, '*is a friend of mine.*'

Zar stepped back, gripping her lance and breathing heavily. There was contempt in Ramilles' voice – Zar could hear it – but as she looked across at Kesh, she realized that the contempt was not directed at her.

A shaft of bright sunlight was streaming into the galleries and catching the kinboy's red hair. Zar smiled at Kesh and was gratified to see him flinch at her gaze as if she'd struck him.

'*I'll leave you to get reacquainted with your friends,*' she said.

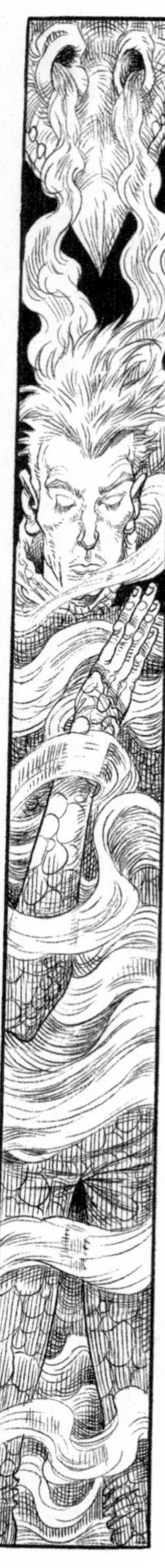

Nine

Over the next few days, other wyrmes and their kin had started to arrive. Many of them. The once silent galleries now sighed and chittered with wyrmetongue.

There were whitewyrmes coiled round the spiral columns of the cavernous central chamber, their riders crouched beneath, conversing in low voices. Others stood in small groups around the walls, the wyrmes inclining their necks and wreathing the kin beside them in coils of aromatic smoke.

Zar made her way across the sandstrewn floor, with Asa, nervous and excited, skittish at her side. They snatched glances at the faces of the strange new arrivals, careful not to let their gaze rest too long, wary of drawing attention to themselves. Zar looked down, and she noticed her soulskin, so white and unsullied compared with those worn by the kin around her.

They had come from all parts of the weald, these

wyrmekin, brought here by their wyrmes, who had answered Aseel's call. And their suits of soulskin – fashioned from the sloughed skin of their individual whitewyrmes – bore the scars of the arduous journeys they had so recently endured. They looked around now. Bemused. Intrigued. None of them had ever seen this place before; a place their wyrmes had been excluded from when they had kinned with them.

Just ahead of her, a large wyrme exhaled a cloud of breath over her kin, a long-limbed youth with spiky blond hair, and Zar watched as the twisting smoke mended his torn and tattered sleeve, restoring it to pristine whiteness as it did so.

Within hours of their arrival, the soulskins of all these kin would be as white as Zar's. But she only had to look into their eyes to know that they had been through things she could hardly even imagine. Beside her, she heard Asa chirr softly.

'*There are so many of them*,' he said, his yellow eyes glowing brightly.

Zar's gaze fell upon two kingirls who had arrived from the jagged ridges a couple of days earlier. Their hair was up, pinned into place with forked slivers of bone, and each of them had a thick black band of sootgrease smeared across their faces from ear to ear, covering their eyes like masks. She watched as they scrutinized their reflections in a shard of polished silverstone and carefully applied fresh grease to their faces with the tips of their fingers.

One of them looked up, her eyes starkwhite against the black mask. Zar quickly looked away, her stomach fluttering.

Above the kingirls, their sleek wyrmes – two young males with daubed black patterns encircling their necks – were wound drowsily round the fluted pillars. Zar and Asa walked past them, their heads down.

Three more kingirls, who had come from the saltflats to the west the day before, stood in the centre of the chamber. They wore lengths of curved willowbark strapped to their feet, that protected their soulskin from the corrosive salt of their territory, but which here in the wyrme gallery clacked on the stone floors. Their wyrmes were old battle-scarred males; one with a splintered foreclaw, another with a jagged tear to his wingtip.

At the base of the columns next to them were four kin from the black pinnacles. They had arrived at the wyrme galleries close on the heels of Kesh's friends from the yellow peaks. Three kingirls, their hair a mass of thin dark plaits, and an older man, who was short and wiry and, it seemed to Zar, never smiled. Their wyrmes – three young males and an older female – were wild-eyed and nervous-looking, and spent most of their time with their long serpentine necks bowed, deep in hushed conversation. Now, though, as Zar and Asa passed by, the wyrmes fell silent and watched them warily until they were out of earshot.

Arriving at the end of the chamber, Zar and Asa stepped between the fluted columns and out onto the broad ledge beyond. They looked up to see two whitewyrmes, riders upon their backs, gliding down through the sky towards the wyrme galleries on rigid outstretched wings.

As they came closer, Zar saw that one kin was a youth with dark hair; the other, a girl, had her hood up and what looked like a coil of rope over one shoulder. Both of them had a kin-lance tucked under their arm that glinted in the early morning sun. Ruddering with their tails and judging the strength of the air currents with the barbels at the corners of their mouths, the two whitewyrmes came in to land on the largest of the jutting rockslabs that lined the ledge.

Zar stepped forwards nervously, aware of Asa trembling at her side. She looked up at the two kin as they slipped from the shoulders of their wyrmes and jumped down deftly onto the ledge in front of her and Asa.

'*Welcome*,' she said, and heard the quaver in her voice.

The kingirl pushed back her hood to reveal a mass of long flaxen hair. She dropped down on one knee till her face was level with Zar's, and Zar was struck by how beautiful she was, with her dark indigo eyes and golden skin.

'*I am Mara. And my companion here is Keel*,' she said, nodding towards the dark-haired youth. '*And who are you, little one?*'

'*This is Zar*,' came a voice. '*And I am Thrace, from the speckled stacks of the valley country to the east. It was my wyrme, Aseel, who sent out the call.*'

Zar and Asa turned to see Thrace standing behind them, her soulskin a dazzling white in the morning sun and fragrant with wyrmesmoke. Her corn-silver hair gleamed and her skin was radiant. Only the delicate smudges of blue below her eyes betrayed the strain she was under.

The black-haired kin looked at Thrace, his eyes as dark and penetrating as his partner's. '*The call took time to reach us,*' he told her. '*Our territory is far to the south – the grasslands where the greywyrmes breed.*' He shook his head. '*Kith gangs have been raiding the wyrmetrails to the east and the herds are thin in number this season.*'

Zar and Asa exchanged glances. Each of the wyrmes and their kin had arrived with similar tales to tell.

'*There are reports of gangs in the saltflats,*' Thrace told them. '*And of scouting parties ranging from the black pinnacles to the yellow peaks.*' Her brow furrowed and, as she continued, a hard edge came into her voice. '*And as for the speckled stacks, they have been overrun, and the wyves of the great whitewyrmes that had been laid there are lost.*' She swept her arm round in a wide arc. '*The colony has abandoned this place,*' she said.

Keel tutted grimly, his dark eyes smouldering.

'*But we shall not,*' Thrace added defiantly. '*That is why Aseel has called you.*'

The kingirl, Mara, straightened up. '*When the fullwinter snows thawed and the returning greywyrmes were so few in number, we went off in search of the cause. And we found it,*' she said, her voice hushed. '*In the passes through the grey mountains. Entire herds, slaughtered and left to rot, and for nothing more than their flameoil.*'

Asa growled deep down in his throat and twists of smoke rose up from his quivering nostrils. Zar reached out and laid a hand on his neck.

'*That was when we saw the kin of the yellow peaks flying high overhead*,' Mara continued, her grip tightening on her kinlance, '*and they passed on your wyrme's call. So we came.*'

'*And Aseel and I thank you for that*,' Thrace told her.

Mara and Keel looked around at the gathered wyrmes and their kin. Behind them, their own wyrmes chittered softly to one another, their eyes amber-flushed with expectation.

'*Up until now we have defended our own territories, and hunted those kith who have encroached upon them*,' Thrace went on. '*But now they are too numerous to resist. Unless we act as one.*'

'*But that is not the kin way*,' Mara objected, and her wyrme inclined his head and opened his jaws.

'*We have always hunted the kith down when and where we've found them*,' he breathed huskily. '*Seeking to deter others from following in their wake . . .*'

'*Yet, unlike kith*,' the female wyrme broke in, '*we have never gloried in death and destruction for its own sake.*' She looked across at the male wyrme, then back at Thrace. '*What you are proposing will mean a great and terrible price shall be paid by the kith when our kin's*' – she hesitated – '*bloodfrenzy is awakened.*' The wyrme's voice was as soft as rain plashing on screefall, but insistent. '*Are you prepared for that, Thrace of the speckled stacks?*'

Thrace trembled, and as the wyrme's eyes glowed a

deepening red she could not hold her gaze. Zar saw the muscles in the kingirl's cheeks twitch as her jaws ground hard together.

'*It is something we must* all *decide*,' Thrace said at length, and she turned and walked away.

Ten

Zar followed Asa up the dark sloping passageway, trailing her fingertips along the clawscratch lines and interlocking circles carved into the walls. The shadows receded behind them, and they emerged into dazzling sunlight.

It was silent, and the heatshimmer air was still. For a moment, Zar thought they were the only ones up there at the top of the wyrme galleries. But then Asa inclined his long neck and Zar turned to see her friend, Thrace.

She was at the far side of the great flat clifftop, staring out across the scrubland towards the mountain ridges far beyond. She was alone.

Zar suddenly felt as if they were intruding and she turned to Asa, who nodded. The pair of them were on the point of slipping away when Thrace spoke.

'*Bloodfrenzy*,' she said. Her voice was soft and soughing. '*It is not in the nature of the great whitewyrmes . . .*'

Zar and Asa exchanged glances.

'But it is *in the nature of humans.'*

She paused and turned. Her dark eyes were stormy and intense. *'Which is why, when they sought a means to fight back against the human invasion of their lands, the most far-sighted of the whitewyrmes kinned with us.'*

Thrace returned her gaze to the distant mountains.

'You see, we wyrmekin are theirs. Body and soul. They find us, the lost or abandoned children of their enemies, and they raise and nurture us. They teach us their ways and their speech. They offer us the gift of flight on their backs, and banish all fear from our lives . . .'

Zar and Asa crossed the clifftop and stood beside Thrace at the edge of the precipitous drop.

'And in return, we show them how to kill.'

She looked down, and Zar saw how Thrace's lower lip trembled. When Thrace spoke again, her windsigh voice had taken on a hard edge, as though a gale was approaching.

'Not as a whitewyrme kills,' she said, *'for food – quickly, cleanly. But as humans do. With cunning and cruelty and a lust for destruction. A frenzy for'* – Thrace paused for a moment – *'blood.'*

She turned away and stared back into the vastness of the weald. Her hair hung down over her face.

'When I think of what Aseel and I are capable of, what all *of us kin and wyrmes, acting together, might be capable of . . .'* Thrace bit her lip. *'It frightens me, Zar, and yet I can see no other way.'*

Zar reached out to take Thrace's hand, but the older kingirl flinched at her touch, shrugged her away.

'I need to talk to Aseel,' Thrace said, her voice constricted and thin. *'Find Aseel for me.'*

Zar and Asa left her standing on the cliff-edge, head bowed, back pokerstraight, kinlance gripped in her hands, and headed back down into the galleries. They descended through the high-ceilinged chambers, with their grooved pillars and slanting shadows now occupied by wyrmes and their kin who quietly tended to them.

Some kin were oiling their wyrmes' feet; others were holding out grubs on the end of their lances for their wyrmes to toast with fiery breath, while still more sat beneath the pillars around which their wyrmes were coiled, and conversed in quiet whispers of wyrmetongue.

There was no sign of Aseel.

Zar and Asa took care to avoid the chamber Kesh and Azura and the yellow peaks kin had made their own, and took the sloping clawscratch tunnel down to the store chambers beneath. At the arched entrance to the stores, Asa craned his neck forward into the darkness and exhaled softly.

Flamelight flickered on the walls as they entered.

It was the first time Zar had been down here since half-summer had filled the weald outside with such an abundance of fresh food. It was cooler than she remembered, and she had forgotten the sweetsour fragrance of smoke and vinegar that laced the air. The ceiling towered far above her head; the walls were rough-hewn and unadorned.

Zar looked at Asa, and the wyrme nodded. They should go a little further.

They crossed the floor of the cavernous underground chamber, the shifting air echoing softly with the sounds of the wyrme galleries above. They walked along the broad storage grooves gouged into the rock that ran the length of the underground cavern, where leathergrubs and flame-dried meat lay stacked in geometric patterns; they picked their way between the deep brine pits cut out of the rock floor and containing pickled stipplebeet and soused damselfly larvae.

Zar paused and peered down into one of the pits. These stores, carefully stocked by the colony, then abandoned, had kept her and Asa alive through that last bitter fullwinter, and she silently gave thanks to the greatwyrmes before continuing.

At the far end of the cavern, they came to a tunnel that led down even deeper below the store chambers. Despite spending the whole of fullwinter in the wyrme galleries, Zar had never ventured beyond this point. The inky blackness of the tunnel had always intimidated her, and did so now, even with Asa beside her.

The young whitewyrme cocked his head to one side, barbels quavering. He stared down the tunnel, then back at her.

'Can you hear it?'

Zar listened, then frowned. She could hear something. Her skin clammed up and goosebumped with unease, and she was relieved to have Asa with her.

Wyrmesounds. Soft breathy whispers. Chittering, like a soft breeze blowing through riverreeds.

Asa turned to Zar, his eyes glowing amber. There were wyrmes down there somewhere, and they were talking. Asa closed his jaws and the flamebreath was extinguished, plunging them into pitch darkness. Zar reached out and took her wyrme's claw in one hand, and Asa led her down the tunnel.

With her free hand trailing along the wall, Zar noted that its surface was scratched with tiny marks, grooves much smaller than those made by the curved claws of a great whitewyrme. She was puzzled for a moment, but then it occurred to her that these clawmarks, crisscrossed and experimental, were the marks of infant wyrmes.

They continued through the darkness in silence. The wyrmesounds grew more distinct.

Asa stopped abruptly and Zar bumped against him. There was a faint glow illuminating the tunnel ahead. The pair of them edged forward and peered round the curving tunnel wall. Beyond was a vast shadowy chamber, illuminated with pale flickering light.

They had found a secret place, far below the open airy galleries above – a place in which to nurture the most precious thing the wyrme colony had possessed. Its young.

For this, Zar realized, was a nursery.

Scarcely daring to breathe, she inched closer. The light was coming from a pool of oil set in a shallow dip in the floor, its surface dancing with purple and yellow flames. It flickered on the walls and high domed ceiling, and on the pearlsheen scales of a whitewyrme sitting on its haunches at the centre of the cave. Zar saw the black zigzag scar that ran down the side of its white neck.

Aseel. It was Aseel. No other whitewyrme had such a distinctive marking.

But what was he doing here?

She looked round at Asa. The light spilling out from the cave tipped the edge of his snout, the tops of his crest; it filled his eyes. He responded to her inquisitive look with the briefest shake of his head. They should not disturb him.

Just beyond Aseel, half-shielded by the curve of his back and folded wings, was another whitewyrme. A female.

She was curled up in a spiral, her tail tucked under her shoulders and her head resting upon the curve of her back. She was looking up at Aseel, thin strings of smoke trickling from her nostrils.

Aseel said something, but his voice was too low for Zar to hear what. He inclined his sinuous neck and the female raised hers. They intertwined gently, until they were muzzle to muzzle and looking into one another's yellow eyes. They whispered to each other in soft lilting words of wyrmetongue, still too quiet for Zar to make out – though their meaning was unmistakeable.

Zar's stomach churned. Aseel had a mate . . .

The female unwound her neck from Aseel's, and Zar caught sight of a small bundle nestling at the centre of her coiled body.

It was a child. An infant boy.

He was sleeping, swaddled in wyrmeslough, his little head peeking out of the swathes of white as the two wyrmes lowered their heads, chirring lightly, and breathed warm sweet smoke over him.

Something stirred inside Zar. Aseel's mate had kinned . . .

She had found herself a defenceless human child and been drawn to enfold him in her coils, bond with him, nurture and protect him. She would clothe him in the skin from her own body and share with him the gift of flight. And one day the time would come when he would give her gifts in return – human cunning and savagery, and the ability to fight and destroy in order to protect not only her, but all wyrmekind, from the predations of kith.

To be kinned. It was wonderful and terrible at the same time. Beside her, Zar felt a tremble ripple through Asa's body. He felt the same way as she did.

This was too intimate a scene on which to intrude. Quietly they withdrew and retraced their footsteps – along the underground stores, up the zigzag passageways and through the chambers above, until they emerged in the topmost gallery to find the place crowded.

The whitewyrmes and their kin had all gathered on the ledges. Their wings were flexed and their kinlances quivered as they looked out across the weald. Zar turned to a kingirl standing close by, her arm wrapped around her wyrme's neck.

'*What's happening?*' she asked.

The kingirl from the jagged ridges turned and shook her head, her eyes flashing white from behind the black mask of sootgrease. Her whitewyrme's barbels quivered as he sniffed at the air

'*The taint*,' the kingirl said. '*There's kith close by.*'

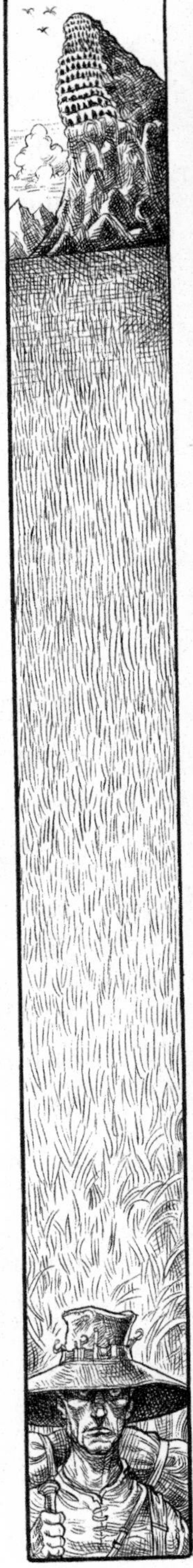

Eleven

'We must get away from here,' Eli announced.

He closed his spyglass and pushed it back inside the pocket of his hacketon jacket.

'Are . . . are we in danger?' Micah asked, staring ahead at the great sandstone cliffs that rose up from the plains in the far distance.

'We are,' Eli replied curtly and turned away, motioning for the others to follow.

The cold misty start to the day became hot and oppressive as the sun rose in the sky. All around them the grasslands seemed to stretch on for ever, with the bluegreen grass swaying languidly as they waded through it. Above their heads, the air thrummed with clouds of midges.

Sometime after midday, banks of high turbulent black cloud rolled in from the west, and the first rain started to fall in the late afternoon. The wind strengthened, the temperature dropped.

Eli neither eased up nor suggested they take shelter. He allowed no rests at all. They gulped water from their gourds and canteens as they walked and, since none of them had anything to eat in their packs, they went hungry.

They kept on in silence. As dusk set in, Eli glanced back at the horizon behind them, then addressed the others.

'We keep on,' he said, his voice edged with defiance, though no one had suggested they should not.

The light faded and the rain eased some, but the wind did not abate. It drove the raindrops needlesharp-cold into their faces, and all five of them were forced to stoop into it, their heads lowered and the brims of their hats tugged down. Night fell, and still they kept on – blindly, one in front of the other, guided by their ears rather than their eyes.

'Damn it to hell!' Cody exclaimed as Ethan kicked his heel, and the both of them went stumbling forward into the darkness. 'That's the third time.'

He bumped into Micah, who was walking just ahead of him, his raised hands shoving his shoulder blades. And Micah blundered into Cara, cussing under his breath. Cara let out a small uncertain gasp, then righted herself. She reached back for Micah, who found her hand and squeezed it reassuringly.

'I'm *sorry*, Cody,' Ethan protested. 'It's so dark and slippy 'n all. And I'm tired . . .'

'Stop your whining,' Cody told him sharply.

'Hush up, *all* of you,' Eli's voice hissed from out of the darkness ahead, his voice clipped with irritation.

'Just hold back a step,' Cody growled at his brother.

'All right, all right,' Ethan whispered back.

The cragclimber kept on. Footsore and boneweary, the others followed. The wind howled like something feral. Midnight came and went, and still Eli kept marching, the others following the steady thud of his footfall and the *tap-tap-tap* of his walking staff in a trance of exhaustion.

Finally Eli did call out for a halt. Micah and Cara stopped in their tracks, and Cody came up behind them, his breath low and rasping.

'Happen we've put as much distance between us and them galleries as we can for now,' Eli told them, and though Micah could not see the expression on the cragclimber's face, he could hear tension in his voice. 'Keep your packs close to hand,' he told them. 'And be ready to move at a moment's notice.'

Micah crouched down in the darkness and slipped his backpack from his shoulders.

'What did you see back there, Eli?' he asked. 'Through the spyglass . . .'

There was a flash, followed by a dull yellow glow that emanated from inside the folds of Eli's leather hacketon as the cragclimber lit the stub of a tallow candle and shielded it from the rain. The pale light illuminated his face, and those of Micah and Cara, and Cody, who was looking around wildly; but not Ethan's face.

For Ethan was not there.

Twelve

'Cody?'

Nothing. Again. Ethan's heart hammered inside his chest.

'Cody?'

Ethan's voice was no more than an urgent whisper. He wanted to shout out for his brother, but dared not, for fear of invoking Eli's ire and his brother's scorn. He'd been rebuked enough for one day. 'Cody . . .'

Still nothing.

Ethan stopped in his tracks. Listened. He'd been guided through the darkness by the sound of his brother's footfalls and rasping breath just up ahead of him. But they were gone now. There was nothing but rainhiss and windhowl. And he was alone.

He wiped the back of his hand across his face, trying to suppress the panic that churned in his stomach, and set off again. A brisk loping walk soon stumbled into a lurching trot. The wet grass was waist-high. It slashed at his legs, bladesharp and needle-tipped. Stones crunched beneath the soles of his heavy boots.

'Cody, Cody, Cody,' he murmured under his breath in time to their clomping.

But Cody did not reply. And Ethan couldn't see him – he couldn't see *anything*. He stopped a second time, his head spinning, scalp itching. He wanted to cry.

What if he was heading off in the wrong direction? What if every step he took was increasing the gap between him and the others?

What should he *do*?

Then he felt it. A blast of air, warm and sulphurous against his cheek. His skin crawled, clammy and chill. His heart thudded harder inside his chest.

It was a gust of wind, was all, he reasoned, just stronger than the rest. It had slammed into his face for a moment, blowing back the brim of his hat, tugging at his jacket, and then was gone. A gust of wind . . .

Suddenly, and without any warning, it was back again. Warm, odorous, buffeting wind. It swirled around him in a powerful updraught. Ethan raised his hands above his head automatically, protectively.

There was a screech. Then another. He heard wingbeats.

Then, abruptly, there was a flurry of noise and movement. Clawscratch. Wingbeat.

Stoneshift.

Something had landed directly in front of him. He peered

unseeing into the blackness. There was something behind him too, and at his sides, left and right.

He could hear them.

Creaking, like old leather. Rustle and scrape. And curious harsh sounds, like driving hail and rumbling thunder – but close by and quite separate from the hiss of the windswept rain.

And then, all at once, he could see them too. Five enormous wyrmes standing around him. Their white-scale bodies were stained red from the glow that emanated from their gaping jaws, fire burning deep in their throats. It was like staring into embered furnaces.

The wyrmes inclined their necks towards him, their wings raised and the scalloped edges disappearing into the darkness. Their eyes pulsed dark amber, and from their gaping jaws came the curious noises of hail and thunder.

The creatures were talking.

From the darkness beyond their upraised wings, there came sharp cries, like dogsnarl and spindrift. The wyrme in front of Ethan folded its wings, and there, sitting at the base of its neck, was a hooded figure.

Ethan stared, wide-eyed, as the figure reached up and lowered the hood. It was a youth. Pale-skinned, younger than him, he judged, with sharp eyes and wisps of red hair plastered to his forehead. His angular body was encased in a tight-fitting suit of white scaly skin, identical to that of the whitewyrme he was seated upon. Gripped in his hand was a long black lance, which he lowered and levelled at Ethan's neck. His eyes narrowed and he hissed venomously, his teeth bared.

From all sides, Ethan heard the harsh hissing sound being echoed. His stomach knotted as he glanced around. Each of the whitewyrmes, he now saw, had a rider upon its back. They were all dressed the same, in clinging suits of wyrmeskin, the hoods raised; they each gripped a long, ferocious-looking lance, which they were pointing at him.

Ethan turned back to the first rider and attempted to smile. But his jaws felt stiff, and his lips tight.

'I . . . I don't mean no harm,' he said. 'My name's Ethan.'

The rider cocked his head to one side and smiled back at Ethan. But it was a cold violent smile, devoid of empathy or friendship or warmth. His lips parted and he let out a keening snarl. The wyrme he was seated on raised its neck and replied in a soft whispering rattle. Ethan swallowed hard, too terrified to imagine what they might be saying.

'He is timorous, this one,' Azura observed, the barbels at her jaws trembling.

'He is kith,' Kesh snarled.

'Travelling alone? They never travel alone.' Timon's small dark eyes darted round from one kin to the other.

'Some do,' his wyrme, Aakhen, corrected him, and Avaar, Amir and Aluris nodded their agreement. *'If you had lived as long as us, you would know that kith come in all sorts . . .'*

'Filth is filth, however they choose to travel,' said Kesh, his voice as harsh as tumbling scree.

'So what shall we do with him?' Ramilles said, prodding the kithyouth in the back with his lance.

Kesh looked across at the older kin. *'Slowdeath,'* he said, and bared his teeth. The word crackled like lightning. *'We should make an example of him, like we did with those hunters up on the northern rises.'* His mouth twisted into a vicious grin. *'We should kill him slowly and with great care. And then display him as a warning to others.'*

'It took them a long time to die,' said Finn, his hooded eyes blinking as he remembered the scene.

'I shall not soon forget it,' Avaar said. Her barbels quivered as she shook her head, and when she spoke again, her voice was soft and fragile. *'To conceive of killing a creature in such a manner . . .'*

She left the words hanging. The other whitewyrmes dipped their heads.

'That's why you have us,' Kesh said, his mouth twisted into a malevolent smile.

Azura turned her head towards him, her eyes flecked with red. *'And you take such delight in it,'* she breathed.

'Perhaps we should dismember this one,' said Timon.

'Or roast him,' said Baal. He ignored the uneasy quivering of his wyrme, Amir, beneath him.

'Certainly we should take his claws and his fangs,' said Finn. *'As they do to wyrmekind . . .'*

Kesh shook his head and fixed Ramilles with a stare. '*I have a better idea,*' he said.

Ethan listened dread-soaked as the strange talk whirled round about him.

All at once, the youth with the red hair lunged forward with his lance, pushing it between Ethan's ankles and twisting, knocking him off balance and sending him sprawling to the ground. With yelps, the other kin jumped from their wyrmes, and planting their lances in the ground, fell on him.

Ethan tried to get up, but one of the kin grabbed his legs while the youth with the thin lips and small darting eyes shoved him hard in the chest, pushing his shoulders back against the ground.

Behind them, one of the wyrmes turned its head and sent out a jet of flame. It scorched the grass to blackened straw, which a second wyrme scythed away with a single sweep of a great curved talon. Ethan felt himself being dragged across onto the bare patch of grassland, which was prickly and still smoking. His arms were pulled straight above his head, his legs were splayed. Bindings were tied round his wrists, his ankles, and secured to spikes that the kin were hammering into the ground with lumps of rock.

Ethan squirmed and writhed, but the bindings held fast. He could not move. The rain splashed into his face, masking the tears that streamed down his cheeks.

The youth stooped down over him. His eyes glittered cold, malignant.

'Wh . . . what are you going to do with me?' Ethan moaned.

The youth's tongue flicked across his lower lip. 'I . . . open you up . . .' he said. The rasped words were faltering and sounded unnatural in his mouth. He pulled his kinlance from the ground and trailed its point from the base of Ethan's neck to the pit of his belly. 'From here . . . to here . . .'

Behind him, the wyrmes trembled. One of them let out a long bleak sigh, smoke coiling up from her flared nostrils. The youth smiled as Ethan began to sob.

'. . . slowly.'

'*It is too much*,' Avaar protested, and the other ancient whitewyrme females nodded their heads in agreement.

Kesh's mouth twisted into a petulant pout as he turned to his wyrme, Azura.

'You *understand, don't you?*' he said, staring into her glowing eyes. '*The kith must fear us if we're to turn them back*.'

Azura looked at the other whitewyrmes, then inclined her head. '*Let our kin do what they must*,' she breathed.

Kesh smiled triumphantly, his sharp crooked teeth glinting in the red light. '*Slowdeath!*' he hissed.

Timon and Baal smiled. Finn nodded. But their whitewyrmes, Aakhen, Amir and Avaar, stepped back and turned away.

'*He glories in the killing, this kin of yours*,' Ramilles' wyrme, Aluris, sighed to Azura.

Azura's eyes flashed red, but she did not disagree.

Kesh raised his lance and pressed it against the skin at Ethan's neck, only for Ramilles to step forward and knock the lance from the younger kin's grasp.

'*No*,' he said. '*Aluris is right. Let this be done quickly*.'

Kesh turned on Ramilles, his eyes burning with hatred, and looked for a moment as if he'd strike him, but stopped when he saw the knife in the older kin's hand. Kesh's snarl turned to a bitter smile.

'*As you wish, Ramilles*,' he said.

Thirteen

'*Stop!*'

The cragclimber's voice rang out across the high grassy plains. His eyes hardened as he peered through the gloom.

There were five whitewyrmes and five riders. The wyrmes were ancient and female, their yellow-stained scales, crisscrossed with scars, suggested to Eli that they came from the sulphur peaks far to the north-east. Their kin were all young males, clad in soulskin and armed with black venom-tipped lances. The brawniest of them, a youth with dark curly hair, was hunkered down over the boy, Ethan, holding a knife to his neck while the others watched.

At his call, all eyes turned to the cragclimber.

The rain had stopped falling and the wind had eased off, leaving the blue-green grass limp and diamond-dropped. The first blush of dawn was giving way to a drab grey of overcast skies, and dense air that was warm and clinging and smelled of bruised leaves.

As he took a step forward, his arms raised and jacket unbuttoned to show he carried no weapons, Eli saw a couple of the wyrmes exchange glances, then look back at him. Three of the kin raised their lances. One of them, wiry and angular with red hair plastered to his forehead, stepped forward, his mouth set in a grim line of hatred. Behind him, his wyrme growled softly, a thin coil of grey smoke twisting up from her nostrils.

'Eli,' Ethan murmured.

The look on the boy's face mirrored the sound of his voice, which was filled with relief and gratitude and hope. And dread. He struggled to move, but the bindings at his arms and legs held him fast. The dark-haired youth pushed him back down.

'Eli?' Ethan said again, quieter, faltering.

Eli did not reply. Instead, he looked over the heads of the kin who had turned to confront him, and into the eyes of their whitewyrmes beyond, each in turn. Inside his chest, he could feel his heart hammering, fit to burst. The wiry kin with the red hair and hate-filled eyes blocked his path, his lips twisted into a malevolent sneer.

Eli did not meet his gaze, but focused rather on the ancient whitewyrme who stood behind the youth. Forcing himself to breathe deeply, evenly, the cragclimber cleared his throat, opened his mouth and spoke in the language of the great whitewyrmes.

Wyrmetongue.

'*I am Eli Halfwinter*,' he said, '*friend to Jura of the green haven, and her wyrme, Asra*.' His voice was harsh and guttural, like meltwater coursing over a gravel bed. '*And as friend of the kin I come to plead for the life of the boy . . .*'

The red-haired youth, lance in hand, thrust his face into Eli's. '*Kith filth*,' he snarled.

Behind him, the whitewyrme's eyes flickered. '*You speak the tongue of the wyrmes*,' she breathed, momentarily impressed before her voice hardened. '*Yet I do not know of this Asra or his kin of whom you speak . . .*'

The red-haired youth dropped down and scythed Eli's legs from under him with a swing of his lance, before leaping onto the cragclimber's chest.

'I rip your heart out!' he screeched in words Eli had no difficulty understanding as he raised the black lance above his head. 'And feed it to the boy!'

The kin with the curly dark hair sprang up from beside Ethan and punched the red-headed youth squarely in the jaw, following the blow with a kick to the ribs that sent him sprawling. Behind the two kin, their respective wyrmes squared up to each other, their eyes blazing red and plumes of smoke rising from their flared nostrils.

'*Ramilles and I know of Asra and Jura of the green haven*,' the dark-haired kin's whitewyrme hissed at the other. '*And we would like to hear more from this kith before your kin ends his life*.'

'*As would I*,' came a clear voice from beyond the circle of wyrmes and kin.

Winded, Eli propped himself up on his elbows and squinted into the early morning light.

'Thrace!' he gasped.

FOURTEEN

'Eli Halfwinter?' the kingirl said softly. She raised a slender hand and pushed her corn-silver hair back behind her ears.

She was seated astride her great whitewyrme, Aseel, her long legs wrapped around the base of his magnificent arched neck. Behind them, coming into land, was a young whitewyrme with a second kingirl on its back.

Eli got slowly to his feet, aware that the kin around him had their eyes on Thrace, and were backing away. 'You have the girl, Hepzibar, with you,' he said. 'And her wyrmeling.'

The kingirl nodded. 'It's Zar now,' she told him, and her whitewyrme trilled softly. 'And Asa is no longer the wyrmeling he once was.'

'Zar,' Eli repeated,

From behind them, there came a snort of disgust. '*You know this kith filth?*' said the kinyouth with the red hair as he rose to his feet. His lip was split from where Ramilles had punched him, and blood had spilled down onto his soulskin, dark red against the sulphur yellow. He bent down and picked up his kinlance, then spat blood onto the ground.

'Do not harm them, Kesh,' Thrace said, her grip tightening on her own lance.

Azura growled, only to be silenced by Aseel's blood-red glare.

'But they brought the taint here,' Kesh said defiantly, backing towards his wyrme, Azura, his eyes fixed on Thrace. *'These* friends *of yours,'* he sneered. *'And anyway, it was us who found them. Their lives are ours!'*

He reached up and placed a hand on his wyrme's back for reassurance. Azura looked down at him, the colour in her eyes changing from deep red to soft amber as she inclined her neck.

Ramilles was standing with his wyrme, Aluris, his face flushed with a mixture of shame and indignation. *'I'm sorry, Thrace,'* he said. *'We wanted to be the first to the kill, to show what the yellow peaks kin could do . . .'*

'You apologize to her!*'* Kesh half shouted, half screamed at the dark-haired youth. *'For hunting down kith! Who is she? She's just kin. Like us. No better, no worse. Her wyrme called and we came, and now they deny us our kill! Are we going to stand for this?'* He turned to the others, who stood, heads bowed, leaning back against their wyrmes. *'We're the yellow peaks kin. And we kill kith our own way. No one tells us what to do . . .'* His voice became pleading, almost tearful. *'Finn, Timon, Baal . . . ?'*

No one spoke.

Ramilles turned his back on Kesh, and his wyrme, Aluris, arched her neck and breathed white smoke over him. The other kin stepped back to their own wyrmes. Kesh looked over and saw Zar watching him, her expression a mixture of pity and contempt. The blood drained from his face.

'*Then to hell with you!*' Kesh screeched. '*To hell with you all!*'

He braced his arm and sprang up onto Azura's back. He gripped on with his legs, his kinlance held tight in one hand while with the other he raised his hood. Azura's eyes blazed red as she looked at Aseel and Thrace.

'*You show my kin no respect*,' she hissed.

Azura raised her wings and beat them back and forth, kicking off with her feet as she did so, and the whitewyrme and her rider rose up into the mist-choked air. Kesh twisted round, his eyes glinting from the shadows inside his hood.

'*I* shall *have my kill*,' he snarled.

Azura's long serpentine tail switched to and fro behind her as she soared higher. Kesh gripped her dorsal ridge, then leaned to one side. The two of them wheeled round in the sky, and flew off towards the clearing mist on the far horizon.

Their long shadows fell before them. They were heading away from the wyrme galleries.

'*Let them go*,' said Ramilles wearily. '*It's like last fullwinter when Kesh quarrelled over our quarters, and stormed off. Azura will bring him back when the fire has left his blood.*'

'*Kesh has an unusual taste for cruelty*,' said Aluris. '*And Azura indulges him.*'

Around her, the other female whitewyrmes nuzzled their kin, enveloping them in wreaths of wyrmesmoke – but said nothing.

Aseel surveyed the four kith and their wyrmes, his eyes dark and barbels trembling at the sides of his mouth. '*If we're going to resist the coming kith we must all act as one*,' he said in a voice as soft and gentle as a sigh. '*You do understand that, don't you?*'

The wyrmes met his gaze; their kin stared down at the ground.

'*We understand*,' said Aluris.

'*Kesh has gone*,' said Thrace, '*but perhaps the rest of you should return to the wyrme galleries.*' She nodded towards Eli and the youth. '*I will deal with these two.*'

Ramilles followed her gaze. He nodded skeptically, but made no objections. '*As you wish*,' he said.

With that, he jumped onto Aluris's back. Beside him, Finn, Timon and Baal climbed up onto the shoulders of their own whitewyrmes, Avaar, Aakhen and Amir. Together, the four whitewyrmes and their riders took to the air and soared back across the sky with slow steady wingbeats toward the distant wyrme galleries.

Thrace swung her leg over Aseel's neck and jumped lightly to the ground. Beside her, Zar did the same. Meanwhile, Eli had waded back through the long grass to the scorched patch where Ethan had been pegged out. He crouched down and began tugging at the knots that bound the boy's ankles and wrists.

'There's a knife at my belt,' Ethan told him.

Eli nodded, shifted Ethan's jacket across and, gripping the handle, pulled it free. He sliced through the tethers one by one. Ethan sat up and rubbed at the chafed skin.

'Thank you, Eli,' he said, and he swallowed uncomfortably. 'For everything. I . . . I sure am sorry I got lost like I did . . .'

The cragclimber shrugged. 'It happens,' he said brusquely.

He looked up to see that Thrace and Zar were standing there looking down at him. He handed Ethan back his knife and climbed to his feet.

'This here is Ethan,' he said, nodding at the boy, who was staring open-mouthed at Thrace. 'We've been sharing the trail. We came west over the jagged ridges, following the blackwing trails.' He frowned. 'We stopped when we saw the whitewyrme galleries. I figured we would not be welcome there.'

Thrace nodded thoughtfully. 'I owe you my life, Eli Halfwinter,' she said. 'So do Zar and Asa. But that means little to my fellow kin. They have come from every corner of the weald to the galleries,' she went on. 'Wyrmes and their kin.' Her voice dropped to an urgent whisper. 'We have gathered to put a stop to the encroachment of the kith once and for all – and you must be far from here when that happens.'

She paused, and looked deep into Eli's eyes, then reached out and rested a hand on his arm. Eli held her gaze.

'You are a good man, Eli Halfwinter,' she said. 'But I cannot protect you if you do not leave this place.'

'I understand,' Eli told her. He nodded earnestly. 'You have just saved my life, Thrace,' he told her. 'And Ethan's. And I consider that a debt repaid. We shall leave now – and may the Maker protect you, and little Zar here.'

'*We will protect our kin*,' said Aseel in a voice like distant thunder. And Asa nodded. '*Whatever is to come*,' he added, looking at Thrace with his bright yellow eyes.

Thrace made no reply. It was like she was staring right through the cragclimber. Eli turned, and he and Ethan followed Thrace's gaze.

The others were approaching from their hiding places in the long plains grass. Cody, Cara and Micah. They had seen the sulphur peaks' kin and their wyrmes flying overhead. And from the looks on their faces, and the loaded spitbolts clutched to their chests, it seemed they were fearing the worst.

Eli glanced back at Thrace. She was standing motionless, her dark eyes pit-black and intense against the deathly pallor of her skin and the wind rippling the ash-gold strands of her hair. Behind her, a shudder rippled through Aseel's great body and his eyes gleamed a darkening red.

As they approached, shielding their eyes from the low sun, Micah, Cara and Cody saw the wyrmes and stopped. Eli waved for them to approach, and both Cara and Cody quickened their pace, but Micah stopped dead in his tracks.

He was not looking at Ethan or Eli. Nor at Zar. Nor at the

two wyrmes who stood beside them, smoke billowing from their mouths. Instead, he was staring at the beautiful kingirl in the shimmering white soulskin, statue-still and open-mouthed.

'You,' he murmured.

Fifteen

'When we left, Aseel and I flew to the high lakes. And when they froze over, we headed for the wyrme galleries that the great whitewyrmes had deserted . . .' Thrace paused. 'We wintered there, with Zar and Asa,' she said, her eyes scanning the rolling plains around them.

Aseel was standing a little way off with Zar and Asa, out of earshot, but with his yellow eyes fixed on his kin.

'You left me,' said Micah, aware of how choked his voice sounded. He stole a glance at Thrace, and immediately wished he hadn't.

She looked so beautiful, her body toned and sleek in the white soulskin and her eyes dark and impossible to read behind the tresses of golden-white hair. It seemed a lifetime ago that they had lain together in the winter den; that they had fought and defeated the winter caller on the snowy cliffside – and Thrace and Aseel had flown off into the marbled grey sky. Yet how long was it since the bite of fullwinter? Three months? Four at most . . .

Micah felt the old familiar pain deep in his chest. The pain he had felt as he watched Thrace leave. The pain he felt whenever he allowed himself to think about this beautiful kingirl.

He turned away from her and stared out across the flat plain of jumbled rocks and swaying grass. In the middle distance, some way to the left of Zar and the two wyrmes, were the others. They were at the makeshift camp where they'd rested up, concealing themselves in the long grass while Eli had gone to beg for Ethan's life. Now they were gathering their kit together.

The lanky fair-haired youth was stooped over his rucksack. Cody was down on his haunches beside him, and the pair of them were exchanging items, making their two packs equal in weight. Eli had just returned from a nearby spring, three watergourds slung from one shoulder and four leather bottles gripped in his hands. Cara was sitting crosslegged, her kit packed and on her back, pretending not to watch Micah and Thrace, but finding it impossible not to.

'I had to go,' said Thrace, and Micah trembled at the sadness in her voice. 'I am kinned with Aseel, and that cannot be broken . . . But it was hard to leave you, Micah.' She fell still, then said, 'What did you do after I left? Where did you go?'

Micah swallowed hard and forced himself not to look at

the kingirl. He was painfully aware how conspicuous they both looked, standing out here, away from the others, talking in whispers. Yet he couldn't tear himself away.

'Eli and I tried to get to Jura's cave in the green haven,' he said, his voice low, 'but fullwinter defeated us. We ended up stumbling across a valley haven called Deephome.' He paused. 'The winter caller wasn't dead. He followed us there. Almost killed us . . .'

The winter caller. A killer, enslaved and trained by the valley keld. Ever since Micah, Eli and Thrace had taken the life of one of their gang – Redmyrtle, a cavern-dwelling cannibal hag – these keld had been out for revenge. The winter caller was dead now but, as Micah knew, the threat of the keld would never die. They inhabited the deep dark places underground, ensnaring the unwary, corrupting the innocent and feeding off the basest instincts of those kith who traded with them. Micah loved the weald, but he hated this evil that lurked beneath its surface . . .

'But you survived,' said Thrace. 'You are here now.'

'It's a long story,' said Micah, looking up and meeting Thrace's gaze. The pain in his chest grew like a bruise.

'I hurt you,' Thrace said softly, reaching out and touching his hand. 'I did not mean to hurt you.'

Despite himself, Micah thrilled at her touch. For a moment neither of them spoke. Then Micah broke the silence.

'I understand,' he said, and swallowed down the lump that was forming in his throat.

And he did understand. It was true. Thrace and Aseel *were* kinned, and there was nothing and no one that could ever come between the two of them. Eli had told him that at the outset, and Micah had learned the truth of it for himself.

He looked up. The great whitewyrme was still watching his kin – watching the pair of them – with those keen yellow eyes of his.

Thrace stepped back and hugged herself, her arms crossed and shoulders hunched. 'The wyrmekin are gathering to resist the kith,' she told Micah. She glanced up at him, her long straight ash-gold hair falling down over her face as she did so. She tossed it back. 'These plains are where we shall make our stand,' she said. 'Soon.'

Micah looked into her eyes. They were tender and full of pain. A tear brimmed and rolled down her smooth flawless cheek.

'Thrace?' he said gently.

The kingirl did not reply.

'Thrace, are y'all right?' He reached out and brushed the tear from her cheek.

Thrace took a step towards him, until they were face to face, almost touching, their breath on each other's skin.

'You remember the hot springs?' she said. 'When you bathed me; when you washed away the blood . . . ?'

'I do,' said Micah. Of course he did. How could he ever forget? Afterwards they had lain together, beside the steaming lake, in each other's arms . . .

'I had come from the gutting tarn,' she said.

'I know that . . .' Micah began, but Thrace silenced him, pressing a finger to his lips.

'We killed many kith that day, Aseel and I. We slaughtered everyone we found in that place.'

Micah nodded. He had seen the carnage with his own eyes. Bodies of kith, burned, broken, butchered . . . A chill tickled at the nape of his neck, making the hairs stand on end.

'It was the bloodfrenzy,' she said. 'It came upon me – and when it took hold, I couldn't stop killing. Men and women. Children . . .'

She faltered, and Micah saw fresh tears welling up in the corners of her dark eyes.

'It's going to happen again, Micah. The bloodfrenzy. I will kill again . . .' She lowered her eyes. 'And when I do, you must be far away from here. You understand?'

Micah nodded slowly, his heart thumping. He could smell the scent of her hair, sweet and fresh and laced with spices, like new-mown grass. The ache in his chest was almost unbearable. He wanted to take this kingirl in his arms. He wanted to kiss her, tell her it was all going to be all right.

But he couldn't.

It wouldn't be all right. He had seen what Thrace was capable of, and it frightened him. Besides, he could feel her wyrme's bright yellow eyes boring into the back of his neck. And Cara was watching too . . .

Cara. With her dark red hair and green eyes, and that band

of freckles that crossed the bridge of her nose. Beautiful, loyal, trusting Cara.

He looked up at Thrace, and her strange, otherworldly beauty struck him with renewed force. The lump in his throat made it impossible to swallow and he didn't trust himself to speak.

'You must go now,' said Thrace. 'Take your kithgirl, Micah, and go far from here.'

Micah nodded dumbly and turned away, hurrying towards Eli, Cara and the others before the tears came.

Behind him, he heard a soft sighing sound, like the wind through plains grass.

It was Thrace, calling to her wyrme.

Sixteen

The oxcart wouldn't be going any further, that much was certain. The back axle had cracked and one of the two drawshafts had shorn right through. Besides, with the ox lying on the ground, wheezing with weald-sickness, there would soon be nothing to pull it.

Seth Fallowfoot looked at his wife, his thin lips a grim line. She shrugged weakly, pushing back a strand of greasy hair that had slipped free from her bonnet. She was standing on the far side of the stricken creature, her hands resting on the shoulders of their younger son, who had buried his head in her apron.

'It's all right, Kyle,' she was saying softly.

Their older son and their daughter were pressed up against her on either side, and she took comfort from the warmth of their bodies. The boy's left knee and elbow were grazed and bleeding from when he'd been thrown from the driving seat of the cart. The girl's cornflower-blue eyes were filled with tears.

Seth knelt down next to the ox and rested a hand on its neck.

'Is he going to die, Daddy?' the girl asked.

'I fear so,' he told her, and sighed.

The ox had grown steadily weaker until the moment when its front legs had finally buckled, upending the cart as it had slammed down onto the rocky ground. Now it lay where it had landed, twitching convulsively, eyeballs rolling and blood trickling from its mouth and nostrils.

Just like their mule before it.

The same symptoms. Collapse and bleeding. Then death.

Back at the new stockade in the middle of the badlands, Seth Fallowfoot had been warned that the weald was no place for low-plains creatures. The old-timer with the crooked teeth who had brought them water had told them that the mule and the ox were sure to weaken and die if they went much further; had said they should proceed on foot. But Seth had been deaf to his warnings.

The old-timer had shrugged.

Time and again, farming folk would leave the low plains and attempt the journey into the high country, he'd said, with a sorrowful shake of his head, their worldly possessions packed onto the back of a wagon or cart, pulled by oxen or mules. And he, Garth Temple, gave them all the same advice he was giving Seth now.

Ditch your cart. Your livestock. Your possessions. The only way into the weald was on your own two feet, with as much water and food as you could carry and a loaded spitbolt on your shoulder. Even then, only those with a constitution suited to the thin air of the weald stood a chance. The others – usually one in five, Garth had noted grimly – went the way of the livestock. They succumbed to wealdsickness and died on the journey. Their bones, picked clean by carrionwyrmes, littered the way, stark and white and marking the trail to the high country.

The bone trail.

Seth had thanked Garth Temple for his advice, but told him he would trust in the Maker to guide him and his family to a new life in the weald. A small homestead. Enough cleared land to plant crops. Perhaps a little orchard . . .

He'd tried to ignore the old-timer's mocking laughter.

The going had been fine at first. Seth drove the oxcart, his wife rode the mule, and the three kids took it in turns to sit with one or other of their parents. But a week later, the mule had collapsed. And now, two days after that, the same thing had happened to the ox.

And Seth wished he'd heeded Garth Temple . . .

Suddenly Kyle broke away from his mother's hands. He picked up the switch that his daddy used to flick the creature's rump, to urge it on, and he slashed at the ox's trembling flank.

'Get up!' he shouted, his voice shrill. 'You gotta get up.' He darted round and struck the creature's neck. 'Get up, get *up*!'

The ox struggled for a moment, eager to comply, then gave a violent shudder. Its head rolled to one side and with its last rasping exhalation of breath it showered Seth's boots with droplets of blood.

Everyone turned and stared blankly at the dead animal. From high above their heads there came the sound of raucous screeching, and they looked up to see black wyrmes with tattered wings tumbling down out of the sky like so many broken umbrellas. They landed some way off, one by one, and snarled at the living creatures that barred their way to the dead one.

Seth climbed to his feet, wincing as he did so. He put his hands to his face and rubbed his temples with his fingertips. Then, seeing his wife and children staring at him, concern in their eyes, he smiled.

'I had hoped the animals would get us further,' he admitted. 'But now we'll have to carry what we can,' he said, 'and keep on.'

It took them the best part of an hour to sort out the food and equipment they would need, and pack it into rucksacks and a small wheelbarrow. The trunks and crates filled with items deemed inessential – each one identifiable by the name *FALLOWFOOT* painted in neat letters on their lids – were abandoned.

Seth told his family they'd come back and collect them when they were settled. The dead ox was left to the scavenging black wyrmes.

The broad expanse of pitted rock shimmered like liquid in the heat as they set off. The landscape was harsh and arid. Apart from the occasional writhing clump of waxy sword-weed, there were no plants. Just rocks and gravel and sand that seemed to stretch on ahead of them for ever.

The sun was down close to the horizon when Seth lowered the wheelbarrow to the ground. The others stopped around him, waiting for him to tell them what to do next. He rubbed his temples. He closed his eyes.

'Y'all right?' his wife asked at length.

'It's this headache,' he told her. 'Can't seem to shift it.' He smiled. 'I'll be fine,' he said. 'If I can just—'

Suddenly his face reddened and his chest convulsed. His hands shot to his mouth to stifle the harsh wheezing cough he could not stop. When it was finally over, he lowered both hands and inspected them warily, each in turn. Then he held them up to his wife, who let out a small cry.

The palms were spattered with blood.

Seventeen

Garth Temple plunged the dip-ladle into the trough, bent forward and tipped the cool water over the back of his head. It turned his lank grey hair several shades darker, and when he straightened up it ran down over his neck and inside his homespun shirt. He rubbed the back of his hand across his forehead and eyed the man standing before him.

'Hot work,' he said and grinned, revealing a mouthful of crooked yellow teeth.

'Evidently,' the merchant observed, with just a trace of sarcasm in his voice.

He was young, but already fleshy and rotund beneath his fine silk robes and fur-trimmed long-coat. And when he had greeted Garth with a handshake, the old wealdtrader had noted with distaste how soft the young merchant's hand was. The mule-drawn carriage that had brought him up from the plains was padded with cushions and covered with an awning of oiled wyrmeleather. Behind it stood five large oxcarts, each one heavy-laden with sawn timber and rolls of roofing felt which their drivers were busy unloading. The young merchant plucked at the fur-trimmed cuffs of his longcoat impatiently as he looked past Garth at the new stockade.

'I had hoped to see greater progress,' he said. 'After all the coin I've spent on workmen and building materials . . .'

'Oh, you can't cut corners,' said Garth. 'Not out here in the badlands.' He turned and followed the merchant's gaze. 'After all, what we're building here is going to transform the high country – and I know only a far-sighted merchant such as your good self can truly appreciate the rewards the new stockade will bring.'

Nathaniel Lint the Younger nodded, ignoring the familiar oily edge that had crept into Garth Temple's voice. It had been the end of fullwinter when he'd last been up to the badlands. At that time, he'd only recently taken up with this scrimshawden master, while the new stockade had been no more than heaps of treetrunks, piles of timber and sacks of nails, and a clutch of plans sketched out on wyrmevellum. Now, so far as he could determine, with fullsummer fast approaching, the place still looked far from complete.

He surveyed the constructions critically. There was a three-storey hay barn with latticed sides. A hexagonal silo. Half a dozen bunkhouses, all but one roofed and glazed. A lookout tower. A cabin. A store. A tavern, with what looked like its own distilling apparatus barnacled onto its side. And downwind to the east, a corral of sorts – pine fencing and a timber gateway enclosing an expanse of dusty ground.

'What about the water?' Nathaniel queried.

'It took a while, but we found it, just as I promised you we would,' said Garth. 'The wellshaft goes down more'n a hundred foot, but the water is pure and sweet.'

The wealdtrader led the young merchant across the unfinished courtyard to the well, where four sick-looking oxen, yoked into the spokes of a giant horizontal wheel, were trudging round in never-ending circles. As the stolid creatures pushed the wheel, an intricate set of cogs and pistons drove a screw-shaped tube, which had been sunk into the ground, round and round on its axis. And as the screw turned, so water was raised from the reservoir deep down beneath the surface. It cascaded out of a wooden spout into a capacious vat, and from there, through a pipe, into the wooden trough.

Garth Temple dabbled his hand in the water. 'This is just the first of a whole series of troughs. All connected with pipes,' he explained. 'We got them rigged up at the bunkhouses, the store, the corral . . .'

'The corral is finished?' The merchant sounded surprised, but gratified.

'A couple days since,' said Garth, turning, the bright sun causing him to frown. 'You care to take a look at it?'

The merchant nodded. 'I surely would,' he said, and allowed himself a small smile. 'See precisely what's become of my investment.'

Again, Garth picked up on the note of sarcasm in the young merchant's voice. This pampered son of wealthy parents clearly had something to prove. Garth had seen the look in his eyes when he'd first met him in that plains tavern a year ago. Sarcastic, calculating and arrogant, but eager to hear about Garth's idea for the new stockade.

Garth had regaled the young merchant with tales of the high country over bottle after bottle of sweet plains wine. He talked of the fertile valleys and the great grasslands beyond, just waiting to be farmed – if only the farmers could get to them. The trouble was that plains creatures like horses and mules and oxen succumbed to wealdsickness up in the thin rarefied air of the high country, just as the wyrmes of the weald sickened and died when brought down to the plains.

Garth Temple's idea was deceptively simple. He proposed to construct a stockade midway between the low plains and the high country in the badlands, a place where both plains animals and weald creatures could survive. Then he, Garth Temple, would stock it with greywyrmes – huge, lumbering, docile creatures, forty-times stronger than an ox and capable of hauling everything an enterprising settler might need to start a new life in the high country.

When they arrived at the stockade, newcomers from the plains would be able to trade their mules and oxen for these wyrmes that would take them up into the weald. And they would pay handsomely for the privilege.

Garth had been gratified at how Nathaniel Lint the Younger's eyes had lit up at the prospect. If the young merchant provided the materials and spread the word down on the plains, Garth Temple had assured him that he would take care of the rest. They had shaken on the deal, which was the first time Garth had noted his new partner's soft fleshy handshake.

With Garth guiding the way, the two of them walked side by side round the back of the well, the oxen snorting and coughing as they passed, and across the mudbake stretch of land on the far side. Standing there were a dozen or so tents and benders, their canvas and animal-skin sides fluttering in the light wind, and close by, the men and women who had put them up.

They were a motley bunch, Nathaniel Lint observed. Grizzled farmhands, fresh-faced ploughboys and hungry-looking labourers. Young newlyweds and old married couples. Brothers and sisters from homes too large to support so many back on the drought-scourged plains. And entire families, some of them spanning four generations, from leathery great-grandparents to swaddled babes-in-arms. What they all shared was the exhausted, sunken-cheeked look of the downtrodden;

that, and a look of desperate hope in their eyes. For these folk had been gripped by landfever.

It had swept through the plains, the talk of every tavern and marketplace, fuelled by stories of a wondrous place in the far west of the high country. This great rolling expanse of grassland was said to be as big as the lowplains themselves. It was empty and just waiting to be settled by those brave enough to attempt the journey. Land for all. Land free from the lords and estate-owners of the plains who had made their lives there a misery.

Who wouldn't be gripped by such a fever? Do anything it took to raise the two gold coins a head that Garth Temple was charging to join his wyrmetrain?

Motley bunch they may be, but they were paying customers, the lot of them, the young merchant noted approvingly.

There was an air of expectation and impatience in the air. Women looked up from their cooking pots, hope in their faces. Old folks stole glances at the two men and muttered to one another under their breath. Children scampered around them as they made their way across the campground.

One man – a tall rangy farmer with string-tied boots and a rabbitskin cap – looked up from the stick he'd been whittling. Beside him his wife, a plump woman with a headscarf tied around her head, nudged him with her elbow. The man nodded, flicked the straw he was chewing from one side of his mouth to the other.

'Garth,' he said, his voice gruff as he nodded his greetings.

'Amos,' said Garth. He did not break his stride, and Amos's wife nudged him a second time.

'Y'any idea how much longer?' he asked.

'Any day now,' said Garth. He strode past. 'Any day now.'

'You been saying that for weeks,' said Amos. 'Hell, you promised us them there wyrmes of yours, and we paid you fair and square up front.' He shook his head. 'Reckon we'll have our money back and take our chances on our own.'

Garth Temple stopped in his tracks. He turned, fixed Amos with a dark look, his lips curling to reveal those crooked teeth of his.

'Amos Greenwood,' he said, 'if you decide to set out with those broken-down mules of yours, there ain't nothing I can do to stop you. And maybe you might just make it.' He shrugged, looked around him. 'Who knows? Maybe them others that decided to set out on their own are doing just fine. That fellow, what's his name? Seth. Seth Fallowfoot. Remember him and his family? Maybe they already found theirselves that little piece of land they always wanted. Ploughed it up. Sowed their first sack of seed. Maybe.' His brow furrowed. 'Or maybe they're lying dead on the trail, their bones picked clean.' He shrugged again. 'Like I say, Amos, who knows?'

He turned away and guided Nathaniel Lint past the settlers.

'That Amos Greenwood,' Garth was muttering. 'Ain't stopped grumbling since the day he arrived.'

'There's no room in the bunkhouses for him?' asked Nathaniel, glancing across at the line of timber buildings.

Garth smiled. 'Full to bursting with paying customers,' he said. 'More arriving every week. Greenwood and his friends are the overspill. Still, I took their money all the same,' he added with a chuckle. He patted the young merchant on the shoulder. 'Your share's tucked away safe and sound in the strongbox in my quarters.'

He stopped beside the sixth bunkhouse. There was hammering coming from up top, and Garth thrust two fingers into his mouth and let out a loud whistle. A shutter flew open and a tousled head appeared at one of the upstairs windows.

'Tyler!' he hollered. 'You and Jonas get yourselves down here. The planks and roofing stuff have arrived.'

'Will do,' the man shouted back, and the shutter slammed shut.

'I want them bunkhouses complete by sundown,' Garth called up. 'The customers are getting restless.'

'A'right,' came the muffled reply.

Garth took Nathaniel by the arm and ushered him on. He gestured to the hay barn and the silo.

'They're both half-full at the moment,' he said. 'Fodder you sent up from the plains.' He smiled. 'But in time we'll be self-sufficient up here. Once the weald starts to get farmed.'

All he needed were the greywyrmes.

Garth Temple led the merchant through a broad gateway and into a vast rectangular yard, open to the sky and fringed on all sides with individual stalls, complete with tether-posts and water troughs. Despite himself, Nathaniel was impressed. He sucked in air noisily over his teeth.

'It's larger than it looks from the outside,' he said.

'There's stalls for nigh on two hundred,' said Garth. 'And that can be increased.'

Nathaniel nodded. He walked slowly across the dusty yard, looking round appraisingly, then stopped before one of the stalls. He put his hands on his hips, looked up at the roofless pen, then down into the broad V-shaped trench in the ground that separated this stall from the one next to it.

'But they're not finished,' he said. 'There's no fences. They need fences.'

He turned to see Garth Temple grinning back at him.

'They *are* finished,' he said, rubbing his hands together eagerly.

Nathaniel frowned. He did not understand.

Garth pointed to the trench. 'Greywyrmes won't cross such a gap,' he explained. 'I guess it's like in their own habitat. They'll walk miles to avoid a wide crack in the rock.'

'And they won't simply jump over it?' said the merchant, looking up, puzzled. 'Or fly?'

'Neither,' said Garth. 'Greywyrmes have wings, but they can't fly no more than a few yards, and then only if they get up to a gallop. These here ditches will keep 'em securely contained.'

The young merchant shrugged. 'All I can do is bow to your expertise,' he said, and his expression hardened. 'But I see no actual wyrmes in these stalls of yours, Temple. I've furnished you with all the timber and tools for this fine stockade, not to mention spread word far and wide amongst the good folk of the plains,' he added with a sneer. 'I've kept my side of the bargain. If this thing's going to work, don't you think it's about time you kept yours?'

'Garth. *Garth!*'

The voice sounded urgent, and Garth turned to see an agitated Amos Greenwood standing in the gateway at the far side of the corral.

'What now, Amos?' Garth snapped. 'Can't you see I'm busy here.'

'I know. Sorry. It's . . .' His voice trailed away.

'Well?'

'Come, look,' Amos told him. 'I think you'll want to see this.'

Garth flashed an exasperated glance at Nathaniel. 'I apologize for this,' he said.

'The merchantman should see too,' Amos said.

Nathaniel shrugged, and the two of them walked over to the gateway. As they approached, Amos turned and pointed off across the shimmering badlands.

'I don't see nothing,' said Garth impatiently.

'There,' said Amos. He jabbed his finger at the air. 'That dustcloud. There's something stirring up the trail – and it looks like it's coming this way. You reckon it could be them packwyrmes of ours?'

Garth reached inside his shirt for the spyglass he had dangling round his neck on a chain. He put it to his eye, held it there for a moment, then turned, his face twitching with the excitement he was trying to contain.

'Reckon it could,' he drawled.

Eighteen

News of the wyrmes' arrival went round the stockade swift as wildfire. Men, women and bands of excited children left their tents and bunkhouses and streamed toward the far side of the corral. They gathered at the split-rail fence, looked out across the blistered rockscape beyond.

And there they were, the promised greywyrmes at last, trudging across the bare earth towards them. Their bodies looked to be fused and liquid, dissolved in the heatshimmer of midday

They had cheered at first, the onlookers. Now they were silent in awe. The greywyrmes were huge; a dozen lumbering monsters, ten times the size of a full-grown ox and slow and deliberate in their movements. Around their massive feet, five men darted to and fro, kith trappers and veterans of the weald, judging by their well-worn clothes and light kit. The sound of their angry cries and cracking bullwhips splintered the afternoon air.

The wyrmes themselves were silent. Their heads were down; their long thick tails were limp and dragging. A sour odour wafted in on the wind.

Garth Temple turned to his head stockman, who was tending to one of the wheezing oxen by the well. 'Ebenezer,' he called out. 'Prepare the stalls. Fresh hay. Water . . . You know the score.'

Ebenezer acknowledged his boss's instructions with a wave. He quickly reharnessed the ox, then headed for the stalls.

'A dozen by my count,' Garth told the merchant. 'Ten full-grown, two calves,' he added, aware that his voice sounded high-pitched and overexcited. He tried hard to mask his relief. 'It's a start, at least,' he said gruffly.

'Indeed,' said Nathaniel Lint the Younger. He frowned, examined his fingernails. 'Remind me how many you said we'd have for this "great journey" of yours, Temple? Three hundred, was it?'

'Two hundred,' said Garth quietly, his face colouring. 'The harpoon gangs promised . . . two hundred,' he said hesitantly, as the young merchant's eyes narrowed. 'With two hundred, we'll clear all our building costs and make a tidy profit with the first wagon train.'

'*Our* building costs,' said Nathaniel, returning his gaze to the hot shimmering rock ahead. 'It is *my* purse that bears the strain of this enterprise.'

The group of wyrmes were no more than a hundred yards

away. They were cresting the last low ridge that separated them and the new stockade, their legs and lower bodies rippling in the intense heat. The excited crowd was getting rowdy again, conversation rising to a babble and the children dancing about, waving and shrieking. The sound of the cracking bull-whips had got louder; the smell of the wyrmes and their drovers more intense . . .

Garth turned to Nathaniel. 'Patience, my friend,' he said. 'These are just the first of many. You'll see. The new stockade will make us both rich.'

'I have every faith in you, Temple,' said the merchant with little enthusiasm. He was fanning his face with his hand, his wrist limp. His face was pinched up with the bad smell. 'If it's all the same to you, Temple,' he said, 'I think I'd like to go and freshen up.'

'Of course,' said Garth, secretly relieved that the merchant was not planning to greet the greywyrme party personally. 'You've had a long journey up here.' He clamped a hand on Nathaniel's shoulder, his fingers grazing the fur collar of his coat. 'My own quarters are at your disposal. Treat them as . . . as . . .'

His voice trailed away as he saw the merchant turn his head, eyebrows arched, and stare down at the hand – which he removed, smiling sheepishly.

'Treat them like your own home,' he said.

'Thank you,' said Nathaniel stiffly, and he turned and strode off, the white handkerchief that he'd plucked from his sleeve clamped to his nose.

Garth watched him go, then turned back to the incoming convoy. The kith wyrmehandlers had neat packs on their backs, with pans, snares and rock-spikes attached to them; a bullwhip in one hand and a steel-tipped prod in the other. They wore broadbrim hats, waistcoats and overjackets, breeches, heavy boots – all made of weathered wyrmeskin – and had the dyed homespun kerchiefs favoured by the harpoon gangs wrapped twice around their necks and tied off with a knot. And they each bore the signs of being a long time on the trail. Stubbled jaws and straggly moustaches. Red eyes. Grime. The sour odour of sweat.

As they got closer, Garth noted the curve-blade knives at their belts and the loaded spitbolts holstered in the flaps of their long overjackets. These were savage high-country kith, accustomed to the unforgiving ways of the weald. They could be unpredictable, prone to sudden bursts of violence; they were interested only in green liquor and returner's wealth, and Garth Temple had dealt with them all his working life.

That young merchant had been wise to go off in search of a perfumed bath, he thought. This lot would skin him alive soon as look at him.

As the convoy approached, Garth eyed the leader of the wyrmehandlers closely.

'Solomon Tallow,' he hailed the hulking kith with the broad shoulders and carefully trimmed stubble, that spoke of a vanity strangely at odds with his worn clothes and battered hat.

'Garth Temple,' the kith replied as the convoy came to a halt just outside the corral.

Behind him, the huge greywyrmes stretched back in a line, breathing heavily. The settlers lining the fence looked on, chattering among themselves. And as the dust cleared, Garth took in the sight of the first greywyrme.

Like the others in the line, its hindlegs had been hobbled with a short length of rope. More rope hadbeen used to clamp its jaws tightly shut, while strapped to its head was a set of oversized horse-blinkers, the stiff wyrmeleather flaps preventing it from seeing sideways. Like the others, it was in a parlous condition that neither the dustswirl nor the heat-shimmer had managed to conceal.

Garth could now see that all the greywyrmes were bone-thin. Lacerations and weeping sores crisscrossed their flanks where they had been brutally whipped. And with their jaws bound shut, Garth didn't like to guess how long the creatures had gone without water.

That had been his idea. The ropes. But then, how else could the men have herded the wyrmes without being burned to death? Tallow's men had neither the skill nor empathy to do what needed to be done. But now Garth would take care of things. He only hoped it wasn't too late. The creatures looked close to collapse.

Not that the crowd seemed to notice. They whooped and hollered and waved their hats in the air. Settler families who had been waiting at the new stockade for weeks embraced each other, delighted that the packwyrmes had finally arrived, men shook each other's hands, while some of the more daring boys reached out over the fence and patted the flank of the huge creature at the head of the line.

'Tell your men to get them into the stalls,' Garth told Solomon Tallow. 'We need to talk.'

Solomon nodded, then waved to the other kith, who proceeded to whip and goad the massive wyrmes back into motion. As they lumbered through the gateway and into the corral yard, Solomon rubbed a meaty hand over his close-cropped scalp and replaced his battered leather hat. He grinned at Garth, his even white teeth stark against the blue-black of his jaw.

'What's on your mind?' he said.

Garth shook his head. 'You sure took your time, Solomon,' he said, looking him squarely in the eye. 'I swear I was beginning to wonder if you'd ever turn up.'

Solomon nodded at the line of plodding wyrmes. 'Not exactly the fastest critters in the world,' he said. His grin broadened. 'Yet we got 'em here in the end.'

Garth frowned. As they limped and shuffled into the stalls, clouds of flies buzzing around their festering sores, he feared they were in an even worse state than he'd first thought. What was more, the two of them had agreed on fifty wyrmes. Shaken hands on it. Yet Solomon had only brought him twelve, and two of them were calves.

'What about the rest of them?' he said evenly. 'Fifty at a time. Wasn't that what we said? In four convoys . . .'

Solomon smiled. 'Now don't be like that,' he said. 'It was as much as I could do to convince my boys not to slaughter the lot of them for their flameoil sacs and have done with the whole damn business. But no,' Solomon continued, his face serious, brow furrowed, 'we had us a deal, you and me. You showed us how to handle 'em, and we did.'

Garth flinched, but said nothing. He certainly hadn't told them to treat the creatures so brutally they might not even survive.

'Only herding these great lumps of wyrmemeat and keeping them alive on the trail is no easy task, Garth,' Solomon went on. He smiled. 'But you were right about them "migratory trails" of theirs. They lead right through the eastern mountains, all the way to those sprawling grasslands in the west.'

'Still,' Garth persisted, 'a dozen wyrmes is a slim haul.'

The last of the line of wyrmes had just passed through the gate, urged on by one of the whipcracking wyrmehands. Solomon and Garth followed it into the corral yard.

'We lost most of 'em on this trip, that's true. But we're learning,' said Tallow. 'And I've got three other gangs out there trapping as we speak – which reminds me . . .'

'You want more money,' said Garth wearily.

Solomon Tallow frowned. 'You ever handled a kith gang, Garth?'

Garth looked down, his face burning.

'No, didn't think so,' Solomon said. He nodded ahead at the other kith. 'I got me a good bunch of men. This gang here worked hard.' His dark eyes gleamed. 'And I reckon they should be adequately rewarded for delivering such goddamn savage creatures up all meek and mild.'

Meek and mild! thought Garth. They looked half-dead.

'I tell you something else,' said Solomon as his wyrme-handlers pushed and prodded the wyrme across the planks laid over the trench, and into its stall.

'What's that?' said Garth.

'Me and the boys have got a hell of a thirst on,' said Solomon, and he laughed. 'I believe you've completed that tavern of yours since my first visit.'

Garth nodded. 'We have,' he said, and he reached into the inside pocket of his jacket for the leather pouch that nestled there. He retrieved it and tossed it across to Solomon. It landed in his outstretched hand with a satisfying jangle. 'It's all there,' he said. 'But I want the full complement of wyrmes next time.'

'I would not have expected otherwise,' said Solomon. He was smiling, but there was an edge to his voice that Garth couldn't fail to notice. The gangleader held out his hand. 'It's a pleasure to do business with . . .' He frowned. 'What the—'

Garth Temple had brushed his hand aside and was dashing full-pelt back along the line of stalls. 'No! No!' he bellowed. 'Stop! Ebenezer, *STOP!*'

In the first of the stalls, the stockhand was loosening the knot that bound the rope round the greywyrme's muzzle to allow it to drink. Feeling its bindings slacken, the wyrme braced its jaws. The knot slipped completely and the rope flew off. The wyrme's mouth opened in a great yawn – and a jet of yellow-white flame roared from its gaping maw.

The fire engulfed Ebenezer, who staggered backwards, arms raised and clothes and hair ablaze. He stumbled, fell.

Over by the split-rail fence, there were horrified screams and the plainsfolk scattered.

'Help him!' Garth cried out.

A wyrmehandler leaped forward and rolled the burning man over in the dust, while a second threw a thick trail-blanket over him to smother the flames. Meanwhile, Garth grabbed a wooden pail and dunked it in the trough, before tossing water into the face of the greywyrme. The air hissed and steamed as its breath was quenched for a moment, before another jet of flame poured from the wyrme's mouth, furnace-hot and pinchnose pungent like molten rock, driving Garth back.

In the neighbouring stalls, the other wyrmes were stamping their feet, rearing up on their hindlegs and pawing at the air. They craned their necks. They rubbed the sides of their heads up against the gateposts or down at the edge of the trench, increasingly desperate to unshackle their own bindings, their frenzy fuelled by the unmuzzled wyrme, whose fiery breath slashed the air like a knife, until . . .

There was a thud.

Garth looked up in dismay. A heavy dullmetal crossbow bolt had embedded itself in the wyrme's left eye.

'Solomon,' Garth gasped, seeing the gangleader lower his sidewinder and holster it in his overjacket.

The mighty creature tottered for a few seconds, then abruptly collapsed. It hit the ground in a cloud of dust, hind-legs stretched out behind it, front legs splayed and head lolling down into the trench.

Garth dropped his pail and hurried across to the stricken stockman. He crouched down, unwrapped the blanket. The smell of burning hair made him retch. Ebenezer was unconscious, the skin on the right side of his face red and raw and already puckering up.

The scars would not be pretty, but at least Ebenezer was alive. Unlike the wyrme. Garth cursed under his breath. It meant the tally was down to eleven.

He looked round to see Solomon Tallow swaggering back across the yard, the other wyrmehandlers following him close behind. Anger and frustration flushed Garth's cheeks and made his hands shake.

'You killed it,' he shouted after him.

'Don't mention it,' Solomon's voice floated back.

Nineteen

The proprietor of the new stockade climbed to his feet. Things surely were not going as smoothly as he'd hoped. Only eleven wyrmes in the corral. His head stockman burned and out of action. And he could already hear the plainsfolk muttering among themselves about these dangerous fire-breathing creatures.

'Muzzled and they die of thirst. Unmuzzled and they burn you to a crisp.'

'Happen we'd have been better off travelling with our oxen after all.'

'Damn fool never thought it through . . .'

But Garth Temple *had* thought it through, to the very last detail. Treated with care and handled properly, these huge greywyrmes could be harnessed and used to transport the settlers up into the thin air of the high country. You just had to know how. And he, Garth Temple, did know how to handle greywyrmes.

Wyrmekind had always fascinated him, right from those earliest days as a trapper in the eastern valley country, and then, later, as a scrimshaw-den owner dealing in flameoil. He had studied their ways, learned how to handle them, and had developed a particular understanding of these great, gentle beasts. Slow to anger but deadly if provoked, the greywyrme needed careful handling, but Garth had the gift, an empathy, a closeness he felt every time he stared into their large doleful eyes.

He brushed the dust from his coat and entered the second of the stalls. His right hand gently rubbed the neck of the creature before him.

The plainsfolk at the split-rail fence were dispersing, going back to the bunkhouses and the tents, to tend cookfires and discuss their options over stewpots of bubbling barleymeal broth. He'd show them. He'd show them all.

Garth continued stroking the greywyrme's neck as he fixed it with a gaze. And, with its vision restricted by the blinkers, the wyrme gazed right back at him.

The death of one of their number had left the remaining wyrmes more subdued, but still jittery. What was more, as Garth knew only too well, they were racked with hunger and thirst, and the smell of the water and sweet hay that they could not get to was driving them all to distraction.

'That's it, my beauty,' Garth whispered to the wyrme standing before him, stroking and crooning and staring into its eyes.

The wyrme stared back. Its neck swayed gently from side to side.

With his free hand, Garth reached into the recesses of his heavy longcoat and took out objects from various pockets. He knelt down and laid them out at his feet. There was a small leather pouch, no larger than a man's fist, a broad belt with a heavy metal buckle, and two peg-like clips that were sprung in the middle, jag-toothed at one end and with a barbed hook at the other. Reaching into a side pocket, Garth drew out a piece of pipe, curved at the top, straight at the bottom and with what looked like a small wooden spigot halfway along its length. He laid it on the ground with the other objects and smiled.

'Easy now, this won't take long,' he crooned to the greywyrme. 'Then I'll get you fed and watered.'

Out of the corner of his eye he caught sight of a small boy, a settler lad, standing at the now deserted fence, staring at him intently. Garth slipped the belt through the tags at the back of the leather pouch.

'Nice and steady,' he whispered as, still holding the wyrme's mesmerized gaze, he reached round the bottom of the creature's long neck. Slowly and carefully he pushed the end of the belt through the buckle, tightened it, then drew back. The pouch hung down over the greywyrme's breast. 'That's the way, my beauty.'

He patted and stroked, patted and stroked. The greywyrme swayed gently.

'Now the hard bit,' Garth told it. 'But it's not going to hurt. Not a great big brave wyrme like you.'

Garth pulled a knife from his belt and tested the sharpness of the blade with his thumb. Then he leaned forward, lulling and crooning the while, and put the point of the blade to the pulsating base of the greywyrme's throat.

'Easy now, my beautiful,' Garth whispered, and as he spoke he gripped the handle of the knife so hard the tendons knotted like rope along his forearm. Then Garth increased the pressure, pushing the blade gently but firmly into the grey scaly skin.

For an instant, the greywyrme seemed distressed. Its eyes rolled back in its head, and it raised and lowered its neck three, four times. The skin around the blade throbbed. But Garth seemed untroubled. He just kept on stroking and patting and whispering, and the wyrme kept on staring back at him with those trusting yellow eyes.

'There we are,' Garth whispered, as a viscous liquid welled up out of the wound that was not blood. Clear and golden it was, like honey. It trickled down over the creature's cracked grey skin.

Garth pulled the blade out of the small wound and inserted the curved end of the pipe smoothly in its place. Then, holding it still, he manoeuvred the straight end of the pipe over the lip of the pouch and pushed it deep inside. The spigot jutted out some way above the top of the leather.

'The clips,' Garth murmured to himself.

One he attached to the top, piercing the wyrme's tough scaly skin with the birdhook and using the grip to hold the pipe in place. The other he attached lower down, so that when the wyrme was walking the pipe could not bounce out of the pouch.

'And we're almost there,' whispered Garth. 'Just turn the little spigot,' he said, doing just that as he spoke, 'and that flameoil of yours will drain out of your sac. And into mine.' He patted the creature's neck affectionately. 'I get the wyrmeoil. And you don't get to burn anyone to a crisp no more.'

Gradually the pouch swelled to about a quarter full, then stopped. Leaving the spigot open, Garth reached up to the wyrme's head. His fingers worried at the knot in the rope that bound its muzzle shut. Untying it, he pulled the rope away. Then he removed the blinkers.

The wyrme caught sight of the boy at the split-rail fence, who was craning forward, his eyes wide with curiosity. It trembled violently and pawed at the ground, and its mouth opened in that yawn-like way it had. But this time there was no fire. Instead, the boy was enveloped in a rush of air that was moist and fetid, and harmless. The wyrme seemed surprised for a moment – but then it turned its neck, plunged its mouth down into the water trough in front of it and drank and drank, long and deep and noisy.

'Without that flameoil of theirs, greywyrmes are just about as meek and mild as you could wish for,' said Garth to the boy. 'Ain't no need to mistreat them.'

He moved round the back of the greywyrme and removed the rope hobbles at its hindlegs to prove it. The creature never even flinched.

'Go tell your folks, son. Garth Temple's got everything under control.'

As the boy ran off, Garth smiled his crooked smile. For the first time in weeks, the uneasy knot in the pit of his stomach relaxed. This enterprise could actually work.

Two hundred wyrmes – each one capable of carrying four settler families, along with their belongings and provisions . . . Two gold pieces a head . . . Given the size of their families – and Maker knows, these settlers certainly held with large families, what with grandfolks and cousins and all. Could be anything up to . . . eighteen . . . twenty thousand gold pieces. And that was just *one* wyrmetrain to the grasslands. With the new stockade up and running, there would be many, many more . . .

Garth whistled softly through his teeth. He and the young merchant would be rich.

And then, of course, there was the flameoil, his own little sideline. All he had to do was fit the spigots, and then organize Tallow and his men to tap the stuff . . .

He looked lovingly at the great greywyrme in the corral in front of him. 'One down,' he said. 'Ten to go.'

Twenty

Nathaniel Lint opened his eyes and stared up at the ceiling, momentarily disorientated. It was late afternoon by the tilt of the shadows. Flies were buzzing round his face.

He was lying on a bed, a hard bed, bathed in sweat. It was ferocious hot. He turned his head to the left. There was a wall of bare boards, a chair beside it with his fur-trimmed coat folded over the back. To his right, there were more bare boards. And a window. He raised his head off the pillow and looked past his booted feet at a door. It was slightly ajar, and Nathaniel suddenly remembered how it had stuck when he'd tried to close it earlier.

Garth Temple's words came back to him. He was to treat the place like his own home.

But this was not Nathaniel Lint's father's mansion down on the plains with its hundred rooms, and this timber shack was not his elegant bedchamber. There were no wardrobes filled with silk robes, no gilt-framed mirrors, no crystal lamps; no curtains at the windows nor rugs upon the floor. And it was hot. Hotter than hell. The air was feverish and stifling. And rank . . .

The new stockade.

Nathaniel pulled himself up, swung his legs off the side of the bed and placed his boots square on the floor. He put his elbows on his knees, lowered his head, scratched his scalp through his matted hair. Then he climbed to his feet.

A shelf beneath the window was set with a pitcher and a cracked bowl. Nathaniel poured some water from one to the other and splashed it over his face. It was refreshing enough, but it would take a sight more than that to wash the stink of this godawful place off him. In the meantime, he would have to content himself with scent. He pulled a small bottle from the front pocket of his buckskin waistcoat, tugged out the cork and splashed perfume over his neck, his wrists and, unbuttoning the collar of his silk shirt, down over his chest. The liquid was cold for a moment, then burned. The air became intoxicating sweet with the fragrance of rose, lavender and honeysuckle, as though a magnificent bouquet of plains flowers had just appeared in the room.

Nathaniel batted away a couple of the more persistent flies. His stomach grumbled, and he crossed to the door and pulled it open.

'Hello?' he called. 'Is anybody there?'

There was no reply. Garth's servant – the woman who had shown him to the room – was either deaf, or had gone out. Nathaniel grunted his irritation. Then, gathering up his coat, he left the room and stepped out into the courtyard.

He'd been right about the time of day. It *was* late afternoon, though the heat hadn't abated none. The badlands was, in Nathaniel Lint's humble opinion, quite the most appalling and inhospitable place he had ever ventured into and he couldn't help asking himself why anyone in their right mind would contemplate leaving the cool rain-kissed plains and venture up into this Maker-forsaken wilderness of bare rock and blistering heat unless they absolutely had to.

But then he did indeed have to. After all, he had a lot riding on this venture – most of the small fortune his father had settled on him. 'Seed money', the old man had called it, his tone gently mocking. He didn't believe his son could make a go of it; he was simply indulging him the way he always did. But he would show Nathaniel Lint the Elder. Oh, yes, he would prove to him just what he could do . . .

Nathaniel paused to get his bearings. The hay barn and silo were behind him. The corral was off to his left, the crowd that had gathered now dispersed. From his right, he heard the sound of loud rowdy voices, raucous laughter, the clatter of drinking mugs. A wheezy squeezebox . . .

It was the tavern.

Nathaniel vaguely remembered Garth pointing it out to him earlier. Not that he'd thought then that he might end up availing himself of its hospitality. He looked at the building uneasily. It might be new, but the door was badly splintered and two of the windows had been boarded over. He rolled his eyes.

Was this really what he was pouring the contents of his purse into? A dusty corral. A fly-blown stockade. A rundown tavern stuck out here in the middle of the badlands . . .

Then again, he told himself, at least the tavern would have something to drink, and if his luck was in, something to eat as well.

With a resigned sigh, he crossed the dusty ground to the door at the front and pushed it half open. A pungent mix of stale liquor and staler bodies struck him like a punch to the face. He recoiled, gathered himself. Then, having set his face in an expression that he hoped indicated that he wasn't someone to mess with, walked inside.

The place was dark and fetid and far worse than Nathaniel had imagined. It was full of men. They were standing in groups, or seated solitary at low tables. He couldn't see their faces. As his presence was noticed, the squeezebox fell silent, the conversation ceased and Nathaniel felt his legs weaken.

'Mister Nathaniel, sir,' came a voice.

He turned and, squinting into the gloom, could just make out a face. A woman's face. The face of Garth's housekeeper. She clearly doubled as the tavern-maid.

With her acknowledgement, the atmosphere seemed to relax and the conversation started up again, but lower now, more furtive. The accordion player squeezed out a few notes.

'Table, sir?' the woman asked, smoothing down her apron. 'A drink? Something to eat?'

'All of those,' said Nathaniel, aiming for heartiness, trying to ignore the thudding of his heart. He felt out of place, conspicuous in his fine plains clothes among these hulking wealdtraders with their wyrmeskin jackets and heavy boots.

The woman showed him to a bench close to the end of a long table. 'Sit yourself down, sir,' she said. 'Mister Garth told me you was to have whatever you wanted.'

'Good of him,' said Nathaniel gruffly.

As he waited for the woman to return, he looked around, his eyes slowly accustoming themselves to the gloom. Oil lamps were burning, he now realized, though their flames seemed to add more smoke to the tavern than light. Faces gleamed in the dull copper glow. Hard, weatherbeaten faces, as immobile and inscrutable as masks. And when he looked across towards the boarded-up window, he recognized the five kith wyrmehandlers who had arrived with the convoy of greywyrmes. Already the worse for wear with drink, they were tottering about, cussing and laughing, and Nathaniel was relieved they paid him no mind.

From close by there came a long loud belch, and Nathaniel looked round to see a bear-like individual seated diagonally opposite him. He was wearing the clothes of an old-style trapper, with birdhooks and snarewire pinned down the lapels of his wyrmeskin halfcoat. A chunk of meat was skewered on the end of his hunting knife, which was gripped in his hand. He raised it in acknowledgment.

'Better out than in,' he mumbled, before tearing off a piece of meat with his yellow teeth. Grease dripped into his thick black beard. He sluiced the chewed meat down with a mouthful of liquor, then belched again. 'To your good health.'

Nathaniel smiled weakly, then looked down. He inspected his fingernails, wishing the woman would get a move on with his meal. The man skitched along the bench a foot or so closer to him, pushing his liquor tankard with him.

'Ain't seen you around here before,' he said, his voice slurring.

'I arrived this morning,' Nathaniel replied.

The trapper nodded thoughtfully, swallowed. He shifted along the bench a tad further, then tore off another hunk of meat.

'One of them settlers, eh?' he enquired, chewing as he spoke.

'No, no,' said Nathaniel, horrified to think that anyone might mistake him, a wealthy merchant, for those abject creatures that poverty and hardship had driven from the plains. 'I . . .' He checked himself. It was never wise to give too much away. 'I have business here.'

The trapper nodded again. He pulled a filthy rag from his pocket and wiped around his mouth, which nestled somewhere beneath his overgrown black moustache.

Nathaniel watched, appalled, intrigued. The man truly was hairy. Like some kind of animal. He had long matted black hair on his head, an unkempt black beard, bushy black eyebrows, and there was more thick black hair sprouting from his cuffs and collar. It would come as little surprise to him if his entire body was covered—

'Business, you say?'

'With Garth Temple,' Nathaniel said, looking around to see what might be holding the woman up with his supper. 'The proprietor of the new stockade . . .'

'I know who Garth Temple is,' the man growled, and shifted along the bench till he was sitting directly opposite Nathaniel.

Despite the heat, a cold sweat broke out on the young merchant's forehead.

The trapper set down his knife, wiped his hand down the grease-stained front of his coat and, half climbing to his feet, leaned across and extended a great paw of a hand. He pumped the merchant's arm up and down, and Nathaniel flinched at the trapper's grip. It was like having his hand crushed in a vice.

'Any friend of Garth Temple's,' he announced, then slumped back down onto the bench.

He skewered yet another lump of meat on the end of his knife, raised it to his mouth – then hesitated. He sniffed at his fingers and his face puckered up behind his beard. He sniffed again. His dark eyes narrowed, and he fixed Nathaniel with a look that was somewhere between amusement and disgust.

'You smell like a girl,' he said. It sounded like an accusation.

Nathaniel's cheeks coloured up. 'It's . . . it's nothing,' he said. 'Just some scent to freshen up . . .'

But the trapper was shaking his head. He took another gulp of liquor. 'You look like a boy but you smell like a girl.'

Nathaniel had the feeling that some of the drinkers close by were listening. The atmosphere of the tavern seemed to shift. The trapper jutted his jaw forward.

'And it ain't right,' he slurred. 'A boy smelling like a girl.' He smiled meanly as he jabbed his knife at Nathaniel. '*Are* ya a girl?'

'Please, I don't want any trouble,' Nathaniel said weakly. 'I'm a guest of Garth Temple's, the proprietor of—'

His words abruptly turned to a strangulated gasp as the trapper lunged towards him and seized him by the front of his fur-trimmed coat. And as he was dragged across the table Nathaniel found himself deeply regretting he had ever entered this establishment.

'Let me go!' he squealed.

But the trapper clearly had no intention of letting him go. With one rock-like fist twisting the merchant's bunched-up fur collar, and the other, drawn back and poised to strike, he lifted him up off the floor. The oily smell of liquor swam around Nathaniel as he was drawn closer to the trapper's smirking face.

'Like I said, any friend of Garth Temple's,' he purred, 'ain't no friend of mine.'

The fist flew forward. Nathaniel closed his eyes. The blow never landed.

Instead, Nathaniel felt the grip on his collar abruptly yield. He dropped back to the floor and, stumbling backwards, looked up to see the trapper being yanked round, his hairy arm, fist still clenched, in the tight grasp of two powerful hands.

Then, with a splintering crack, his assailant head-butted him. Blood erupted from the trapper's nose. A thudding blow landed in his stomach. He grunted, doubled up. Two uppercuts jerked his head back first one way, then the other. The third sent him crashing to the floor.

The victor watched him, breathing noisily, his hands on his hips. The dull lampglow gleamed on his shaven scalp, in his hard dark eyes. He wiped the sweat from his brow on the back of his hand, then turned to the other wyrmehands.

'Get him out of here,' he snarled.

Taking an arm and a leg each, the four of them dragged the unconscious trapper across the floor. Nathaniel turned to his rescuer, who was reaching out a hand towards him.

'The name's Solomon Tallow,' he said.

Nathaniel took the hand and shook it warmly. 'Nathaniel Lint the Younger. I'm a guest of—'

'Garth Temple,' said Solomon, and smiled. 'I heard.'

Behind them, there was the sound of the door being

kicked open, and Nathaniel turned to see the heavy body of the trapper flumping down onto the ground outside. A cheer of derision went up. He turned back to Solomon.

'I am in your debt, Solomon Tallow,' he said. 'I don't know how to thank you.'

The gangmaster's even white teeth flashed in the gloom of the tavern. 'Happen I might think of something,' he said.

Twenty-One

It took Garth more than four hours to finish tapping the greywyrmes, by which time the last dregs of sunlight were draining away. He looked up into the starflicker indigo sky, head back, arms out, and stretched. He was exhausted – but it had been worth it. Not only were the greywyrmes no longer a danger unmuzzled, but they were now able to eat and drink their fill.

Plus there was the flameoil itself. The last greywyrme he'd tapped was a large male. A whole pouch had been filled, and still the priceless liquid had kept coming. Garth bent down and picked up the earthenware flagon he'd decanted the wyrmeoil into. Full, and it would bring him a small fortune down on the plains.

As Garth turned to go, he was aware of the sound of steady breathing as the eleven greywyrmes slept, their necks curved round to meet their tails in the broad coil that wyrmes formed when at rest. He had applied salves and ointments to their festering sores and oiled the split skin of their feet, and was gratified to see that their condition was not quite as bad as he'd feared.

He rubbed his hands together and headed off to his cabin, clutching the flagon of flameoil. He would collect more from the pouches of the others in the morning. Pure profit, just for himself. His deal with Nathaniel Lint had been to build the stockade, to stock the corral with packwyrmes and fleece the settlers for passage up to the high country. The flameoil was his little sideline. No need to trouble the young merchant's head with things that needn't concern him.

As Garth crossed the dusty courtyard, passing the oxen toiling at the well pump, he glanced over to see the merchant stumbling out of the tavern. Grease and spilled drink stained the front of his fine silk shirt, and there was more matting the fur of his collar. His eyes glittered. He paused in the open doorway and smiled lopsidedly.

'Temple,' he said, and Garth could smell the liquor on the merchant's breath.

'Been well looked after?' Garth enquired.

'No complaints,' Nathaniel said. 'Got fed. Watered . . .' He hiccupped, then giggled. 'Watered a bit more than I should of.'

Garth looked in through the doorway. The tavern was full, but his gaze fell at once upon the five wyrmehands who were standing in a group over by the shuttered windows, looking back at him. Solomon smiled and raised his tankard in greeting. Beside Garth, Nathaniel giggled again.

'Fascinating man, that Solomon Tallow,' he said.

Garth Temple nodded thoughtfully. For all his arrogant swagger the young merchant was weak and suggestible. Garth did not want Tallow getting his hooks into him. He would have to watch them. Watch them carefully.

Twenty-Two

'She sure was pretty,' Ethan muttered, and he let out a soft appreciative whistle.

'Who?' said Cody, though he knew full well who Ethan meant.

'Why that kingirl, of course. Thrace. Don't tell me you didn't notice how' – Ethan checked himself – 'pretty she was. Well, not pretty exactly,' he said. 'Pretty's the wrong word. Beautiful.' He frowned. '*Fierce* beautiful,' he said, settling on the words.

'Fierce beautiful is just about right,' said Cody. 'She'd eat a scrawny little jackrabbit like you alive. That's if she gave you a second look,' he added dismissively. 'Which I doubt.'

'Unlike a big hunk like you, eh, Code?' Ethan grinned. 'Fancy your chances, do you?'

'She ain't my type. Far as I'm concerned, Cara's ten times more beautiful,' Cody replied, and his smile broadened. 'A hundred times.'

'I tell you what,' Ethan continued, and Cody held his breath, wondering what fool thing his brother was about to come out with now. 'I can't imagine her living in no winter den with Eli and Micah. It must have been like trying to cage the wind.'

Cody nodded. He knew what his brother meant. The kingirl was as wild-seeming as she was beautiful, more wyrme than human . . .

'Stop your dawdling and keep up!'

The cragclimber's shout echoed back across the grassy plains, and the two of them looked up to see Eli standing facing them, his hands on his hips.

'I intend to make it to them mountains yonder,' he called, and pointed to the high ridge of purple rock far ahead, 'and find me a den there. With you, or without you.'

'Cara,' Micah said and, for the first time, he seemed to notice how far ahead the others were. He squeezed her hands. 'You waited for me.'

Of course I waited for you. I would wait a thousand years for you. An eternity. The thoughts jabbered and jostled inside Cara's head, but remained unspoken. She shrugged.

'Didn't want to lose you,' she said lightly.

Micah nodded. 'I . . .' He fell still.

Cara looked into his eyes, wondering whether he was going to finish his thought – and when he did not, she let go of one of his hands and tugged him into motion with the other.

'Come on,' she said, pulling him along with her as she strode ahead. She nodded into the distance. 'Eli seems determined to reach those mountains by sundown.'

Micah observed them. 'They're not as close as they look,' he said.

Cara nodded.

'And if I know Eli Halfwinter,' Micah went on, 'he won't be content with just reaching them. Happen he'll be fixing to press on through them before darkness forces us to rest up.'

'Then come *on*,' said Cara, tugging his arm again.

They continued after the others, walking in silence for several minutes, before Cara spoke again.

'Thrace . . .' she began.

'Thrace?' Micah said warily. 'What about Thrace?'

Cara sighed miserably.

'What about Thrace?' he repeated.

'Nothing, I . . .' Cara instantly regretted speaking the kin-girl's name, suddenly afraid she would hear things she didn't want to know. 'The pair of you shared a winter den.' She hesitated. 'You must have been very close.'

Micah shrugged. 'Thrace is kinned,' he said matter-of-factly. 'Like them other wyrmes and their riders that captured Ethan.' He swallowed. 'Her bond is with Aseel, her wyrme.'

Micah realized how low his voice had become, how fractured – and he realized too the effect his words were having on Cara. She nodded and tried to smile, but she looked tense and shrunken into herself. He smiled back at her, hoping to make her feel better.

'Thrace and I could never have stayed together,' he said.

Cara shivered, her thoughts colliding with one another inside her head. She was glad they could never have stayed together. More than glad. But Micah wasn't. Despite the smile he'd managed, that much was clear. And the obvious pain in his eyes filled Cara with a nagging desperation. Oh, she could do her best to wash away his pain, and would do. But what then? Thrace would always be someone missing from his life; a part of him that he could not have. And she, Cara, would forever be second best.

'Y'all right?' Micah asked her tentatively.

Cara looked at him, nodded, a small fragile smile on her lips. 'I'm all right,' she said.

They arrived in the foothills of the mountain range soon after the sun had disappeared behind the tall purple crags. The sky was still light and the cragclimber proposed that they press on.

Ethan and Cody exchanged glances. The pair of them would have preferred to rest, but were not about to speak up.

'Think we can find a way through?' Micah asked.

Eli shrugged. 'Happen there's only one way to find out.'

They set off into a likely-looking pass, a small stream coursing through a narrow, steep-sided valley, the lower rock walls thick with broad ferns and pale stubby succulents. Half an hour in and a sheer rockface with water cascading over it from high above forced them back the way they'd come. They fared no better at their second attempt, while the third cleft in the rock closed up before they'd gone more than a hundred yards. Darkness was beginning to close in.

Micah scanned the landscape around them. The foothills seemed, to his mind at least, uncommon fertile. The further south away from the wyrme galleries they'd travelled, the greener the landscape had become. And here the low mounds and outcrops of rock that fringed the grasslands and abutted the soaring mountains beyond were thick with low trees and berried shrubs and clumps of herbs, that scented the still-warm air with rich tangy smells. There were the telltale signs of a valley to his right – a broad stream, dense foliage; mander-wyrme and bluewing nests clinging to the vertical cliffsides.

'How about that one?' he suggested.

Eli nodded. 'Go ahead and scout it. We'll follow.' He stopped to tighten the straps of his backpack. Micah and Cara went on ahead, while Ethan and Cody stayed with Eli.

The gloom wrapped itself around them. The air was pungent and moist. Dense tumblemoss clung to the rocks. Micah stumbled ahead, the scene before him almost seeming to flash on and off as the colours peaked and faded, and his night vision of black and white and grey took hold. They'd advanced into the valley some three hundred yards or so, climbing the while, when Micah caught sight of what he took to be a large grey boulder up ahead. Unlike all the others, though, there were no ferns clinging to it; no lichen, no moss.

As he got closer Micah saw that it wasn't a boulder at all. It was a greywyrme, lying dead and desiccated on the ground, its tail half-curled, body twisted with legs to one side, and long neck outstretched. The creature looked as though it had been fighting. There were deep wounds and gashes on its back and flanks, and one of the stubby wings was torn and hanging on by a dark bloody tendon.

Micah approached the corpse and frowned, nonplussed.

There was a rope shackling the greywyrme's back legs together. He moved round to the front of the creature. More rope had been used to clamp the jaws tight shut, while attached to its head was something that to Micah resembled horse-blinkers. He stepped away from the dead wyrme, turned back and peered into the shadowy darkness behind him.

'Eli!' he called. 'Eli! There's something up here you need to see.'

Twenty-Three

Nathaniel's mouth tasted foul. He sat up on one elbow, reached out and poured himself a mug of water. Took a sip.

The water was sugary, citric, and he gulped it to the bottom of the glass, then poured himself another from the jug beside the bed. He sat up and leaned back against the wall behind him till the hammering in his head subsided some.

He was back in Garth Temple's quarters, the mean little timber cabin with the earthen floor and hard bed, yet he had no memory of getting there. Not for the first time, he asked himself what he was doing in this flyblown hell-hole.

'So the young merchant adventurer is off to seek his fortune in the high country,' his father had said, when Nathaniel had finally got up the courage to outline his plans. 'And all based on the magnificent theories of a scrimshaw den trader.'

Nathaniel grimaced. He could see that look on his father's face now, a look of patronizing contempt; he could hear the sarcasm that loaded his words.

Scrimshaw den *master* he was. And more than that, Garth Temple was a man with a vision – a vision that made sense to Nathaniel, of a great train of greywyrmes, each with an immense load strapped to its back and whole families of settlers following behind their great swishing tails. From the badlands up to the weald and back again they would plough a trail, taking settlers one way and weald goods the other. At the new stockade, the weald goods would be unloaded and sent on down tothe plains in ox carts which, in turn, would bring fresh settlers up to the new stockade.

There was a fortune to be made, Garth Temple had declared, for men of vision. Like themselves.

Nathaniel's pulse quickened just thinking about it. Holding a hand to his head, he climbed gingerly to his feet, crossed to the window and looked out.

Construction of the bunkhouses was continuing apace, with the foundations of three more buildings already in place. He watched the carpenters and joiners and tilers hard at work, their faces glistening in the swelter of the mid-morning sun.

He had to hand it to Garth Temple. The stockade was beginning to look like a proper settlement. But Nathaniel was paying for it all, and he wanted a return on his investment as soon as possible. The settlers wouldn't pay up until the corral was full and Garth Temple's 'great journey' to the weald could finally set off. Then Nathaniel could return to the plains, his purse bulging, to wipe that contemptuous smile of his father's face once and for all.

'Morning, Nat!'

The rough yet jovial voice broke into his thoughts, though Nathaniel did not associate it with himself. At least, not at first. It was only when he saw the burly kith wyrmehandler with the shaved head grinning up at him from the courtyard outside, that he realized Solomon Tallow had intended his greeting for him.

And it all came back to Nathaniel. The tavern. The trapper. The fight. And the long hard drinking session that he had had with Tallow and his wyrmehandlers.

They'd had trouble with his name – or feigned it, calling him Nestor, or Nicodemus, or Nebuchadnezzar, and roaring with laughter each time he'd corrected them. Laughing himself, Nathaniel had spelled it out.

'N-A-T . . .' – which was as far as he got before Tallow had raised a hand to stop him.

'Nat,' he'd said. 'Nat is good. Nat we can remember, eh, boys?' And he'd raised his tankard of ale and toasted him. 'To Nat!' he'd said.

And the others had raised their own tankards in response. 'To Nat!'

As the ale took hold, Nathaniel had begun to relax. It had felt good being accepted by these rough, weald-seasoned kith. The drink had flowed. More tankards of ale, accompanied by shots of green liquor that tasted of tar and anise, and, as he gulped them down, each one burned his throat a little less than the one before. When the others had become rowdy, with backslapping and hearty laughter; sharing stories, breaking into song, Solomon had taken him to one side.

Nathaniel remembered how he'd fixed him with those dark eyes of his. And when he'd spoken, Solomon's voice was low and intimate, like he was taking the young merchant into his confidence.

'You seem like an enterprising young fellow,' he'd said. 'Well-connected down on the plains, according to Lizzie the tavern-maid over there, and doing fine work recruiting would-be settlers.'

Nathaniel had nodded, his brow furrowed.

'Well, *I'm* well connected up in the weald,' Solomon had continued. 'Got the harpoon gangs organized and working for me. Rounding up greywyrmes ready to herd down here to the new stockade. Already a new batch on its way, or should be.'

Nathaniel had tried to concentrate, but his head was swimming, and it was all he could do to follow Tallow's words.

'Thing is,' the kith gangmaster had added, 'with you at one end of this here operation and me at the other, my question to you is . . .' Solomon had paused and held the young merchant's gaze, unblinking, for what seemed like an age.

'What?' Nathaniel had said. His voice was slurring and Solomon seemed to have four eyes.

'Do we need a middle-man?' Solomon had said. Then he'd grinned, placed a hand on Nathaniel's shoulder. 'Do we need Garth Temple?'

Now, in the dry and dusty courtyard outside his window, Solomon had stopped and was looking at Nathaniel amiably, his teeth bared and hands on his hips.

'Thought about my question from last night?' he asked.

The colour drained from the young merchant's cheeks and, in the presence of the rough bluff kith, he suddenly felt callow, effete.

'Just thinking it over now,' he replied, his voice barely more than a whisper.

Twenty-Four

It was six days later when a distant dustcloud heralded the arrival of a second convoy of greywyrmes. It might have been sooner than that, but for the violent lightning storms that had gripped the badlands in between.

Forked lightning bolts had hurtled down out of a glowering sky for three days and three nights solid, striking the parched ground and skewering anything in their way. The greywyrmes in the stalls bucked and bellowed. The silo was damaged, and one of the newly completed bunkhouses was struck and set ablaze. Word had gone up at once, and the plainsfolk had organized a human chain from the well to the burning building, passing buckets back and forth, while the roughneck kith trappers watched from the tavern porch, shouting raucous encouragement, but making no move to help.

Each day, fresh would-be settlers had arrived from the low plains, their worldly possessions packed onto the backs of carts and wagons and pulled by exhausted oxen and wheezing, half-starved mules. The plainsfolk were grateful for the shelter the new stockade afforded up here in the badlands, and they huddled in groups in the lee of its buildings and beside the corral. Finally, the lightning storms passed, and when the cry went up that more greywyrmes were approaching, the newcomers joined the others of the stockade to greet the incoming convoy.

Garth Temple was at the head of the crowd, his eyes wide with astonishment. More greywyrmes. He could scarce believe it. Solomon Tallow had been as good as his word. Those harpoon gangs of his had indeed been busy and now a second convoy had arrived.

And what a second convoy!

The proprietor of the new stockade raised his spyglass to his eye. There must be a hundred of the creatures. At least.

He looked round, searching the crowd for any sign of Solomon or his men. Or Nathaniel Lint, for that matter.

The young merchant had kept himself to himself since the first greywyrmes had arrived, hardly leaving his room in Garth's quarters. And for Garth Temple himself – whose time was taken up tending to the poor mistreated creatures – this had suited him just fine.

The convoy came closer. Garth called to his head stockman, Ebenezer, who came hurrying over, the burnt side of his face and neck still wrapped in salve-soaked bandages.

'Prepare the corral,' he instructed.

Ebenezer nodded, and he and the other stockmen headed over to the corral, where they set to work forking straw and shifting hay bales, and laying down the heavy planks of wood over the trenches that led into the stalls. Garth realized his heart was racing.

One hundred greywyrmes! Enough for the great journey! The money would come pouring in from settlers eager to secure their places. And then, of course, there was his lucrative sideline – all that flameoil to be tapped.

It occurred to Garth that he would have his hands full. It was all he could do to tap the eleven wyrmes from the first convoy. Clearly he would need help – though only from those he could trust . . .

He looked round again. There was no sign of either Solomon Tallow or Nathaniel Lint, and he wondered at it. Surely they must have heard the commotion the incoming convoy of wyrmes was causing.

And then he saw them.

The pair of them were standing over by the well. Tallow had his back to him, but his brawny shoulders and shaven scalp were unmistakable. The young merchant was frowning, shaking his head. The pair of them were deep in conversation.

And Garth Temple's heart raced a little bit faster.

'I figured you'd been avoiding me,' Solomon said, his casual drawl belied by the intensity of his gaze. That, and the tight grip he had on Nathaniel's arm.

'Avoiding you?' Nathaniel said innocently.

'Avoiding me,' Solomon repeated.

It was true. Nathaniel *had* been avoiding Solomon Tallow. The fact was, despite Tallow's casual manner and easy smile, Nathaniel found the gangmaster intimidating. He'd been a fool to get drunk with him and his men that night in the tavern, and he bitterly regretted it.

Since then, the young merchant had spent most of his time holed up in Garth Temple's quarters, hiding. He would have slipped away and returned to the low plains if he could. But the lightning storms had started up, and Nathaniel Lint was even more frightened of lightning than he was of Solomon Tallow and his gang.

But now there were more greywyrmes coming in. Nathaniel had ventured out of his room and headed across the new stockade, hoping to find Garth Temple – only to run into Solomon Tallow himself.

'I believe you and me had a deal,' he told him, his tone a shade light of gruff. 'And a deal's a deal.'

'In . . . indeed it is,' said Nathaniel. Unable to meet the kith's penetrating gaze, his eyes darted around uneasily. 'I'm sorry. I've . . .'

He fell still, knowing that appealing to ill health – head-pain, belly-ache, fever; excuses that would have worked down on the plains – would not cut it here. Not with this pitiless kith from the high country.

'Thing is,' said Solomon, 'it would be bad for business to

scare the settlers. We agreed that, didn't we?' He thrust his face into the young merchant's, but his voice remained calm, quiet. 'This has got to be handled . . . delicately,' Solomon went on. 'And someone utterly above suspicion has to handle it.'

Nathaniel trembled at the words.

Solomon frowned, and when he spoke again his voice was low, almost intimate. 'And we talked about how to achieve our ends, did we not? You remember?'

And Nathaniel did remember. It came back to him, cold and clear and real, like a bucket of cold water being dashed in his face. Solomon's proposal, spoken the morning after that drunken night in the tavern. Words whispered through an open window; words he had listened to and had failed to contradict.

Nathaniel nodded meekly.

'Good,' said Solomon, his eyes thin dark strips as he stared into the young merchant's face. 'Then see to it. I swear I ain't fixing to remind you again.'

'Watch and learn,' Garth told Ebenezer and the other stockmen when they had joined him in the stall.

Garth demonstrated how to attach the leather pouch round a greywyrme's neck, and where to make the incision for the tapping-pipe. Then he stood back and watched as, first Ebenezer, then the others, tried the procedure for themselves.

They found it difficult. The wyrmes were wary, jittery, and though they were muzzled, the blows from their powerful swaying necks sent stockmen sprawling more than once.

'Excellent,' Garth conceded when the last of them had successfully attached a pouch and spigot to a wyrme. 'I want the whole herd tapped by sundown,' he added, turning away.

The rest of the huge creatures shuffled in their stalls, and the air in the corral was thick with their warm loamy odour. Muffled grunts and groans seeped from their muzzled jaws.

Garth left the greywyrmes and the stockmen who were seeing to them. He crossed back over the yard of the corral, and was surprised to see Nathaniel Lint loitering at the split-rail fence. The young merchant was deep in thought, and when Garth greeted him, he looked up, the expression on his face oddly shifty, Garth thought. Nathaniel raised a hand in acknowledgement, only to turn away immediately afterwards and hurry off, back hunched and head down.

Garth frowned thoughtfully, then shrugged. The young merchant was an odd one, all right.

He paused at one of the troughs, unhooked a dip-ladle and plunged it into the water. He drank long and deep, satisfying his thirst, then returned the ladle to its hook and strode over to the store-shack for an empty earthenware pot. He hurried across to the line of wyrmestalls on the far side of the corral where he had put the first arrivals.

The greywyrmes there looked magnificent now. Sleek, vigorous and well-fed, they bore no sign of the rigours of the arduous journey they'd endured from the high plains, driven on by the callous kith wyrmehandlers.

'Not a moment too soon,' Garth muttered to himself as

he observed the bulging leather pouch at the neck of the first creature.

He tipped the contents of the pouch into the pot, taking care not to spill a single drop. The flameoil sloshed about satisfactorily. He moved on to the second wyrme.

The creatures were used to him now. There was no more rolling of eyes or scratching at the dust with their claws. Instead, with the flameoil constantly draining away, they were left placid and malleable. Content, even.

'That's it, my beauty,' Garth murmured softly. 'That's the way.'

At the sixth wyrme in the line, Garth hesitated, puzzled. He reached out and cupped the leather pouch in both hands. There was barely anything in it. He checked the pouch for any sign of a split in the leather, and the dusty ground beneath, to see whether any of the precious flameoil had dripped away.

The wyrme juddered and swayed, and Garth looked up to see that its eyes had darkened to a deep fiery red.

Then he noticed the spigot.

His heart gave a lurch. The little wooden tap had been screwed down, closing off the tapping-pipe and preventing the flameoil from draining away.

The greywyrme leaned forward, its long neck craning. A yellow-white plume of searing flame billowed from its yawning mouth.

Garth's screams were extinguished in an instant as the flames enveloped him. He crumpled to the ground in a ball of fire. And when, half an hour later, Ebenezer found him, it was too late. Garth's curled-up body was charred and smoking and quite quite dead.

Nathaniel Lint found Solomon Tallow standing outside Garth Temple's quarters. He looked up, his dark eyes filled with sorrow.

'Terrible accident,' he observed, and his mouth twitched into something that looked almost like a smile.

Nathaniel's stomach was churning. His head spun. The kith gangmaster reached out and gripped him by the shoulders.

'Y'all right?' he said.

Nathaniel nodded dumbly.

Solomon's eyes narrowed against the glare of the late afternoon sun.

'Guess these quarters belong to you now.' He paused. 'Since you're now the proprietor of the new stockade.'

Nathaniel lowered his head – only for Solomon to put his fingers beneath his chin and lift it again, till the two of them were staring at one another.

'Cheer up, Nat,' he said, fixing him with a stare. 'The first murder always hits hardest.' He frowned. 'If you're to prosper in the weald, it won't be your last.'

Nathaniel Lint the Younger trembled beneath the brutal gaze of the kith gangmaster. Garth Temple had been in the way; the 'middle-man' as Solomon had put it – and when an inquisitive settler-boy had provided him with some very useful information about the wyrmes and their flameoil, he had passed it on to Nathaniel.

And now Garth Temple was out of the way.

Nathaniel had lost one partner and gained another – a ruthless weald-hardened gangmaster. He had a sinking feeling in the pit of his stomach.

'We split the settlers' fares, but I keep the flameoil.' Solomon flashed that broad white-toothed smile of his. 'Any objections?'

He extended his hand to Nathaniel.

'Let's shake on it,' he said. 'Partner.'

Twenty-Five

Cara leaned forward, her eyes fixed on the sky. She'd never seen anything like it.

Jagged forks of lightning, too numerous to count, hissed and crackled down out of the vaulted indigo heavens one after the other. They were still for a moment, like a forest of dazzling stalactites, then vanished – only to be replaced by countless more a heartbeat later. Thunder crashed and rumbled in an endless tumult of percussion. The air smelled charred. The curtain of night pulsated and flashed, and when Cara blinked, afterglowed pink and green.

She looked down at Micah, who was lying on his side, head in her lap, staring up into the sky as intently as she herself had been. Her fingers played idly with his hair, brushing the thick strands back and forwards. She traced the whorls of his ear with her fingertips.

The pair of them were resting on a spread wyrme-skin pelt, Cara crosslegged, Micah sprawled out.

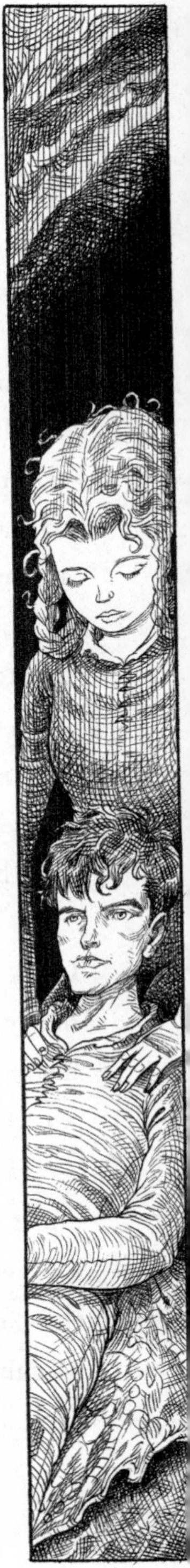

Above their heads was a broad slab of jutting rock. They were high up the north face of a steep cliffside, above the tree-line. The cave was shallow, scarcely more than a recess in the rock, but at least it afforded them some shelter from the dry lightning storm that had swept in with such speed and lack of warning.

'It ain't what we're looking for long-term,' Eli had observed. He looked round, head stooped forward so as not to graze his scalp on the low rock. 'But I reckon it'll do till this storm eases off.'

Cody and Ethan had looked at each other, and Ethan had had to stifle a grin. It certainly would do. Very nicely. They'd been travelling without respite through the east mountains and beyond for twelve days now, and any rest was welcome.

'Get a fire going,' Eli had told them. 'I'll fetch some water and then we'll try to get us some shut-eye.'

Cody could not sleep. Despite the plentiful supper he'd eaten; despite the lateness of the hour; despite being half-dead on his feet, he was unable to drift off. He wondered whether he was the only one.

He looked at his younger brother enviously, watching his chest rhythmically rising and falling. And Eli was snoring, a regular throat-rattle and soft whistle that seemed to fill the cave. Micah and Cara were curled up spoonwise, with Micah's arm draped around Cara's body. Their breathing came low and even.

No, he thought. Just me.

Beyond the cave, the electric storm raged on loud and bright and violent. Cody wrapped an arm round his head.

He hated lightning. Hated and feared it. Always had, for as far back as he could remember. He crushed his folded arm into his ear. He screwed his eyes shut.

'Let it be over,' he whispered. 'Please, make it stop . . .'

Cody brought his knees up and curled into a tight ball, his arms still wrapped tight and protective round his head. He recalled the greywyrme that Micah had discovered in the mountain pass, hobbled and blinkered, its jaws bound with ropes.

Eli had not said anything at first, but Cody had noted by the way his eyes hardened and his jaw clenched that the crag-climber was disturbed. He'd crouched down and examined the blinkers closely, tugging at the buckles and straps.

'This weren't made for no ox or mule,' he'd observed at length. 'It's been special designed for a greywyrme. And them ropes, stopping it from running fast or breathing fire. Or drinking,' he'd added, his voice low, thoughtful. 'Happen that's what must have killed it most like. Lest it was the brutality of its treatment . . .'

Cody vividly remembered the crisscross of welts cut into the leathery skin of the creature's back. It looked like it had taken a vicious beating. And he remembered too the scorn in Eli's voice when he had finally spoken up.

'Kith business,' he'd said.

As they'd continued up the valley through the mountains, Eli had spotted other evidence of kith. To Cody the place looked untouched, but time and again the cragclimber would point out stuff to them. Rocks set on rocks. Knotted clumps of bluegrass. Scratches in the rock, that looked like they might have been of natural cause but that Eli interpreted as man-made.

'Kith signs,' he'd said. 'Someone's been marking a trail through these mountains.'

Cody allowed himself to open his eyes. The dazzling lightning display had not abated, and when he shifted his arm he heard the thunder crashing and cracking louder than ever. He raised his head and looked across to where Micah and Cara were curled up together on the wyrmehide at the far side of the low emberglow fire. As the lightning flashed in the sky, it illuminated the pair of them. The curve of their shoulders. Their heads – Micah's fair hair looking darker than it was; Cara's hanging in delicate twisting curls. Micah's arm was folded round Cara's slender waist, and Cody's stomach cramped up at the sight of it.

His gaze lingered on Cara's body, her face; on the arch of an eyebrow, and the full, soft, slightly-parted lips. She was beautiful. Cody didn't think he'd ever seen a girl so beautiful.

He closed his eyes again, shutting out the storm – and shutting out the sight of the two of them nuzzling up close.

* * *

The storm was still raging at sun-up. Cody had finally dropped off to sleep, and was woken by Eli, who arose as the sky began to lighten, stoked the fire and stirred it back into life.

'We best remain here,' Eli counselled, 'and see to our kit.'

Ethan and Cody washed their clothes in the pool of water at the side of the cave entrance and laid them out to dry, with Cody skittish as a colt as he went about his chores, one eye on the sky. Micah sharpened his hackdagger on a chunk of powderstone he'd found on the cave floor, while Cara repaired a tear in her wyrmeskin cloak.

All at once, with a deafening crack that set the floor of the cave quaking, a bolt of lightning struck the jutting slab of rock above their heads. From the shadow-filled recesses of the shallow cave, there came the soft hiss of trickling sand and an ominous rumble. Everyone held their breath.

The next moment, with an almighty thud and boom and clatter, rocks began to fall. Eli leaped to his feet just in time as a massive boulder crashed down where he had been sitting. Cody and Ethan scrambled forward, out of the dust-filled darkness and towards the opening of the cave, while Micah crouched down over Cara, shielding her protectively. As the noise subsided and the dust settled, the continuing flash and dazzle of the lightning outside illuminated the cave.

Rocks lay in a jumbled heap. And there, at the back of the cave, was a jagged crack in the rock wall.

Eli pulled a stubby dip-torch from his backpack and lit it. The flame flickered for a moment, then caught. The cragclimber held the flaming torch before him and approached the dark opening. He climbed up onto a displaced slab of rock, then thrust the dip-torch inside the crevice.

Micah squeezed Cara's hand, then crossed the cave after Eli, fallen grit and gravel crunching under his boots. Eli disappeared through the hole. Cody watched the flamelight flicker inside, then turned to Cara, who looked set to follow Micah, and he reached out and stayed her with his arm.

'Best stay here,' he told her softly, 'till we know it's safe.'

'See anything?' Micah called through the hole.

There was a moment's silence, then Eli's voice floated back. It sounded deep and echoey. 'Come see for yourself,' he said.

Micah scrambled up the fallen rocks and manoeuvred himself through the hole. He jumped down onto the floor on the other side and looked around. Eli was standing on the far side of a vast cavern. There were stalactites and stalagmites to one side, and water trickled down over a jutting overhang. On the other side of the cavern, the wall was studded with half a dozen gaps in the rock, some that seemed to lead into smaller chambers; one that twisted up into the ceiling. In the light of the dip-torch flames, motes of dust could be seen coursing down from the vertical hole on an incoming draught of pure sweet air.

Eli turned to the youth. His face looked more at ease with itself than Micah had seen it in weeks.

'Happen we might have found us a winter den after all,' he said.

* * *

'Fresh water. Clean air. Wood close by to burn, and space enough both for the five of us and all the stores we'll need to survive fullwinter.' Eli poked at the embers of the fire, which crackled and pulsed and sent sparks flying up into the darkening sky. 'Reckon this den could really work out for us.'

At the cragclimber's instruction, they had already cleared the newly fallen rocks and rigged up a slab of sandstone inside the cavern that, when the time came, they would be able to use to seal the den. They had also emptied their backpacks.

All the stuff they had gathered along the trail was lying in different piles. Fibrous bollweed that would yield up string and yarn; wyrme-carcasses, to be stripped for their skin and bones. A full pouch of salt. Roots, funguses and a range of pungent herbs that the cragclimber identified either as having medicinal properties or tasting good. And there was also the knife – a folding affair with a jag-blade and a small saw attachment – which Ethan had spotted in the valley pass through the east mountains. One of the kith must have dropped it and, to Ethan's delight, the cragclimber had allowed him to keep it.

'Course, it ain't going to be easy getting set up,' Eli was saying, his face earnest as he looked at them each in turn. 'We're going to have to work hard. Fullwinter's always closer than it seems.'

The lightning storm had finally passed overhead and the air felt cool and fresh.

'First off, we'll need to start laying up stocks from hereabouts. Fish to be smoked. Any fruit and edible roots we can find. And firewood. Lots of firewood. It gets bitter cold inside a winter den in the depths of fullwinter,' he said, looking at the two brothers, each in turn. 'Then there's stuff we can't forage and can't do without. Flameoil, green liquor, spitbolts and medicine.' He shrugged. 'Items that can mean the difference twixt life and death.'

Eli turned to the others. 'We're gonna have to journey back east and trade for such things in a scrimshaw den,' he said. His eyes narrowed. 'And when we do, we'll need to keep our wits about us – as Micah can attest.'

Eli sat back and smiled. The others searched Micah's face for his reaction, but he merely acknowledged the cragclimber's words with a nod.

'Now get this lot packed away,' Eli told them. 'We'll begin our preparations tomorrow.'

The others nodded and set to work. Eli left them to it. He climbed to his feet and shambled out of the cave, then perched down on a rocky outcrop, high above the ravine that fell away below the cave. He reached into the pocket of his heavy hacketon and drew out the huge claw he'd secreted there. It was blue-grey and heavy in his hand, the point vicious sharp – the larger of the two he'd found at the scene of the massacred kith.

He surveyed the sky. Whatever creature this massive claw belonged to was out there somewhere, and the prospect of running into such a beast filled the cragclimber with foreboding. He turned the claw over in his hand thoughtfully. Greywyrmes in harness. Kith marking trails through the mountains. And these massive unknown wyrmes roaming the weald . . .

These were strange times in the high country. And Eli Halfwinter did not like them; did not like them one little bit.

Twenty-Six

The night-foragers were out. They were hunting round the dewponds, where swarms of insects were at their most plentiful.

There were tufted skitterwyrmes, their shaggy crests flaring like struck matches as the sporadic moonlight came and went. There were bearded rockwyrmes and silver snapwings, and a pair of night-wyrmes, with angular snouts and huge black eyes. Some were scratching at the ground for grubs; some flapped low over the rocks and grass, snatching bugs and beetles from the air.

A warm breeze blew across the grasslands, rippling the wild barley and plains vetch and bringing with it a sweet yet acrid odour. The wyrmes twitched and tasted the air, then scattered, chittering and screeching into the night.

High above, the clouds parted momentarily and the moon shone down on a line of figures moving silently through the long plains grass – tall, heavily-armed men in wyrmescale armour and bleachedbone masks.

The valley keld were on the move. They had left their subterranean caverns and were moving silently through the night.

The first carried a woven basket strapped to his shoulders, containing the small wizened figure of Blue Slake the poisoner, in his grubby high-collared coat of faded velvet. As the basket swayed, he scanned the trail ahead, one clawlike hand gripping a spyglass, the other dabbing at the hole in his ruined face, where a nose had once been.

Following behind came four hulking slaves, a hammock of lakewyrmeskin slung between them. In its folds there reclined the eel-mother, an immensely fat woman with serpentine curls and sharp broken teeth, two plump crevicewyrmes coiled around her shoulders.

Next came two more slaves, in heavy black cloaks, carrying a padded chair on two poles. The occupant of the chair was Cutter Daniel the distiller. He wore a spiked skullcap pulled down low over his pallid grey face, and a leather coat that had small bottles attached to it, each one individually wrapped in a wad of gauze so they would not knock together and clink their wearer's presence. As he raised his hand, the moonlight glinted on the needlepoints of his filed nails, and on the long knotted whip of plaited wyrmeskin he held.

A dozen more heavily-armed slaves followed, axes, flails and intricately barbed gutting tools gripped in their huge fists. The bone masks at their faces made them as grotesque and inscrutable as demons in a nightmare. They moved stealthily on moccasined feet, peering this way and that as they crept through the grass.

At the back of the column, seated on a cushioned bench that was slung between two more bone-masked men, a black-hooded figure rocked gently back and forth.

'They came this way,' Blue Slake called back from the front of the line.

'Yes. And they're close. I sense it.'

The voice from beneath the hood was soft and honeyed, with a silky musical lilt, little more than a whisper. The keld mistress pushed her hood back, and her alabaster-white face, white hair, white eyelashes, seemed almost to glow in the moonlight. Her turquoise eyes sparkled; bloodless lips parted to reveal small sharpened teeth.

'Eli Halfwinter . . . and the boy . . .'

Twenty-Seven

Micah looked ahead, his eyes narrowed against the low morning sun. They were on the western fringes of the valley country. A hundred yards or so further ahead, the ridge they were standing on dropped sharply away into a broad valley with pine-pocked sides and a barley-fringed river that meandered along its floor. On the far side – maybe half a mile or so off, where the mountains rose up again – was a cluster of man-made constructions.

A roof, fashioned from long straight logs, jutted out from the rock close to the bottom of the cliff-face, and beyond its shaded cover were low stone-wall pens and runty outhouses. To one side stood a tall pine, stripped, dead, a tattered banner fluttering limply at its top.

Micah turned to Eli, who had his spyglass to his eye and was taking it all in. Behind them, Cara, Ethan and Cody remained silent, shifting their heavy backpacks on their shoulders and exchanging weary looks. They had been on the trail for seventeen days, and they were footsore and bone-tired and desperate for some sort of respite.

It was Cody who spoke up. 'Eli?' he said, his voice flat, blunt. 'Have we found us a scrimshaw den or not?'

The cragclimber lowered his spyglass and turned to him, then to the others. He tipped back his broadbrim hat, mopped his brow on the back of his hand.

'It's a scrimshaw den all right,' he said. 'But not the one I was heading for. Seems to be a new operation by the look of it. The Deadpine Den it proclaims itself.' He paused, nodded, and a small smile cracked his dour expression when he saw Cara's expectant face staring back at him. 'Fancy heading on down to take a look?'

Cara smiled back at him. 'You try stopping us,' she said.

'Greetings, strangers,' came a voice.

Eli stopped in his tracks. The others came to a halt behind him. A man was crouched at the edge of the jutting log roof, peering down at them. He was sunbrowned and wiry, with greying hair, salt-and-pepper to his grizzled jaw, and eyes that looked in two directions at the same time. It was difficult to see where his gaze was fixed, but Micah assumed it was on them.

'Come for trade?' he said. 'Or do you want lodging?'

'Trade,' said Eli. 'We ain't fixing to stay longer than we have to, friend.'

The man nodded. He was chewing lazily on cudleaf, and

his mouth slipped into an easy smile to reveal brown-stained teeth. He scrambled to his feet, then slid down one of the thick uprights that supported the roof. He was more agile than his age might have allowed. He thrust out a hand to Eli that was lean and bony, the skin as loose as an old leather glove.

'Fletcher Crow,' he announced. 'Denkeeper of the Deadpine.'

'Eli,' the cragclimber told him. 'Eli Halfwinter.'

He shook the scrimshaw den owner's hand stiffly, his shoulders hunched and his eyes impassive, and Micah was aware that the cragclimber was on his guard, and that he should be too. He glanced around at the entrance to the den.

There were empty pens, covered in netting and intended for rockwyrmes, flitterwyrmes and the like. Beside them stood several shacks with drystone walls and half-anchored tarpaulin covers that flapped in the wind to reveal drying racks and gutting slabs for the curing of wyrmepelts. These too were empty. The sturdy roof over the cave entrance was constructed from bleached logs that were sunk into holes cut in the sandstone at one end, fixed with crossbeams along their length, and supported on stout uprights at the other. A wooden sign hung from one of the crossbeams, its carved letters announcing *The Deadpine Scrimshaw Den – Victuals, Liquor and Goods for Trade.*

Eli looked up at the sign, then back at the man called Fletcher Crow. 'Been here long?' he enquired.

'Long enough,' Fletcher Crow replied, and spat a jet of cudleaf juice onto the dirt at his feet. 'Had a pitch in a den down near rooster rock. Back east of here. Happen you might know it.'

'I know it,' Eli confirmed.

'Owned by Garth Temple.' Crow frowned. 'Took fifty percent of everything I made. Happen you might know him too,' he added. 'Old fellow. Face like a sack of weasels. I figured I'd do better if I struck out alone, so I came out here and found myself a likely spot.'

He turned and headed back into the cool shade beneath the log roof. Eli followed him, but not before shooting Micah a backwards glance. Micah nodded, and fingered the spitbolt holstered at his side. Cara noticed the movement and her eyes grew wide.

'Stay close,' Micah whispered, taking her hand and following Eli.

Behind them, Cody and Ethan stepped forward.

'What the hell you doing?' Cody muttered, trying and failing to shake off Ethan's hand, which had suddenly gripped a hold of his shoulder.

'Lead me,' said Ethan.

Cody turned, to see that his younger brother had his eyes clamped tightly shut.

'What foolishness is this now?' he said.

Ethan smiled, but kept his eyes shut. 'I ain't never seen the inside of a scrimshaw den before,' he said, as though that were explanation enough. 'You tell me when to open my eyes.'

Cody hesitated, and for a moment Ethan thought he was going to refuse. But then Cody grunted and walked on, and Ethan knew he was being indulged.

'You're still just a big kid, ain't yer?' he grumbled, but there was affection in his voice.

'Just as well I've got you to look after me, then,' said Ethan.

They stepped over the threshold.

'You can open them eyes of yours now,' Cody announced, his voice shrouded with echo.

Ethan hesitated a moment, enjoying the anticipation. Over two weeks on the trail – weeks of barleymeal, hardtack and dried wyrmemeat, and a rucksack for a pillow. But now he was finally here, in a scrimshaw den, where all the riches of the weald were to be found. Leastways, that was the way Micah had told it. He sniffed long and deep.

The air was moist and steeped in odours. Stale liquor, woodsmoke, and something sweet and pungent that Ethan could not place. And from the echoing tone to the various noises he could hear – scratching and scraping, footfall, voices and such – the place sounded enormous.

Ethan opened his eyes and blinked, and could not help but be disappointed. The promised hustle and bustle and cornucopia of items for sale was so much less than he had been led to believe. Certainly the place was large, but that only served to diminish the scale of its contents.

Like an amphitheatre, the cavernous den fanned out from the entrance, rising up in broad semi-circular, stonecut terraces. To the far right, a stream of water trickled down over the copper-stained rock and collected in a large pool. Dip-torches in iron brackets cast shadows over the high ceiling of the cavern, from which dozens of metal cages of various shapes and sizes hung down on chains. But like the abandoned pens and the squat shacks outside, the cages were empty.

Figures sat hunched in small groups on the terraces, gathered around ill-stocked wyrmepelts spread out on the floor. An old man lay on a moth-eaten blanket, fast asleep and snoring. A way to his left, a couple – toothless and bony – were slumped up against one another, shoulder to shoulder, deep in slurred muttering. A straggle-bearded man, knelt beside a length of uncured wyrmeskin, was scraping the fat from the rough underside with a ridged block of pumice. Occasionally he would look up, eyes ablaze, to continue an argument with a second man, who seemed to be offering advice but little practical help. And a group of raggedy feral-looking children with tangled hair and grimy faces dodged and darted around the groups in what looked like a never-ending game of tag.

Fletcher Crow waved a hand at the terraces in a broad sweep. 'Business is a bit slow,' he admitted. 'Seems a lot of kith are heading back east into the badlands to trade these days . . .'

'The badlands?' said Eli, and Micah noticed the surprise in his voice.

To his left, Ethan let out a rueful whistle. 'Wouldn't catch me going back there, not for anything, eh, Cody?'

Cody ignored him. His eyes were fixed on an elderly woman in a filthy apron who was squatting beside a wyrmepelt covered with pieces of delicately carved wyrmebone.

'It's where the new settlement is,' Fletcher said bitterly,

and spat. 'Folks say there ain't nothing they can't trade there for twenty times what they'd get here in the weald.' He glanced up at the empty cages above their heads. 'Even buying live wyrmes down there, according to the harpoon gangs.'

Micah saw Eli flinch, and he remembered the dead grey-wyrme they'd found shackled and bound in the pass.

Fletcher smiled. 'So it sure is good to welcome kith such as yourselves, with heavy packs and an eye for a good trade.'

Eli nodded, but did not return the den owner's smile. Instead, Micah saw his pale-blue eyes scan the terraces above them, picking out the kith in the shadows; lean, half-starved men in tattered cloaks who looked back hungrily.

Fletcher Crow bowed and headed back to the entrance, and Micah noticed several of the raggedy kith follow him. He suddenly had a panicky trapped feeling in the pit of his stomach. There was limebark, dried salsify roots, cudleaf and wyrmepelts in the pack on Micah's back; goods he would trade for the tools and medicine they needed for the winter – if, that is, he could find them in this poorly-stocked scrimshaw den. And, more importantly, so long as they managed to get out again without being robbed blind.

Twenty-Eight

Cody leaned forward, picked up one of the pieces of scrimshaw laid out on the wyrmepelt before him and turned it over in his hands. Then he replaced it.

'Looking for something in particular?' the old woman croaked.

Cody did not look up. 'Don't rightly know,' he mumbled hesitantly and blushed.

He picked up another piece. It was round and delicate, and made from flawless, cream-white wyrme-bone. A whitewyrme had been carved in an oval, its serpentine tail coiling and wings raised. A leather cord was threaded through the wingtips.

'You fixing to trade for that or not?' The woman sounded querulous and impatient.

Cody looked up, the carving nestling in the palm of his large calloused hand. The woman was eyeing him suspiciously, as though she expected him to slip the medallion into his pocket and make a run for it.

'Well?' she rasped.

Cody stared down at the scrimshaw carving, then back at the woman, and he nodded, the slightest incline of his head. He reached into the side pocket of his breeches and removed two silver coins, which he held out.

'Not enough,' the woman snapped, her face crimped and scowling.

Cody shrugged. 'It's all I have,' he said, putting the medallion down and making to stand up.

'Not so hasty,' the old woman said, the harshness to her voice softening a tad. 'What you got in there, boy?' She pointed at the backpack slung over Cody's shoulder.

'Barleyseed,' he said, and heard her tut dismissively. 'Red fungus.' He swung the backpack to the ground and opened it, looked inside. 'Some heads of bollcotton . . . Oh, and these.' He pulled out a bundle of bones, the length and thickness of his middle finger. 'Wyrmebones.' He handed them to her.

The woman's interest was unmistakable. She undid the knot in the twine that bound them together and inspected the bones carefully; holding them up to the lamplight, putting them to her nose and sniffing.

'Wingbones of a mistwyrme,' she murmured. 'I'll take them. Along with the silver.'

Cody slipped the scrimshaw medallion into his breeches pocket and concluded the deal with the two silver coins before climbing to his feet. It was the last of his hard-earned plains money, the two worn silver coins. The other four –

gold pieces – he'd used to buy kit and provisions in a dusty little village, the last plains outpost before the badlands.

His fingers traced the carving in his pocket. There was no going back. Not ever.

He looked up at the next terrace. Eli was trading wyrmepelts for crossbow bolts with an armourer in a grease-stained apron and, judging by the man's waving arms and shrugging shoulders, was getting the best of the deal. Ethan was standing next to him, trying to look knowledgeable and seasoned, holding up the pelts when Eli nodded to him. But his eyes were wary and his smile faltering. Like Cody, he was aware of the kith in the shadows watching their every move.

Micah was further up the rising terraces, on his knees. He had traded the flameoil and wyrmeteeth for a new copper pot and a useful-looking rock-pick, and seemed pleased with his bargain, and Cody cursed under his breath. *He* was meant to be trading their dried goods for a flintbox, and a whetstone if there was one to be had, and he had allowed himself to get distracted by the trinkets of a scrimshaw pedlar.

Still, the mistwyrme bones were his to do with as he liked – Eli had said as much. And the silver coins he'd earned himself through back-breaking toil back there on the plains.

Cody looked around at the traders crouched down on the terraces in front of spread wyrmepelts, on which their wares were displayed. There was a distiller with small vials of green liquor, a herbalist with bunches of aromatic grasses and dark rockmoss, a knife-sharpener . . . And there on the wyrmepelt before him, a couple of whetstones. Cody smiled and made his way over, only to see Cara kneeling in front of an old kith woman who was trading weald medicine.

Cara. Cody felt his chest tighten just looking at her.

'Is that soap?' she was asking.

'Finest soap in all the weald,' the old woman replied, her tone flatter than her words. She picked up a pale-green block, the size of a brick, and passed it to Cara, who raised it to her nose.

'Myrtle,' she said.

'Finest myrtle,' the woman agreed.

Cara placed it down and inspected the other items spread out across the wyrmepelt. There was whiterot cream and leech salve, and various sticky ointments for cuts, burns and chilblains, together with rolls of cloth bandages. Cara surveyed them for a moment, then looked up at the woman. She opened her backpack and took out the pungent dried cudleaf they had gathered several weeks back on the steep banks of a mountain creek. There were five small bales, and Cody noted how the old woman's eyes lit up at the sight of them.

'I'll take all you have,' said Cara simply.

It was a good trade and the old woman knew it. She reached out and shook Cara's hand greedily.

'You got yourself a deal,' she cackled.

Cody knelt down beside Cara and helped her put the medicines into her pack.

'Seen a whetstone over there,' he told her. 'I'm fixing to trade our dried goods for it . . .' he started to say, before stopping, his face draining of all colour.

His eyes were fixed on the medallion that nestled against Cara's sunblush skin at the base of her throat. It was a piece of scrimshaw work. Round. Ornately carved.

Cara caught him staring and glanced down. She smiled, her nose crinkling up and freckles crowding together. 'Pretty, isn't it?' she said.

Cody nodded dumbly.

'Micah gave it to me,' Cara said and smiled. 'Traded the black salsify roots for two flintboxes, and got this into the bargain.'

Cody's fingers closed crushtight round the medallion in his pocket till his fingers throbbed. 'Mighty fine,' he mumbled.

'Give me the dried goods, Cody,' came a voice. It was Eli. Ethan and Micah were standing beside him looking down at Cody and Cara. 'There's a whetstone over there,' he said.

'I know, I—' Cody began, handing his pack to the crag-climber, only to be cut short.

'No time for haggling,' Eli muttered. 'We need to get out of this place.' He took Cody's pack over to the knife-sharpener and tipped its contents out in front of him. There was a brief muttered exchange and Eli returned with the smaller of the two whetstones. 'Let's go,' he said.

He turned and strode off down the terraced steps towards the cavern entrance. The others followed.

Outside, Eli paused in the shade of the jutting log roof and his eyes narrowed against the late afternoon dazzle beyond. Three men were there.

One was sitting on the low drystone wall of an empty wyrmepen, his hands on his thighs; the other two were leaning up against the wall on either side of him. They each wore broad-brimmed wyrmeskin hats, waistcoats and breeches, and had dyed homespun kerchiefs knotted around their necks. And they were armed.

Eli noted their holstered spitbolts, the knives at their belts. As he stepped slowly out from the shadow, he glanced up to see Fletcher Crow reclining in a simple wooden rocking chair that was set atop the log roof. The scrimshaw den owner shrugged as if to say this was none of his business – though Eli suspected it not to be the case.

The three men stared back at them like carrionwyrmes waiting to feast. Then a fourth man emerged from behind the back of one of the tarpaulin covered shacks, a large knife at his belt and a heavy sidewinder slung over his shoulder that glinted in the sunlight. He eyed Eli up and down with something akin to insolence.

'All done with your trading?' he said, and though his voice was amiable enough there was menace in the way he blocked the cragclimber's path.

Eli tipped his hat down till the shadow from the brim lay across his narrowed eyes. 'Happen we have, friend,' he said.

His own voice was measured, and sounded amiable enough,

but Micah noticed how the cragclimber's hand moved closer to the handle of his own holstered spitbolt. Micah did the same.

'Well, that is sure a pity,' said the man, blacknail fingers scratching at his chin. He turned to the others. 'Ain't it, boys?'

'Sure is,' they drawled back, and they ambled over to flank him, two on one side, one on the other.

The man turned back to Eli. 'See, the thing is,' he said, 'you got something that we'd be interested in trading you for.' His eyes creased at the corners as his face broke into a yellow-toothed smile. 'More than interested.'

He reached into his back pocket and pulled a hip-flask from it, which he tossed to Eli, who caught it automatically. 'Fair exchange.'

Eli glanced at the hipflask. It was silver. Half full by the feel of it. He looked up.

'Fair exchange for what?' he said.

The man jerked his head forward. 'The girl,' he said, and Micah's stomach lurched.

Cara flushed crimson.

On the rooftop, Fletcher Crow kept on rocking but did not look down. His narrowed gaze was fixed on the far horizon.

'She ain't for trade,' said Eli levelly.

The man's grin grew broader. 'I don't believe you have a choice in the matter,' he said, a soft lilt to his voice.

Eli's pale eyes darkened. He opened his hand and the hip-flask fell to the ground with a clatter. He kicked it back over the dust toward the man.

'Take your liquor and let us pass, friend,' he said.

The man stared back at him, the smile fading from his face. 'You ain't no friend of mine.'

All at once, and with no warning, he swung the heavy primed sidewinder from his shoulder and took aim – only for the cragclimber to beat him to it. The spitbolt jumped in Eli's hand as he squeezed the trigger.

The man fell to the ground, screaming with pain and clutching at the top of his thigh. Beside him, the three others leaped forward, the first landing on Eli and bringing him crashing to the ground, the second firing a spitbolt at Micah, and the third knocking Cody and Ethan to one side. A bolt hummed past Micah's head and struck a wooden crossbeam behind him as he fumbled with his own spitbolt, raising it to his eyes, firing it, hoping for the best.

The bolt buried itself in the kith's chest. The man dropped to his knees before toppling forwards and landing face down in the dust.

'Micah!'

Cara's voice cut through the air, shrill, fear-filled. Eli was grappling with the kith who had brought him down. Cody and Ethan were scrambling to their feet, white-faced and staring.

The third kith had grabbed Cara and was backing away, a muscular arm wrapped tightly round her neck and a broad-blade knife in his hand.

'Don't do anything stupid,' he hissed. 'The girl's coming with me.'

Micah froze. So did Eli. The kith he'd been wrestling with slumped over onto his side, Eli's knife in his throat and dark blood staining the ground round his head like a black halo.

The man grinned unpleasantly as he pulled Cara backwards, the blade of his knife softly caressing the side of the girl's cheek. Up and down. Up and down. Cara trembled. Up and down . . .

With a long low animal-like bellow, Cody erupted from the shade beneath the log roof and barrelled into the man bullhard, his right shoulder crunching into the man's ribs and head cracking his chin as he tore Cara from his grasp. The kith fell backwards, winded, blind with pain. Cara landed heavily in a heap. The kith slammed down on his back and Cody was upon him. He bunched his fist and punched him repeatedly in the face.

Blood spurted from a shattered nose. Teeth broke and bone crunched as he kept on punching. Hard brutal blows, without respite, that turned the man's face to a bloody pulp.

'Cody, Cody.' It was Ethan. He was tugging at his brother's collar. 'Cody, enough!'

Cody let go of the kith and fell back. He was panting and his eyes were glazed. He was somewhere else. Back on the plains, protecting his brother from another attack in the only way he knew how. Sobs racked his body as he raised his bloodied hands to cover his face.

Micah helped Cara to her feet. The sleeve of her blouse was torn and there was a thin cut on her cheek from the kith's knife. Micah reached out to wipe away the blood, but she broke away from him and knelt down beside Cody. She took him in her arms and cradled his head, whispering to him soothingly until, at last, he fell still.

The surviving kith was still rolling around in the dust, clutching his leg and moaning softly.

'Come on,' Eli said to the others. 'Let's hit the trail.'

Micah nodded numbly, retrieved his rucksack and slung it back onto his shoulders. Ethan did the same. Cara helped Cody to his feet, handed him his backpack and Cody returned the favour. Eli adjusted the straps of his own pack before reloading his spitbolt and levelling it at Fletcher Crow up on the log roof.

The denkeeper's wall-eyed stare widened. The rocking chair came to a halt. Eli shifted the spitbolt to the right and sent the bolt thudding into the dead pine.

'I find you here next time I come this way,' he said, his voice gruff with threat and promise, 'and I swear you're gonna end up deader than that tree.'

Twenty-Nine

The moon shone down on the sharp tips of the rock ridges, on scrubby pale-leafed bushes and glossy succulents, and on the small band camped beneath a high outcrop. The cragclimber and the boy. And the three others.

The keld mistress turned to the rest of the valley keld crouched down in the shadows: Cutter Daniel, Blue Slake and the eel-mother. Behind them were their keld fighters, their coldfire eyes glinting behind wyrmebone masks. The bone armour they wore was spattered with dried bloodspray and soot and, as well as the bone-hammers, rockspikes, sidewinders and knives they bore, each of them had a heavily laden forage sack at his side.

The scrimshaw den had been too tempting a target to pass up, the keld mistress acknowledged. The blood feud with the man, Eli Halfwinter, and the boy, Micah, was one thing, but a scrimshaw den, poorly defended and vulnerable out here on the fringes of kith habitation, was quite another.

The valley keld had moved in at nightfall after the keld mistress had sent a pair of scouts to keep track of Halfwinter and his band. They would deal with them soon enough.

What they found at the scrimshaw den had intrigued the keld mistress. There had been a fight the day before. It had left three kith dead and one badly wounded, and the den owner himself shaken and distracted. The keld mistress had allowed Cutter Daniel to roast him slowly over a fire while her keld dispatched the other den traders and filled their forage sacks.

It was a decent haul. What was more, between his pleadings for mercy and agonized oaths, the keld mistress learned some interesting things from Fletcher Crow – before she had finally put him out of his misery.

Once again Halfwinter and the boy had left a familiar trail of bloodshed in their wake. Just like the winter caller and the Deephome keld before him, Crow had underestimated these two, and paid the price. The keld mistress vowed not to make the same mistake . . .

But that was not all Fletcher Crow had had to say. He'd babbled on about some great journey being undertaken. It seemed that thousands of plainsfolk were gathering in the badlands, at a place they called the new stockade, with the intention of setting out for the high country in a vast wyrme-drawn wagontrain.

Crow had seen the greed glinting in the keld mistress's eyes, and perhaps hoped the embellishing of his story might buy him his life.

A grizzled kith by the name of Garth Temple was behind this great enterprise, he'd told her, and explained how Temple had recruited the harpoon gangs of the East Ridges to trap the greywyrmes for him.

Certainly the keld mistress had heard the rumours of sack-loads of harnesses and tethers being made in the gutting tarns and scrimshaw dens. She had wondered about it at the time. Now it was making some sort of sense.

There was an opportunity here, the keld mistress conceded as she unsheathed her knife of polished obsidian and slit the den owner's throat. Settlers from the plains would be easy prey compared to the seasoned kith the keld usually dealt with – and there were thousands of them into the bargain.

Naturally, the skull keld to the south and the west-dwelling deep-cavern keld would want their cut, but it seemed the valley keld had the chance to steal a march on them. The keld mistress turned, her ice-white face pinched with determination, and gave the signal to her keld.

But first, Halfwinter and the boy . . .

Thirty

Kesh ate greedily, tearing at the soft succulent flesh of the rustfly larva with sharp teeth. His wyrme Azura breathed out. Fragrant white smoke billowed from her parted jaws and enfolded the crouching youth beside her. Her yellow eyes glowed. She enjoyed watching him eat – the fierce concentration he had as he tore at the food; biting, chewing, swallowing, in swift convulsive movements.

Just like a wyrme.

When she had found him, Kesh had been two years old, maybe less. He was crouched over his dead mother, beating her with small hard fists, screeching at her to wake up. A rockfall had crushed her legs and pinned her there at the foot of the steep gulley where, from the agonized look on her sunken face, she had taken her time to die.

Azura had seen plenty of dead kith like this one. Their bodies were strewn throughout the valley country – victims of disease, mishap and hunger. And when they died, they left their young; tiny and fragile and defenceless in the harshness of the weald. The whitewyrme had felt the intense pang of kinship twice in her long life. Once with Kale, and she had shared many fullwinters with him until a kith bolt had robbed him of his life.

And now with Kesh.

Where Kale had been quiet and watchful, hesitant in his thoughts and actions, no matter how much encouragement Azura gave him, Kesh was impulsive, almost reckless. There was a savage anger in him that had grown more keen with each season. And Azura had taken care to nourish it. Kesh was too skilful, too agile, too clever to fall victim to the kith the way Kale had done. He knew how to track and hunt them, how to lay in wait and how to attack – and, most important of all, how to prolong the distress and agony of the two-hides he caught.

Slowdeath. At that, Kesh had shown real talent.

Azura knew this cruelty appalled the others. Avaar, Aakhen, Amir, Aluris. And their kin. But it thrilled her – thrilled her more than she liked to admit. Kesh was her weapon, merciless and intractable. When they flew together, the long years of mourning Kale seemed to melt away and she felt young again.

It had been painful leaving the others back there in the grasslands, but Azura hadn't hesitated for a moment. She had felt Kesh's anger and his humiliation in front of the wyrme, Aseel, and his kin, Thrace. They had denied him his kill and

Azura understood that Kesh could never accept this. He was proud, wilful, driven. He would not rest until he had taken the lives of these kith.

So they had left the other wyrmekin and set out, back to the east, to lie in wait for the band of kith whose deaths belonged to them.

For weeks they had tracked them – the man, the girl, the three youths – through the grasslands, into the peaks and further east, heading back to the edge of the valley country. And they had bided their time.

Kesh wanted to take them all in one strike, and that was difficult when they were strung out along the trail. He might catch two, three if he was lucky, but the others would escape. And that would be a shame, for Kesh intended that they should watch each other die.

Slowly.

Nighttime had proved no easier to launch an assault, for when they rested up the man was skilful at choosing defensive, hard-to-attack places. The previous week, Kesh and Azura had been about to strike when a violent lightning storm had broken and the kith had found shelter in a crevice deep in the rock. A couple of days after that, they had set out foraging in twos and threes.

And they had waited. And as they did so, Azura had realized that they weren't the only ones on the trail of the kith. There were others. Loathsome, stinking creatures, wearing tattered clothes and bone masks, and the stench of death.

Keld.

If kith were vile, then the keld were a thousand times worse. A kith might kill a wyrme. A keld would capture it, enslave it, torture it, stunt it . . .

Kesh and she were of the same mind. They would rid the weald not only of these kith who had humiliated him, but also of the keld following them, whose very presence in the high country was an abomination.

Finally, when all five kith had set off further eastwards, and with the keld still in silent nighttime pursuit, Kesh and Azura went with them. The packs on the kiths' backs were bulging and looked heavy, and Azura had guessed they were seeking out their own kind to trade and barter with. She and Kesh had tracked them, keeping to the high peaks, staying low on the horizon, out of view.

The kith *had* found a trading place – though they did not stay there for long. And before the five of them returned on a westward trail, Azura had smelled blood on them.

Whatever had happened, the kith were clearly shaken. The man, who was always so careful in his choice of camp, had called a halt in the foothills of the ridge country in a shallow gulch beneath a high outcrop – oblivious to the fact that, as the sun set, their keld pursuers were emerging from cracks and crevices in the rocks and taking up positions on the outcrop above them.

The kith were down there now, huddled around a small fire, talking in low voices. All five of them. Together. And no watcher had been posted.

As clouds scudded feverishly across the bright gibbous moon, Azura could sense Kesh's keen excitement. He swallowed the last of the rustfly larvae and wiped his mouth, before climbing to his feet and peering down from their vantage point on the ridge-top opposite. When he spoke, his wyrmetongue was guttural and hard-edged, yet little more than a whisper.

'Slowdeath to them all.'

Thirty-One

The air had chilled, the wind had dropped. The moon was large and plump and almost full, and when something flickered blinkfast across its face, Micah flinched.

Broadspread wings. A long sinuous neck. A black lance, stark against the silver disc . . .

A whitewyrme was circling high overhead. A whitewyrme with a rider.

Micah turned to the others sitting around the campfire. Eli must also have seen the wyrme and rider, for he had his spitbolt ready in his hands and was kicking dust and gravel into the fire to extinguish it. Behind him, Ethan let out a stifled cry of alarm, while Cody scrambled to his feet. Cara reached out for Micah, but he barely noticed the touch of her hand. His stomach was turning somersaults.

The whitewyrme folded back its wings and arrowed down through the air. A bright white jet of flame roared from parted jaws as it plunged earthwards.

But not at Micah. Not at any of them.

Instead, as they watched, the wyrme and rider swooped down towards the ridge of rocks above them, where a number of figures had just appeared, their outlines dark and jagged against the moonlit sky. They wore facemasks and breastplates of bone-armour, and carried weapons that glinted in the silver moonlight. Bone-hammers and rockspikes. Jaghook flails. Cudgels, sidewinders, longknives . . .

'Keld,' Eli muttered. He backed away from the smoking remains of the fire, his blue eyes fixed on the crag above, and Micah and the others followed. 'Dozens of them . . . I should have spotted them before. How could I have been so careless?'

'You mean they've been following us?' said Micah, his voice taut and breathless.

Eli nodded grimly. 'Sure as hell ain't no coincidence they're here. You mess with the keld, lad, and they don't ever forget it.'

Micah felt Cara's grip on his arm tighten as the whitewyrme hovered over the ridge and spat jets of flame down at the cowering figures, forcing them to scatter for cover. In the fiery light he could see a woman in a black cloak. She was standing her ground, her eerie snow-white features impassive as she stared up at the wyrme. A group of keld formed a protective shield around her.

With quick darting movements, the kin on the wyrme's back stabbed downwards with the black lance. Three keld screamed and toppled forwards, their cream-white bone-armour punctured and spurting blood as they fell from the crag. A fourth followed, body ablaze and flailing about uselessly as he plunged. They landed in a clatter of bone-splinter and twisted weaponry around the campfire where, moments before, Micah and the others had sat hunched and exhausted and oblivious to the impending danger.

The cloying smell of cave-mould and crevice-must filled Micah's nostrils, followed by the acrid stench of burning hair and flesh. Sweeping Cara along with him, Micah fled, following Eli, Ethan and Cody down into a narrow, shadow-filled gulch some way off.

Above the crag, the wyrme and its rider dodged and ducked in the air as the keld sent a fusillade of rockspikes and sidewinder bolts up at them. With twisting movements and scything claws, the wyrme deflected the missiles as best it could, spitting out jets of hissing flame, while the hooded kin on its back wielded the black lance with deadly accuracy.

In the darkness of the gulch, Micah could hear Cara breathing heavily close beside him. Ethan's voice sounded, croaky, quavering.

'The wyrme and the rider,' he whispered, as half a dozen more keld fell in flaming arcs down towards the camp fire. 'I recognize them . . . They're the ones that tried to kill me.'

'Happen you're right, lad,' came Eli's voice. 'Reckon they were tracking us too. Him and his wyrme. And would have finished off what they started, had they not spotted them there keld about to do the same thing. Kin hate keld worse even than kith, which is to our good fortune.'

Micah looked up. The top of the crag was firebright illuminated by the human torches of burning keld, and in the flickering light Micah could see that the wyrme had been hit in several places. The white scales on the chest and flanks were streaked with rivulets of dark blood – though hovering above the ridge, the creature seemed oblivious to the wounds.

The kin had pulled back his hood, and Micah now saw that Ethan had been right. It was the kinyouth with the flame-red hair. His thin narrow face stared down below at the devastation he and his whitewyrme had wrought.

Keld fighters, bleeding, smouldering. The corpse of an obese keld woman, squabbling crevicewyrmes tearing strips of flesh from her belly. Two dead figures lying side by side, one wearing a high collared velvet coat; one without a nose, his ruined face fixed in a rictus of horror and surprise: both with thick gleaming blood on their chests where the kin's blackpine lance had skewered their keld hearts.

In among them was the woman in the black cloak, standing hunched over the bodies of her followers. The kin was taunting her with delicate thrusts of his razor-sharp lance and high chittering burst of wyrmetongue as his wyrme circled low overhead. All at once, the woman straightened up, her white face twisted and contorted with hate. From the folds of her cloak she drew out something round and metallic and the size of a clenched fist. And as the short sparking fuse fizzed at the top of the globe, Micah recognized it as a keld grenade – the same sort of weapon the winter caller had used . . .

Kesh thrust down with his kinlance. The blood roared in his ears and a savage delight made his heart race.

The bloodfrenzy was upon him.

Azura sensed it as she opened wide her jaws and sent a jet of flame hurtling down at the white-faced keld woman below. She was holding a smooth pebble, shiny and silver, in her outstretched hand, but recoiled as the flames hit the rock at her feet.

The rest of the keld lay dead or dying around her. Despite their fearsome weaponry and hideous appearance, these cave dwellers had proved no match for a battle-hardened wyrme and its kin. Up here in the open air Kesh and Azura had skewered and roasted the subterranean creatures like so many fat damsel grubs.

Dead, they were all dead – all except for the white-faced hag. And she had nothing left but this stone to throw at him. Kesh tossed his head back and let out a shriek of triumphant laughter. He would finish her now. Run her through with his lance. And then he and Azura would take their sweet time with the kith who were cowering in the gulch below . . .

Micah watched the keld woman swing her arm and hurl the grenade.

It arced up over the wyrme's head and, with a dazzling

flash and a head-splitting crack, exploded in mid-air. A cloud of dirty yellow smoke, as dense as bollcotton, bubbled and billowed and rolled over and over itself as it expanded.

Twisting and writhing, the wyrme came tumbling out of the boiling pall of smoke, her wings beating and neck arched, before regaining her balance and steadying herself in the sky.

There was no rider upon her back.

The smoke cleared. There was no sign of the keld woman in the black cloak either – but among the smoking remains of the keld dead on the ridge-top, Micah saw the white gleam of soulskin. The kinyouth lay in a twisted heap, like a settler child's discarded ragdoll, his broken limbs bent at grotesque angles; his face a bloody mask of red.

The whitewyrme had spotted the body too. She came down to land on the crag, silently, in the way of whitewyrmes, folding her great wings as her hindlegs touched the rock. She stood tall, her sinuous neck bent in a graceful curve and yellow eyes fixed on the dead youth at her feet.

'*Kesh. My Kesh . . .*' Her voice was like the wind soughing through pinnacle pines. Slowly, gently, the whitewyrme inclined her neck and nudged the corpse with her muzzle. Then, eyes pale yellow with sorrow, she rose back to her full height, stretched her wings and let out a piercing cry of grief that made Micah shrink back into the shadows of the dry gulch.

Beside him, Cara was shivering uncontrollably, and Micah reached out and drew her close to him, folding his arms round her trembling body. He could feel her breath, quavering and warm, against his neck.

When he looked up, the whitewyrme had launched herself back into the air and was flapping slowly away to the west, the limp body of her dead kin cradled in her foreclaws.

Eli had risen to his feet and was walking back over to the charred remnants of the campfire, followed by Ethan and Cody, who were picking their way carefully through the dead keld.

'Maker knows, we've been lucky,' Eli said, retrieving his rucksack and dusting it off.

'Lucky!' Ethan exclaimed. 'You call being hunted by wyrme-kin, shot at by scrimshaw thieves and tracked down by these . . . these . . . bone-faced monsters lucky?'

Eli pulled the pack onto his shoulders with a shrug. 'No, lad,' he told him, 'but being alive to tell the tale surely is.'

Thirty-Two

Far to the west, a full season's flight away from the valley country and the galleries they had abandoned, the whitewyrme colony was stirring. Sick, forlorn and out of place in this strange land, they awoke to face another day as the sun rose over a landscape of basalt blocks and obsidian flow; a landscape crisscrossed by lava-glow crevices and deep ravines.

At the lip of the greatest of them – a broad V-shaped chasm – dark shapes were moving back and forth against a backdrop of crimson smoke and great spewing gobs of liquid rock that turned from white to yellow to red. Thunderstorms rumbled and growled on the horizon as they teetered on spindly legs of lightning around the ring of mountains, while sulphurous smoke twisted up from the ravines below and hung over the rockscape like swathes of yellow-stain muslin.

Standing on a rock bluff, Alsasse, the leader of the

colony, extended his snow-white neck stiffly and surveyed the world around him. It seemed half-formed and unknowable. His nostrils flared at the pungent odours of phosphorus and sulphur and molten ores.

It was furnace-hot here, far from his beloved valley country – a land of highstacks and deeplakes, plateaulands of swaying grass, waterfalls and green havens and sweet babbling snowmelt streams. There, the air was cool and the sky was clear and blue, unblurred by smoke or steam. And rising above the rolling grasslands was the glistening sandstone fortress of the wyrme galleries . . .

The air seemed to tremble like boiling water and, immersed inside its searing heat, the dark shapes of the blueblackwyrmes moved over the landscape like basalt boulders come to life. And all the while, from the great chasm which glowed and throbbed like a raw wound, more blueblackwyrmes were emerging. This was their home, and the whitewyrmes were their guests – but unwelcome, barely tolerated.

The ancient whitewyrme craned his neck, wincing as he did so, and peered down into the chasm. Hardbake mud galleries lined the curving walls of the glowing abyss; landing-perches and fluted uprights scored the rock. And from them the blueblackwyrmes were launching themselves into the air, slicing through the wreaths of smoke on knife-edge wings as they rose on thermals that carried them up to the lip of the chasm.

The whitewyrme was about to turn away when his attention was caught by a blueblackwyrme standing braced at the edge of a steaming, algae-fringed pool close by. It was a wyrmeling, little more than half grown, yet already larger than the whitewyrme himself, with huge black talons and powerful jaws. Its stout muscular neck was stuck out rigid over the bubbling water, and it was watching attentively, oblivious to the toxic fumes. Saltflies and sulphur bugs buzzed round its unblinking gem-blue eyes and parted muzzle.

All at once, there was a flash of orange and red as a small pot-bellied wyrme launched itself off the far side of the pool. It flapped its angular wings and snatched a brace of plump damsel flies from the air.

At the selfsame moment, the blueblackwyrmeling lunged forward, wings raised for balance. It clamped its jaws round the pot-bellied wyrme, puncturing its gut, and shook its head sharply. Then, with an odd delicacy, it removed the limp creature from its mouth with its foreclaws.

From the other side of the pool, there came a grunt of approval, and the whitewyrme saw one of the black boulders stand up and reveal itself to be a full-grown blueblackwyrme. It inclined its head as the wyrmeling held up its dead prey.

'*Tear the head off, then the wings*,' the blueblackwyrme growled.

'*Like this?*' the wyrmeling said as it obeyed its parent's instruction.

'*That's the way*,' the full-grown blueblack encouraged. '*Now eat the rest*.'

The whitewyrme had to concentrate to understand their harsh guttural words, yet their intent was clear. These great lumbering creatures were no different from the whitewyrmes. Like them, they were devoted to their young, teaching them, nurturing and nourishing them.

And yet, of course, there *was* a difference. For unlike this robust wyrmeling, with its bright blue eyes and gleaming blue-black scales, the pale wyrmelings of the whitewyrmes were failing to thrive.

The ancient whitewyrme turned his head and looked back across the savage landscape to the sulphur lakes where the whitewyrme colony was roosting, far from the glowing chasm. They had chosen to settle away from the furnace heat of the chasm. Yet they could not escape the miasmal air, nor the sulphurous water, and the prey they consumed – though it eased their hunger – made them sick. Every day, more of their number were dying.

From his vantage point, the whitewyrme could see the colony in the distance responding to the rising sun – glitters of white that flecked the black shores of the sulphur lakes. He stepped down from the rock bluff, scree shifting between his clawed feet. His legs felt heavy. His head swam. And as he stretched out his great wings and launched himself into the air, he let out a low groan.

The thermals took the whitewyrme effortlessly over

the dark landscape, his ruddering tail guiding him down towards the bubbling lakes. He circled over the colony on the shore of the largest lake, his yellow eyes bright and glowing.

An ancient female below him bent her head and plucked listlessly at scales that were coming loose on her breast and haunches. Two males had to help each other to stand. Their necks hung low, inverse arches, and their legs bowed. A female nuzzled her motionless wyrmeling before letting out a long, low, keening cry of anguish. The cry was taken up by others close by.

The whitewyrme came in to land a little way off.

'*We lost another last night, Alsasse*,' came a rainswirl voice, and Alsasse turned to see a second wyrme approaching him, deep sorrow in his eyes.

Alsasse felt his stomach cramp. '*Another?*' he said. '*Who this time, Alucius?*'

The wyrme dipped his head. He was the second of the host, the largest and strongest of their number, yet as he came closer Alsasse noted that even he was being laid low by their surroundings. He was walking with a hinking limp, there were open cankers at the side of his mouth and when he spoke, his voice was weak and reedy.

'*Alwynia.*'

Alsasse let out a small moan of despair. Alwynia. One of the young females. Alucius's mate.

'*She laid a wyve in the nest we had prepared together – on the bluffs above the lake,*' said Alucius. He inclined his head, as though the weight of his words were pulling it down. '*She was greatly weakened,*' he added, '*and died shortly before day-break.*'

'*Alucius, I am sorry . . .*'

But the second in the host looked away. '*The wyve perished also,*' he continued, and he shook his head. '*Like all those others we brought with us, it needed the gentle warmth of the highstacks back in the valley country, not the searing heat of this volcanic inferno.*' He fixed the ancient leader of the colony with his amber-shot eyes. '*Alsasse, we are sick. Our young are dying and our eggs are barren. There is no future for the colony in this place . . .*'

Just then, from behind them, there came the sound of raised guttural voices. Alsasse and Alucius turned their heads and looked back towards the great abyss in the distance, where groups of blueblackwyrmes were gathering, heads back and necks craned, staring up at the sky. The two whitewyrmes followed their gaze.

A small group, four black dots in the overcast sky, was approaching from the east.

'*The raiding party,*' said Alucius.

Alsasse groaned. '*I must go,*' he said wearily.

He scanned the incoming flock of wyrmes for a sight of the whitewyrme, Aylsa, who, several weeks earlier, had led the party of four blueblacks back to the valley country. But so far as he could see, she was not among them.

Without another word, Alsasse spread his wings and launched off from the ground. He allowed the thermals to lift his aching body up into the glowering sky once more, and rode the air currents in a wide arc round the mountain peaks and down towards the blueblackwyrme colony, the searing heat burning his eyes as he flew closer to the fiery chasm. He touched down on the chasm's edge amid a large gathering of blueblacks, who glanced at him dismissively as he landed, before returning their attention to the sky.

Alsasse caught sight of movement, and turned to see a massive clawed hand appear out of the chasm and grip its edge. It was followed a moment later by a head, broad-jawed and one-eyed; muscular shoulders, a robust torso. Then, with a grunt, a huge blueblackwyrme pulled itself up onto the lip of rock and rose to its feet.

Alsasse shrank back before the bulk and vigour of the mighty leader of the blueblackwyrmes. Like the heat from the chasm's depths, Beveesh-gar radiated a burning power that was dominating and intense. His teeth and claws glinted in the blood-red light, while the milky white glow of his blind eye only seemed to enhance his brutal strength. And unlike Alsasse, whose skin was dull and yellow-stained by sulphurous lake water, the blueblackwyrme's scales gleamed like burnished metal.

Beveesh-gar threw back his head and stared up at the sky with his one good eye.

'*At last*,' he grunted.

One by one the approaching blueblackwyrmes came in to land before him. They looked weary and bore evidence of a fight – half-healed wounds on their flanks and necks, torn wings. One of them had lost the tip of a tail; another, two claws from his left hand. Beveesh-gar acknowledged their arrival in silence, his inquisitive gaze resting for a moment on each in turn as they bowed their heads respectfully. The last of the four wyrmes was carrying a bundle in its foreclaws, which it laid at the leader's feet.

Beveesh-gar's single eye grew wide with surprise. '*Is that it?*' he asked, the guttural words tinged with a low growling contempt.

The blueblackwyrme looked down at the body as if seeing it for the first time, then nodded. '*We caught it in the valley lands.*'

Alsasse recognized the voice. It belonged to Hasheev-gul, Beveesh-gar's sixth son.

'*Far to the east,*' he went on. '*There were five of them, seated around a fire. We attacked and killed them all. This one was the biggest.*'

He nodded at the dead body at his father's feet. The head was twisted to one side, the tongue lolling. One outstretched arm was jutting out, and Hasheev-gul pushed it back snug against the body.

The leader of the blueblackwyrmes took a step forward. The others hung back deferentially. He looked down for a moment, then lowered his head and sniffed.

'*It stinks*,' he said, his voice harsh and grating.

From around him, the blueblackwyrmes growled their agreement. Alsasse remained silent. The taint of the two-hides was nothing new to him.

Grimacing, Beveesh-gar flicked the head from side to side with an outstretched claw. He thrust his muzzle into the corpse's belly, then pulled back, perplexed . . .

'*It is a* two-*hides*,' said Alsasse.

A hundred bright blue eyes stared at the slender whitewyrme in their midst. Beveesh-gar drew back from the body and turned to him.

Alsasse stepped forward, his head lowered. '*As you know, I . . . I have knowledge of these creatures*.'

For a moment, the towering blueblackwyrme glared back at him. Then, with a low snort that filled the air with sour odour, he moved to one side. Alsasse approached the body of the two-hides.

Hasheev-gul was right. It was a large specimen. A male. And it looked as though it had been in good health before it had been killed.

Holding his breath, Alsasse stooped forward over the corpse. Then, trying hard to keep his arm from shaking, he sliced through the front of the jacket with a single razor-sharp claw.

'*This is the outer hide I told you about*,' he explained. '*It protects them. From the sun. From thorns . . .*' He slowly peeled back the thick scaly material to reveal the inner hide, that was thin and pale and downy with dark curling hair. '*And this is the inner hide of the creature,'* he said. '*The true hide. The hide it was born with, which burns in the sun and tears so easily . . .*'

'*And the other?*' Beveesh-gar enquired.

'*Wyrmeskin,*' said Alsasse, and flinched at the sound of the great blueblackwyrme leader's sharp intake of breath.

'*Let me,*' Beveesh-gar said gruffly, brushing the whitewyrme aside. '*I want to see for myself just how easily it tears.*'

As Alsasse watched, the blueblackwyrme leaned forward. Then, with the lightest of touches, he punctured this inner hide with the tip of his dark claw and drew a line down the creature's breast. The flesh beneath opened up, pink and fibrous, and Beveesh-gar looked round at the others in the circle, his face incredulous.

'*Its hide is softer than that of a sulphur grub,*' he said. '*If it wasn't for the outer hide . . .*' He growled softly. '*The* wyrme *hide . . .*'

Returning his attention to the corpse, Beveesh-gar reached down and tore off its foot-coverings with his teeth one by one, and spat them aside. He tilted his head and examined the nails at the tips of the creature's toes, then at its fingers, prodding them delicately with his own massive black claw. He snorted. Then, switching his attention to the dead creature's mouth, he pulled the top lip up and peered closely at the two rows of teeth that were small and worn and brown-stained.

He straightened up and turned to Alsasse. '*These two-hides you fear so much are weak,*' he said.

'Do not be fooled, Beveesh-gar, venerable leader of the blue-black host,' said Alsasse, pulling himself up to his full height and looking the blueblackwyrme squarely in the eye. *'As I told you before, what the two-hides lack in strength, they more than make up for in cunning – snares and traps and weapons that spit thorns . . . They have even found ways to steal our fire and turn it against us.'*

Beveesh-gar's one good eye narrowed *'Can this be true?'* He looked at his son, then at the others. At the wounds on the blueblackwyrmes' flanks and neck, the torn wings, the missing claws . . .

'Five of the two-hides did this to your raiding party,' Alsasse continued. *'And there are thousands more following their trail. Spreading further west with each passing season. That is why we whitewyrmes left the valley country, home of our ancestors, nesting place of our wyves . . .'*

'And yet,' said Beveesh-gar, his voice as dark and menacing as the thunder that still rumbled round the smoking landscape, *'you have also told us that there are those among you snowwyrmes who allow these stinking creatures to ride upon their backs.'*

Alsasse faltered. He turned away, unable to hold the penetrating gaze of the leader of the blueblackwyrmes.

'It is true,' he said at last. *'Some whitewyrmes have kinned with the two-hides' young. They rear them, nurture them. They clothe them in their own wyrmeslough,'* he said, and tried to ignore the expression of disgust that spread across Beveesh-gar's face. *'They believe that it is only by understanding the two-hides and using*

their cunning against them that they can be defeated.' He paused. '*It is not a way that the rest of us can accept . . .*'

'*You are right to reject it, snowwyrme. Such wyrmes are a disgrace to all wyrmekind,*' the blueblackwyrme said bluntly, cutting Alsasse short. '*Yet we blueblacks cannot accept your way either.*'

Beveesh-gar's gaze bore into Alsasse's.

'*You abandoned the land of your ancestors,*' said Beveesh-gar, his guttural voice softer now, '*and came here.*' He shook his heavy head from side to side. '*But you do not belong here, snow-wyrme. This is not your home.*'

The words tolled inside Alsasse's head. He stared down shakily at the ground, knowing that Beveesh-gar was right.

'*Yet we had to escape the taint of the two-hides,*' he explained. '*The destruction they cause wherever they go. The stench of death they spread. We had no choice but to get as far away from them as possible . . .*'

'*There* is *another way,*' the leader of the blueblackwyrmes said slowly.

'*There is?*' said Alsasse, aware more than ever of the great blueblackwyrmes towering over him. He felt small, lost and alone.

'*A return to the valley country.*'

Alsasse looked up. '*You want us to leave? To go back there? Back to the taint of the two-hides and the wyrmekin we shunned?*'

'*Wyrmekin!*' Beveesh-gar spat the words in his guttural wyrmetongue. '*They deserve death even more than the two-*

hides . . . But the answer to your question, snowwyrme, is yes.' He paused. *'But you will not go alone.'*

The leader of the blueblackwyrme's jewel-bright eye widened.

'We *shall return with you.'*

Thirty-Three

Thrace had never been so far down beneath the whitewyrme galleries before. She'd visited the stores, of course, with their stocks of dried leathergrubs and soused damselfly larvae that the colony had abandoned when they fled, but had gone no further.

She hadn't wanted to. There seemed to be something private about the tunnels that wormed their way through the deep rock; something intimate.

These dark subterranean depths were where the great whitewyrmes had nursed their young for centuries. Coiled around the wyrmelings they had carried from the hatchery in the highstacks to the nursery cavern below the colony, the great whitewyrmes would wreath their young in smoke, whispering the secrets and wisdom of their kind to them as they did so. Then, just after their first sloughing – when they were already fluent in wyrmetongue and ready to take their first flight – the wyrmelings would be led up into the light airy galleries above to join the bustling life of the colony.

It hadn't seemed right to Thrace to intrude into this, the most secret of places – especially now, when the highstacks had been lost and the nursery cavern had fallen silent. But then Zar had come to her, and Thrace had put her reservations aside. It had been impossible for her to continue to stay away.

She stood now at the entrance to the nursery cavern. Her delicate fingers trailed over the clawscratch walls as she stared at the female whitewyrme who was curled up on the ground before her, just as Zar had said she would be. A circle of indentations in the floor, filled with flameoil and set alight, cast a flickering light over her white scales.

'*You are Aylsa*,' said Thrace.

It was a statement, not a question, and it was responded to in kind.

'*And you are Thrace.*'

The kingirl flinched.

'*You thought I would not have heard of you?*' Aylsa said, her eyes glittering.

Thrace shrugged. '*I . . . I gave it little thought*,' she said.

Aylsa raised her head and fixed Thrace with her intense yellow eyes. She said nothing. She didn't need to. Both of them knew she was lying. And Thrace remembered that when Aseel had answered Aylsa's mating call four seasons earlier, she had thought of little else but who this whitewyrme might be, whose hold over him had been so powerful that Aseel had left his kin standing on the highstack, alone and vulnerable.

Thrace's belly cramped just thinking about it – and the terrible things that had followed. But Aseel had returned to Thrace, and together they had taken their revenge on the kith . . .

'*Long before he kinned with you, when Aseel and I were still wyrmelings, we were paired,*' the great whitewyrme said in soft lilting wyrmetongue. Wisps of white smoke curled up from her nostrils as she spoke, and her eyes did not leave Thrace's. '*And then he chose to kin,*' she said, '*and the colony rejected him.*'

Aylsa inclined her neck and her eyes glowed amber. Thrace felt her stomach churning.

'*But when the time came to mate,*' the whitewyrme said softly, '*I called – and Aseel came to me.*' She sighed. '*Afterwards, though, I could not persuade him to stay.*' Aylsa's eyes flared to acid yellow once more, bright and accusing, as she stared at the kingirl. '*He left and I flew alone to the highstacks and laid a wyve.*'

Thrace's eyes grew wider. '*A wyve?*'

Aylsa lowered her gaze. '*It should still be there, warmed by the smoke-vents, waiting to hatch . . .*' A harsh edge came into her voice. '*Unless one of your kind has taken it.*'

'*My kind?*' said Thrace, her voice low and even as anger rose inside her.

'*Two-hides,*' said Aylsa simply.

'*The skin I wear next to my own is wyrmeslough, freely given, not the hide of a slaughtered wyrme,*' said Thrace hotly. '*I am kin, not kith.*'

She took a step into the nursery cavern and noticed the great whitewyrme's coiled body flinch.

'*Ever since we kinned, for as far back as I can remember,*' Thrace continued, '*Aseel and I have defended the highstacks, and the wyves they contain.*' She stared back at the whitewyrme defiantly. '*Even as the kith swarm through the valley country, we kin stay and fight. Unlike you and your colony. Who reject us,*' she added.

Thrace crouched down beside the circle of flickering flame and looked intently at the whitewyrme.

'*Tell me, Aylsa,*' she said, nursing her anger. '*Where did the colony go? And why aren't you with them?*'

'*The colony is far from the taint of the two-hides,*' Aylsa said, relaxing the coils of her tail and drawing back her wings. '*And* this *is why I'm not with them.*'

Aylsa twisted her sinuous neck and stared down lovingly at the small child, who was nestled in the coils of her body. A boy. More than two years old, less than five; the oil-glow flickered on the wyrmeslough that swaddled his small body.

Zar had told her about the whitewyrme in the nursery cavern that she'd seen Aseel visit, and Thrace guessed from what Zar had said – from the way they nuzzled, their necks entwined and eyes glowing amber – that this wyrme was Aseel's mate, Aylsa. But there had been no mention of a child. '*You have kinned . . .*'

Thrace's words were cut short by the sound of a low growl

and, realizing that they were no longer alone, both Thrace and Aylsa turned to the entrance of the cavern. A tall whitewyrme, body rigid, the black zigzag scar at the neck pulsing, stood looking at them.

'*Aseel*,' said Thrace, scrambling to her feet. '*How long have you been there?*'

'*Long enough*,' Aseel replied. He strode into the cavern and stopped in front of Aylsa. '*We have a wyve?*' His voice was as harsh as splitting timber. '*Why didn't you tell me?*'

But before Aylsa could answer, the infant awoke. His face crumpled and he began to wail, fat tears sliding down his cheeks. Aylsa tightened her coiled body around him and inclined her neck, comforting him with lulling chitters and warm aromatic breath.

Aseel straightened up and turned to Thrace. '*We must return to the highstacks*,' he said.

THIRTY-FOUR

Cody took the length of canegrass, turned it over in his hand, then laid it flat on the slab of rock before him. He clipped off the leaves with his knife and peeled away the dark outer layer, then chopped the remaining stem into six pieces, each the width of his hand. The blade was coated thick with yellow syrup. He reached for another stem and cut it likewise.

'You lost something, Cara?' he said.

The two of them were sitting crosslegged on the grass-stubbled ground, an earthenware pot and a pile of green canegrass between them.

Cara was muttering something under her breath, but it was to herself, not to him. She reached up and pushed her hair back from her face, feeling beneath the folds of her cloak as she did so, before returning her attention to the side pockets of the backpack. Then, with a small gasp of exasperation, she clutched at the front of her blouse and peeked down inside.

Cody watched her, intrigued, colouring up momentarily at the thought of the view she must have, then looked away guiltily.

'Where *is* it?' Cara sighed.

And at that moment, Cody knew exactly what it was she was searching for. The carved medallion Micah had given her – and he was about to say as much when Micah himself returned, his outstretched arms weighed down beneath a fresh bundle of the woody green stems, which he dropped down on top of the rest. He glanced inside the earthenware pot, which was already close to half-full.

'Happen this'll be enough to fill it,' he said and, pulling his hackdagger from his belt, he crouched down between Cody and Cara.

Cody slapped at a midge on the back of his neck, avoiding his gaze. He looked flushed, uncomfortable. Cara smiled back at Micah, but weakly, with her mouth but not her eyes. Then she pushed her backpack to one side and picked up her own knife. The yellow syrup had started to coagulate on the blade.

Micah shifted forwards onto his knees and picked up a pair of bone-crushers; two hinged metal clamps with a tightening screw. He gripped a stem of chopped canegrass in the jaws of the cumbersome tool and steadily tightened the screw. Viscous yellow syrup streamed down into the top of the pot. He held the canegrass in place till the syrup came in drips, then stopped completely. Finally, undoing the screw, he tossed the crushed fibres into the grass behind him.

Cody slapped at another midge, on his forearm this time, and brushed the black smear away with his fingertips.

'I remember the first time Eli showed me how to harvest the sweetness in canegrass,' Micah said. 'It was by a gulch near the blackwater falls. Had Thrace and me gather us up a mountain of the stuff before he revealed its secret . . .'

Micah gazed up into the sky, a faraway look in his eyes. It was the look he always got when he mentioned the kingirl – or so it seemed to Cody. Cara had noticed it too. Cody could tell that by the way she busied herself with the canegrass, her head down. And he did the same, aware of her ill-ease and wanting to comfort it away with sympathetic words.

How could Micah be so insensitive? he wondered as anger boiled up inside him.

He glanced up at the beautiful kithgirl. He had to be careful.

The episode outside the scrimshaw had unnerved her, he knew that. Of course, she'd been grateful when he'd rescued her from that filthy kith with the knife at her throat, but when he'd smashed the man's ribs and jaw with his fists, and beaten his face to a bloody pulp, unable to stop himself pummelling, pummelling, Cara had watched, shocked and frightened, then turned away.

True, he'd proved that he could protect her. But it had come at a cost. For she was wary of him now. His brute strength. His hot-headedness. Cody knew that Cara feared for the next time he might lose control.

Then again, so did he.

Cody saw Cara glance up at Micah again, a welling sadness in her turquoise eyes, and he felt his fists bunch up. Given half a chance, he'd beat Micah's thoughtlessness out of him. He breathed in long and deep, then out.

Stay calm, he cautioned himself. Keep a hold of yourself.

He turned to Micah, who was still staring out at the far horizon, lost in his own thoughts. 'You seen Eli and my brother?' he asked, and wondered whether Cara could hear he was talking through gritted teeth.

Micah turned to him. 'Said something about scouting out those cliffs to the south,' he said distantly. 'Foraging for redcaps . . .'

'Redcaps?' said Cara brightly, her nose crinkling up questioningly as she seized on his words. 'What are they?'

'Giant mushrooms,' said Micah. 'Biggest I've ever seen. They grow on the ledges below manderwyrme colonies. Hard to get to though.' He crushed another of the lengths of cane-grass into the pot. 'But they make for good eating.'

He reached for another stem. Cara and Cody resumed their cutting. The conversation ceased.

The midges thrummed, the wind sighed and the trickling of the syrup rose in pitch as the earthenware pot steadily filled. Low in the sky now, the sun had turned slowly from white to red, colouring the thin streaks of cloud vermilion, then purple, as it did so.

All at once there came a loud noise – like hands clapping

in applause – and all three of them looked round to see a small flock of mistwyrmes rising up from the clumps of grass and ratty scrub. They flapped hard their pale-blue wings, and wheeled off, ungainly and screeching, towards the sinking sun. And below them, silhouetted against the fading colours, were Eli and Ethan.

'*There* they are,' said Cody unnecessarily. He climbed to his feet.

Ethan waved to him, and Cody waved back, noting, not for the first time, how much his brother had grown since the pair of them had first entered the weald. He watched the two of them approach, his eyes thin slits against the brightness.

Eli, tall, rangy, his gait loose-limbed and purposeful. He barely seemed to notice the rucksack on his back. And Ethan beside him, stumbling forward, tilted to one side by the heavy bag slung over first one shoulder, then the other. He was chattering by the look of him, and glancing round at the cragclimber for approval.

'. . . and I could have got that big one if I hadn't slipped,' Ethan was saying, his voice breathless and excited as he and Eli drew closer. 'But I held onto what I had, Eli. Reckon I'm getting a head for heights, like you,' he said, looking up at the cragclimber. 'Do you reckon I'm getting a head for heights?'

'Maybe,' said Eli indulgently.

'It was that manderwyrme,' said Ethan, smiling. 'Flapping up like that and scaring me half to death.'

The pair of them stopped in front of the pile of shredded canegrass.

'We got us a whole load of redhats,' Ethan announced proudly, swinging the heavy bag off his shoulder and setting it down on the ground.

'Redcaps,' said Eli.

'Redcaps,' Ethan repeated without missing a beat. 'Some for now. Some for later.'

Eli removed his rucksack and nodded towards the earthenware pot. 'Looks like you're just about finished here,' he said with approval.

Micah nodded and, picking up a cork stopper, sealed the pot.

'Reckon we've earned ourselves a good campfire tonight,' said Eli. 'Spotted some brushwood over yonder, Micah,' he added, with a jerk of his head. 'Care to help Ethan and me gather it?'

Micah nodded again, and followed Ethan and Eli off across the dusk-shadowed grass plain, but Cody could tell his thoughts were still on that kingirl of his. Opposite him, Cara was equally distracted as she rummaged through her rucksack once more.

'Reckon you've lost it,' he told her calmly.

'What?' said Cara sharply. She looked up, her blue-green eyes flashing.

'That scrimshaw medallion,' said Cody. 'The one Micah gave you.'

He reached into his pocket and pulled out the scrimshaw carving he'd bought. Bought for her. Cara. He held it out.

'You found it!' she exclaimed.

Cody dropped the medallion into her outstretched hand and watched as she examined it. A look of confusion passed across her face. She looked up.

'But . . . but this is a wyrme in flight,' she said. 'My one was carved different, curled up in a spiral, its wings folded.'

Cody shrugged, hoping he wouldn't blush. His stomach knotted.

'Just put it on,' he said, holding her gaze.

For a moment Cara did not move. Then, to Cody's relief, she reached up and knotted the thong behind her neck.

'Where did you get it?' she asked.

'Same place as Micah,' Cody replied. 'The scrimshaw den.'

Cara nodded slowly, then; 'Why?'

For you, Cara! For you! the words shrieked inside Cody's head.

He shrugged again. 'No reason,' he said, and wanted to bite off his own tongue for the lie he'd told. 'I just liked it was all.'

Cara smiled uncertainly, then lowered her gaze. She undid the top two buttons of her blouse and let the small medallion fall back against her skin.

'It looks real pretty,' said Cody. The knotted fist inside his stomach clenched all the tighter. 'And . . . and Micah'll never notice the difference.'

Cara eyed him warily for a moment, then smiled again. 'You don't think so?'

Cody shook his head.

Ever since Micah had clapped eyes on that kingirl, Thrace, back in the grasslands, it was like he only had thoughts for her. Cara – sweet, beautiful Cara – seemed invisible to him.

No, Micah would not notice.

But Cody would. Every time he looked at Cara, he'd know that it was now *his* medallion that she was wearing, nestling against her skin, so close to her heart. Not Micah's.

And that made Cody happy. Very happy.

Thirty-Five

Nathaniel Lint the Younger nursed the half-empty tumbler before him, turning it round and round with his fingers, spoking out blades of light from the angles of glass that slid over the barewood walls of the tavern as he did so. There was a clock in the corner. White enamelled face, fancy numbers and ornate hands, and a ponderous brass pendulum, all clad in polished mahogany. Like Nathaniel himself, it was fresh from the plains and out of place; like him, it was counting off the seconds.

Outside, greywyrmes bellowed and bucked, tugging at their harnesses. Bullwhips cracked as the wyrmehandlers struggled to hold them in check. Voices were raised, urgent, excited. Filled with fear, with hope. Barking out commands, instructions, keeping errant children close by. There was clatter and crash, the noise of wood on wood, metal on metal. The air was brown with scuffed-up dust, and through it, the fuzzed sun rose inexorably to its noontime zenith, the scheduled time of their departure.

The minutes passed and the frenzied activity grew, the cacophony of man and beast reaching a tumultuous crescendo.

'Secure that tarpaulin.'

'Get them seedsacks loaded.'

'Aaron. *Aaron!* You come here *now*, d'ya hear? I don't want you out of my sight.'

It had started early, with the would-be settlers from the plains rising hours before the sun, emerging from their rooms in the bunkhouses, from their tents and benders, and packing up their belongings. After weeks of waiting, the moment was almost upon them – the moment the great expedition would set off from the badlands and trek westwards towards the grasslands and the promise of a new life in the high weald.

Nathaniel Lint glanced up at the clock. High noon was less than an hour away.

The feverish activity outside was everything he had hoped for and dreamed of for so long. Finally, those plans – hatched in a tavern over a bottle of finest wine down on the plains and painstakingly honed here in the badlands – were coming to fruition. The not inconsiderable sum of money that his father had given him, and that he had invested in the enterprise, had not been wasted after all. The new stockade, with its pumps and well, its haylofts and silos, its bunkhouses and corrals – its tavern, had come into being; the settlers had arrived from the plains in droves. Now they were all but ready to depart.

And Nathaniel had never felt worse.

'You require a top-up, sir?'

Nathaniel looked up. Lizzie the tavern-maid was wiping her chapped hands on a rag, staring at him levelly.

He wondered whether she had her suspicions about how he, a young merchant, had become sole owner of the new stockade. Each day in the cabin, when she brought him his breakfast on a tray, Nathaniel searched her face for any trace of blame for that 'dreadful business', as she'd called it. He'd yet to find any, but remained uneasy nonetheless.

She raised her eyebrows questioningly, and he nodded.

'A jug,' he said morosely, raising his tumbler and tossing back the last of the green liquor in one gulp.

Lizzie nodded, pushed back a greasy strand of lank hair behind her ear and turned away. Moments later, she was back, a bulbous pewter jug in her hand. She filled the tumbler to the brim, then set the jug down beside it. Nathaniel nodded his thanks, then waited for her to go before raising the glass.

'To you, Garth Temple,' he muttered to himself, and knocked back the whole tumbler in one. He slammed it back down on the table, wincing as the burning liquor coursed down his insides.

Garth Temple. The kindest, truest, most trusting friend a young merchant could ever wish for. The weald would never see his like again . . .

He poured himself another shot of liquor.

Nathaniel had hoped a drink or two might make him

feel better, to ease the guilt. Instead, it was turning him maudlin. He looked back at the clock ticking steadily in the corner.

If only he could turn back time, he thought bitterly. But what was done was done, and no amount of remorse would change that. And then there were the voices he couldn't get out of his head.

There's a fortune to be made for men of vision. Men like ourselves.

Nathaniel recalled the look of fervent belief in Garth Temple's eyes as they had shaken hands on the deal. It had gone better than either of them might have imagined.

Thing is, with you at one end of this here operation and me at the other . . . Solomon Tallow's voice had been smooth, persuasive, with that hint of menace Nathaniel had got to know so well. *Do we need anyone in the middle? Do we need Garth Temple?*

Nathaniel poured and downed another shot of the green liquor.

All you got to do is turn the spigot off . . .

And that was what he'd done. He had tampered with Garth Temple's extraordinary contraption for taming the greywyrmes' fiery breath. And when Garth had gone to decant the flameoil that had should have collected in the leather pouch buckled round the great creature's neck, it had opened its gaping mouth and incinerated him in an instant.

Garth Temple was dead. And he, Nathaniel, was the cause. He was a killer. A murderer . . .

Cheer up, Nat.

Tallow's words. Goading. Scornful.

The first murder always hits hardest.

Nathaniel shuddered.

It won't be your last.

Oh, but it would. It would. As the Maker was his witness, Nathaniel swore that never, ever again would he cause the death of another man.

It won't be your last. It won't be your last . . .

Nathaniel groaned.

Solomon Tallow had got his hooks into him and wasn't about to let go. Now he and those henchmen of his strutted around the place, calling the shots, while he, Nathaniel Lint the Younger, the owner of the new stockade, had to skulk in the tavern to keep out of their way.

Nathaniel looked up at the ticking clock and smiled. As soon as Tallow and his thugs had departed, he would see about getting himself bodyguards of his own. Big, brawny, fearless men that he would pay handsomely to protect him. And when Solomon Tallow returned, it would be his turn to take orders.

'Get them boxes loaded!'

He could hear him now, shouting. The bullying voice was louder than all the other noises put together, and conjured up the sight of the man; his brutish muscular bulk, his bunched fists and shaved head; the dark calculating eyes.

'Move it!'

Nathaniel drained his tumbler, set it aside. He rested his elbows on the table, put his hands to his ears and pressed, endeavouring to shut out the man's voice.

'Fall into line!'

But Solomon Tallow would not be shut out . . .

Thirty-Six

'Fall into line!' Solomon bellowed, jabbing at the flanks of a straying greywyrme with a long spike-tipped pole.

The heavy-laden creature lumbered forward, roaring flamelessly. The sacks and boxes roped to its back swayed from side to side, and its driver, perched atop the neck-saddle, tugged hard at the reins to hold the wyrme steady. Solomon strutted past.

'Move it along here, folks,' he called out as he continued along the line of greywyrmes towards the head of the column. The heavy bullwhip in his fist twitched impatiently as he walked. 'I ain't fixing to wait for no stragglers.'

The column of greywyrmes extended right the way across the new stockade, from the bunkhouses at one end to the corral at the other, and off a ways into the dustblown rockflats beyond. There was a greywyrme for each group of settlers. One hundred and one in all.

They were tethered up in lines of eight or nine, a broad neck-saddle attached to each of the lead wyrmes, and all loaded with possessions and provisions of every kind, secured with ropes and nets and lengths of oilcloth. There were leather chests and nailed-down crates; pots and pans; boxes, bales and bed-rolls; sacks of seed and coils of wire, and timber planks for the homesteads the settlers planned to construct, as well as the chairs, beds and bathtubs they would furnish them with.

It made for an odd sight, the wyrmes and their loads; like cluttered houses on legs. And to complete the illusion of a small town on the move were the saplings – apples, pears, cherries and plums; walnut and pine – tethered into place by those hoping to establish orchards up in the fertile grasslands, and creating the appearance of small copses nestling in among the buildings.

Solomon cracked his bullwhip, and a grin plucked at the corners of his mouth. He was enjoying himself. There was a carnival atmosphere to the air. The travelling show was about to leave town, and he, Solomon Tallow, was its ringmaster, in charge of every last detail.

'I said, *move* it!'

The settlers had packed up their gear quickly and cheerfully, that much he had to concede. Chivvied both by him and his men, and their own desire to get underway, they had stowed their tents, separated out gear for the journey from gear for when they arrived, and roped the whole lot to their allotted greywyrmes.

Truth be told, the settlers had been so biddable that Solomon had barely had to raise his voice at all, and the bullwhip was good as redundant. Yet he had shouted and threatened and cussed, and that bullwhip of his had cracked the air like thunderclaps. It was required. The settlers wouldn't have expected anything less.

They wanted to know that there was someone in charge. Someone capable and strong. Someone they could depend upon to guide them through the unknown wilderness ahead, who would take care of their needs and protect them from attack, should it come to that. And if that meant being cussed at and menaced, then so be it. It was for their own good, and they were grateful to accept this rough kith as their leader.

And for himself, Solomon Tallow was more than happy to take on the role.

He'd had a shave that morning in preparation for their departure. Maker knew, there'd be little enough opportunity for primping and preening when they were on the trail. He'd shaved his face, his head, and buffed up his scalp with wyrmegrease that would protect it from the sun some, and that marked him out as someone who was not to be messed with.

They admired him, these settlers, Solomon could tell that; could see it in their eyes. He observed how they looked askance at him as he strode past, tree trunk legs splayed and heavy boots kicking up the dust. They noted his gleaming skull, his bull neck and barrel chest, his massive arms that looked to be carved from dark seasoned wood. Once or twice, someone's gaze would linger a mite too long. A callow youth, envious of his physique; a pretty girl, weak-kneed with longing in his presence; a stocky former ploughhand, fists clenched, sizing him up. And Solomon would hold that gaze until they looked away.

They always did.

He could also be considerate though, gracious. In a lesser man, it might have been seen as weakness rather than strength.

But not in Solomon Tallow.

Halfway along the shuffling column, he paused to help an old-timer and his hunched wife to secure a rope they'd been struggling with to the flanks of a greywyrme already festooned with the belongings of their extended family. His forearms bunched like iron hawsers as he cinched the rope and pulled hard on the knot, while the greywyrme shifted from one massive foot to the other and rolled its eyes.

The old man tipped his hat. 'Appreciate it,' he said.

'You're welcome,' Solomon told him, and his natural swagger intensified as he continued along the line.

Further on a ways, a harassed-looking woman with a boy and an old lady who might have been her mother, or possibly even her grandmother, was finding it hard to cope. Solomon stopped beside them, and showed the woman how to pleat the edges of her flapping tarpaulin, then he double-knotted the ends of the rope tight to hold it shut. Another family, who were sharing the wyrme, had taken most of the available space on the creature's back and were waiting patiently for the signal to move.

'That weald dust gets in everywhere if'n you don't take precautions to keep it out,' Solomon told the woman. He turned and admired his handiwork, patting the side of the bulging waxed cloth. 'This should see you right.'

'Thank you, sir,' said the woman, smiling up at him shyly, and Solomon saw that beneath her anxious expression there lurked a pale and beguiling beauty. Her green eyes sparkled as she swept back her thick chestnut hair. 'It ain't easy, with my husband passed and all.'

Solomon cocked his head to one side, boyish, and smiled back at her. His even white teeth gleamed in the sunlight, reassuring and ravenous in equal measure. Behind him, the boy was bickering with the son of the other family. The youth was several years older than him, but the boy was tenacious.

The woman turned on them.

'You hush now, Josiah,' she scolded her son. 'And leave Zeb alone.'

Instead of easing up, the squabbling grew louder and more physical. The younger boy took a swing at the older, who shoved him hard in the chest and kicked at his shins as he stumbled backwards.

'Hey, there!' Solomon said sharply, irritated that the boys' behaviour had stolen the mother's attention from him. His eyes darkened. 'This is no time for scrapping.'

But by now the boys were too far gone to heed anyone.

The younger boy had fallen to the ground, the older one had dropped down onto him, and the pair of them were rolling over and over in the dust, fists flying and voices shrill with indignation.

'Stop it, now!' the woman cried, stooping down and tugging at first one, then the other, with as much success as she'd had with the tarpaulin.

Solomon strode forward, eased her gently aside and seized the pair of them, one in each hand. He held them up.

'Do I have your full attention?' he asked.

They nodded meekly, their anger spent and fear taking over as they began to understand their predicament. Solomon hesitated.

'Don't I know you?' he said, looking at the younger boy.

'Reckon so, Mr Tallow, sir,' said the boy, looking back at him steadily.

The older boy looked close to crying, and bit his lower lip to ensure he did not.

'I was the one who told you what that gentleman did to drain the firebreath out of these here wyrmes.' The boy smiled slyly. 'And you gave me a silver piece. Still have it, safe and sound,' he said, patting his tunic.

Tallow let go of the older boy, who fled round to the other side of the laden wyrme to rejoin his family. He set the younger boy down, and smiled.

'You're an observant lad,' he said. 'Reckon I could do with some help out on the trail ahead. What do you say?'

'Gladly,' the boy said, looking over at his mother. 'Long as you look out for Ma and me.'

Solomon winked at the woman, who smiled coyly and lowered her eyes. His gaze lingered on her face a moment longer than was necessary, then he looked back at the boy.

'Be glad to, Josiah,' he said, and turned away.

He raised his head and squinted into the sun, high in the sky, directly above his head. It was noon, or near as damn it.

'Get ready to move out!' he bellowed, his hands cupped to his mouth as he strode purposefully on up to the front of the column. He turned and peered back down the line of heavily-laden greywyrmes. 'I said, get ready!'

At his command, the wyrmehandlers gripped the harnesses of their greywyrmes, pulled themselves up into their neck-saddles and took a hold of the reins, while beneath them the settlers hitched backpacks onto their shoulders. A muttering of voices rose to an expectant babble.

Feeling better than ever, Solomon approached his own greywyrme, which as befitted his status was the biggest and strongest of the hundred and one creatures. A leader, like himself. The covered load upon its back towered half as high again as any of the other wyrmes, while the padded neck-saddle had an impressive harpoon-loaded sidewinder mounted on its pommel.

'All set?' Solomon called back.

'All set, boss,' the wyrmehandlers called out along the line.

Solomon looked up at the greywyrme, and marvelled at just how much the creature was able to carry. Bundles of harpoon bolts; sidewinders, greased and wrapped in tarpaulin; wyrmeharnesses by the dozen; whips, spikes, axes and swords – enough to equip a small army, which was exactly what Solomon intended to do once he'd dumped these settlers out in the grasslands to fend for themselves. Then he'd meet up with Israel Dagg and his gang, and return to the new stockade with more kith, more wyrmes, and repeat the process.

Soon, Solomon Tallow reckoned, he'd be top man in the high country, as powerful as any of the lords back down on the plains.

He was about to climb up into the neck-saddle when he paused. Something was missing.

Or rather, some*one*.

'Where's Lint?' he demanded to one of the wyrmehandlers, the good humour draining out of him like water from a tub.

The handler turned, shrugged, his grimy fingernails scratching through his matted hair. 'He ain't here,' he said.

'I can see that,' Solomon snapped. 'Question is, why not?' He looked back along the line, seeking in vain for a sight of the young merchant. Then he fixed his hard angry gaze on the wyrmehandler. 'Find him, Enoch, and fetch him.'

THIRTY-SEVEN

Nathaniel Lint reached for the pewter jug and, trying to steady his shaking hands, tipped the dregs of the green liquor into his tumbler. He raised it and surveyed it blearily, then closed one eye in an attempt to make the double-image fuse into one – and, when it would not, he drained the liquor anyhow.

'I'm drunk,' he admitted to himself, and giggled.

His inebriation had gone through various stages, shifting from remorse to self-pity, to a burning rage that Garth Temple had been so foolish. It was his own fault that he hadn't noticed the spigot had been tampered with. Maker above, the man was supposed to be an expert. *He* was the one to blame for his death – and for leaving him, Nathaniel, at the mercy of that monster Tallow. Then his mood had shifted again, and he'd laughed out loud, aware of Lizzie the tavern-woman staring at him, and not caring.

'Let them do their worst,' he muttered. 'Damn them to hell, the lot of them . . .'

He turned his head and looked out of the window, wincing at the brightness. He groaned.

They were still there, the greywyrmes, the long column stretching out across the new stockade. He raked his fingers through his hair.

Surely it was noon by now . . .

Just then, the door of the tavern burst open and slammed back hard against the wall behind. A hefty-looking figure stood silhouetted in the doorway, legs apart, arms raised.

'At last,' came a gruff voice. 'I been looking for you all over.'

Nathaniel frowned. 'I'm here,' he said, and chuckled throatily that someone might not know his whereabouts when it was so clear to him.

'Sol wants you,' the voice continued. 'And he ain't happy.'

Nathaniel sighed. He wasn't feeling too good himself. 'I . . . I was about to go get me a lie-down,' he said. 'A little sleep . . .'

Muttering something under his breath, the man strode into the tavern, his heavy boots clomping on the bare boards and as he moved away from the blinding light at the doorway, Nathaniel saw him. He wasn't as big as Solomon Tallow, but he was big enough. And ugly. His face looked swollen and misshapen, like he'd been punched repeatedly back when he was a baby. He had greasy blond hair, tied up at the back, a stringy moustache and small hateful black eyes that narrowed menacingly as he came closer.

He didn't look too happy either, Nathaniel noted, and he shrank back nervously in his chair, his erstwhile bravado quite gone.

The man stopped beside him. 'Get up,' he snarled.

Nathaniel looked up and attempted a smile, but the man did not smile back. His eyebrows drew together. His small black eyes all but disappeared.

'Get up,' he repeated, his voice quieter now, almost sing-song.

Nathaniel half rose, pushed back his chair, which screeched on the floorboards as it lurched backwards. He lost his balance, slumped back down and giggled foolishly.

The man reached out and grabbed Nathaniel's jacket, his fist bunching up a wad of fur-trim overmantle and finely embroidered silk. He dragged the young merchant to his feet and thrust his face close. Nathaniel smelled his foul breath. Rank meat. Stale liquor. Contempt.

'Sol don't like to be kept waiting,' he purred. Then, altering his hold, the man gripped the scruff of the young merchant's collar and shoved him unceremoniously across the tavern floor and out the door.

The noonday brightness struck Nathaniel hard. His head hammered and he screwed his eyes shut as the man marched him across the baked clay of the stockade. When he opened them again, peeking gingerly through slitted eyelids, he saw he was being escorted along the line of huge creatures.

Greywyrme after greywyrme, great packs on their backs,

tied up like parcels – and were those trees? And people. Lots of people. Men, women, children; old and young. They seemed to be waiting for him.

Perhaps, thought Nathaniel muzzily, Tallow expected him to make some sort of speech, as owner of the new stockade. Bid them farewell. Say a few hope-filled words about the new life that awaited them out west; sensitive, but not cloying . . .

All at once, the man released his hold. Nathaniel stumbled, momentum driving him forwards a couple of steps, then fell to his knees. When he looked up, he saw that he was at the very front of the column, and that Solomon Tallow was towering high above him, seated in the neck-saddle of a gigantic greywyrme and staring down at him.

'I . . . I'm sorry,' Nathaniel said, climbing shakily to his feet. He swallowed down a mouthful of bile and tried to sober up, at least enough to speak coherently. If he had to give a speech, he wanted it to be memorable. Or at least understandable. He turned around, one hand on the flank of Solomon's greywyrme for support. 'My friends—'

Solomon cut him short. 'What the hell you think you're doing?' he hissed.

Nathaniel looked up, puzzled, and winced at the bright sun that shone down on the kith's gleaming scalp. And his confusion grew when Solomon reached across and patted the seat of the neck-saddle.

'Climb up,' he said.

'Climb up?' Nathaniel repeated numbly. 'But . . . the new stockade . . .'

'It'll be fine,' Solomon reassured him. 'I'm leaving a few of my boys to take care of things here.' His even white teeth flashed. 'You're coming with me.'

Thirty-Eight

The flat ground fell away, sheer and abrupt, like a massive trapdoor had opened up before them. Micah gasped and grabbed at Cara's arm, tugging her away from the edge. They were standing on the lip of a vast canyon, an unexpected chasm that crossed their path. Cody came to a lurching halt beside them, windmilling his arms for balance. A dislodged rock fell, taking sand and gravel with it, and landed far below with a muffled thud and a circular puff of dust.

Cody whistled. 'Glad that weren't me,' he observed shakily. He ran his hand over his cropped scalp, sending up a fine spray of sweat that blushed pink against the low red sun.

Cara laughed uneasily.

'Of course,' Micah chided himself hotly. 'I should have known.' He nodded towards the chaos of orange and brown striped wyrmes that darted through the air overhead, snapping at insects, dodging one another as they wheeled and dived. 'Favourite roost of manderwyrmes, hidden canyons such as these.'

'What now, then?' Cody asked. He moved away from the precipitous drop and squinted back the way they'd come. The tall rearing-bear shaped boulder they'd set off from an hour or so earlier was glowing like a fiery beacon in the distance, across the flat plateau. 'Reckon we ought to head back?'

Micah frowned.

They'd come south, foraging for food, while Eli and Ethan had headed north. Originally, the cragclimber had suggested both brothers accompany him, mindful that Cara and Micah might want time alone; said he was fixing to find him some watershrimp or sweetwater crabs at the dewponds he'd sighted through his spyglass. For supper, he'd added. But Cody had declined.

'Happen Ethan would prefer it if he had you all to himself,' he'd said, and chuckled, making light of it.

Eli had looked across at Micah, but if he had minded, it did not show. So he left with Ethan, and Cody had set off with Cara and Micah. They were all to meet up back at bear rock at sundown to compare their finds.

Thus far, the three of them had pitiful little to show for their endeavours. Pickings had been slim. Apart from the skeletal remains of a mistwyrme, a couple of sulphur-rocks and a clump of aromatic herbs that Cara had crushed between her fingers and declared to be rockthyme, they'd found nothing worth adding to their backpacks, and though Micah kept telling himself they had nothing to prove he wanted to return to Eli with something more substantial.

'Happen there might be some redcaps within reach,' he suggested, leaning out over the yawning drop and scanning the rockside for the telltale crimson blotches.

'We had redcaps the other night,' Cara reminded him.

'And bitter they were too, to my taste,' Cody added.

'And mine,' Cara said, nodding, and they traded quick glances.

Cody was grimacing, his tongue sticking out and nose screwed up. Cara grinned back at him, amused by this display of boyish revulsion. As a rule the young kith's face was set hard, impassive and unreadable, like he was holding stuff back; like he was acting the way he thought a man ought to act. Tough and unflinching. With studied disinterest. A hint of menace. The memory of the redcaps had washed all that away, leaving him temporarily off guard.

'I ever have to eat them again it'll be too soon,' he laughed, holding Cara's gaze.

And Cara laughed with him, the moment of light-heartedness they were sharing permitting her to return his gaze. He had beautiful eyes, she thought. They were the same shape and shade of green as his brother's, but while Ethan's flashed and sparkled, everything on show, Cody's were deep and still and mysterious as dark limpid pools. She looked away, flushing in her cheeks, the front of her neck, and she glanced at Micah, hoping that he hadn't noticed.

He hadn't. Of course he hadn't. He was staring off into the sky – the way he did – and Cara wondered somewhat bitterly what might have triggered his memories of the kingirl this time. The manderwyrmes maybe? Tumbling over a cliff-face . . .

'What about the eggs?' said Cody.

Micah turned, frowned, rubbed a hand over the back of his head. 'Eggs?'

Cody jerked his chin toward to the flitting manderwyrmes. 'I take it they're roosting for a purpose.'

Micah nodded. 'It's a hatchery,' he confirmed. 'They nest in dug-out hollows, but—'

'I love manderwyrme eggs,' Cara broke in. 'Back in Deephome, certain times of year, the brothers would return from sentinel watch with sackloads of the things. We'd have them breakfast, dinner and supper.' She licked her lips at the memory from her lost home at the bottom of the wooded chasm in the valley country. 'And any left over got pickled in great glazed demijohns . . .'

Cody laughed. 'Manderwyrme eggs it is, then.'

'I don't think we should,' said Micah. 'Eli, he wouldn't like it. He don't hold with killing wyrmes and such, you know that.'

'Eggs,' said Cody slowly, like he was talking to a child, or an idiot. 'I ain't talking 'bout killing no wyrmes, I'm saying we take a few of their eggs. Hell, Micah, back on the plains people eat duck eggs, chicken eggs. Don't do no harm to the ducks or chickens, do it?'

'No, but—'

'Well, there you go then. We take us a few and fry them up tonight in the skillet.' He smacked his lips theatrically. 'Dee-licious.'

Cara laughed, cocked her head to one side. 'Oh, Micah,' she said, cajoling him sweetly. 'It can't do any harm, surely.'

Cody snorted. 'You know Micah, Cara,' he said. 'He's a good boy. He wouldn't never do nothing to upset old Eli, now would he?'

Cara flinched at the taunting words, but though she stopped laughing she could not entirely wipe the smile from her face. Micah was bristling. Cody stared at him, loose-shouldered, fists half-bunched. They were all but squaring up to one another, eyes locked. The tense silence between them seemed to throb. Cara wanted to say that the eggs didn't matter; that they should just forget them. But she could not.

Micah's cheeks trembled as his jaws clenched.

'I intend to get us some,' said Cody matter-of-factly. His top lip curled. 'You have any problems with that, Micah, you can always tell Eli you was out-voted.'

Micah swallowed. Cara reached out and touched his arm.

'How many do they lay?' she asked.

Micah turned to her, his brow furrowed. 'Lay?' he said.

'In one batch,' she said. 'How many eggs?'

Micah shrugged. 'Five. Six.'

Cara smiled. 'Then, so long as we don't take more than one a nest, they're not even gonna notice.'

Micah nodded, but looked unconvinced. 'What if we get one about to hatch?' he said. 'You crack out a close-eye wyrmeling into a sizzling skillet, and Eli *is* going to object, I can promise you that.'

Cara nodded. 'So would I,' she said, then smiled. 'But it's easy. We'll have to take the eggs from a nest that's got maybe three or four just. That way, we'll know they're fresh laid.'

Cody chuckled softly at her logic, and Cara flushed up all over again at his appreciation of her. Micah was looking down at the ground, scuffing his boots.

'Well, all right, then,' he said. 'You two go ahead.' He looked up again, his face a mixture of hurt and defiance. 'But *I* ain't getting any.'

'Of course you ain't,' said Cody lightly. 'We'll need you to watch the ropes.'

'You . . . you got ropes?' said Micah.

'I got ropes, Micah. I got everything that I need,' said Cody. He smiled at Cara. 'That *we* need.'

He swung his rucksack off his shoulders, set it down on the ground and loosened the drawstrings. Moving closer, Cara stooped over and watched as Cody retrieved from the bag four coils of rope – two long and two short – metal rings, two rock-spikes with threading holes and a rockhammer. His fingers moved quick and efficient over the ropes as he checked them, and Cara noticed the dark hair at his wrists and on the back of his hand, and how it caught the fading light as his muscles flexed.

'Down on the plains, I did my fair share of well digging,' he explained, noting with satisfaction the look of interest in Cara's eyes. 'Used these lowering ropes . . . I'll show you how.'

He climbed to his feet and, gathering up the rockspikes and hammer and slinging the ropes over his shoulder, looked along the line of the cliff, one way, then the other. He strode over to the edge of the canyon and, taking the hammer, drove the two spikes deep into the rock, side by side.

Cara and Micah watched him. Cara sensed Micah's unease, but said nothing.

'You attach the rope like so,' said Cody, unravelling one of the long lengths and kneeling down to thread it through the first rockspike. 'It's forty yards long,' he said. 'Which gives us twenty yards of descent.' Cody tied off both ends of the rope with large figure-of-eight knots and climbed to his feet. 'You want to give it a go, Cara?'

Micah looked at her, and Cara was gratified to note that she had his full attention now. She nodded. There were butterflies in her stomach and her scalp itched. It was a long, long way down to the bottom of the canyon, and she occupied her thoughts busying herself – removing her backpack from her shoulders and putting it back on at her front.

'OK,' said Cody, taking one of the short ropes, threading on a ring, and tying it securely round her waist. 'I'll attach the rope to you, like this . . .'

Cara stepped forward and held her arms up, and Cody pushed the rope up through the ring. Cara flushed as his fingers inadvertently touched her thigh, her hips; pressed against her stomach. Then – perhaps not so inadvertently – brushed against her breasts as he looped the rope over her shoulder.

'That should do you,' he said at last, taking hold of the bottom of the rope. 'You hold this end at all times,' he told her, 'with your left hand, feeding it through. These, you hold onto with your right.' He handed her the doubled lengths of rope. 'Release your grip a tad when you want to go down. Grip it tight when you want to stop. You got that?'

'I think so,' said Cara uncertainly.

'Don't worry,' he told her, and grinned lop-sided. 'There ain't nothing to it, you'll see.' He looked over at Micah. 'You watch the spikes,' he said, handing him the rockhammer. 'And make sure them ropes don't tangle. Think you can manage that?'

Micah's face coloured, but he bit his tongue and nodded.

When Cody had attached himself to the second set of ropes to his satisfaction, he stepped backwards to the edge of the cliff. Then, with one hand behind him, holding one end of the rope and the two clamped together in his other hand at his side, he leaned back till he was stuck out over the drop beneath him, back straight and legs bent at the knees. He looked round at Cara, saw her wide-eyed expression and grinned.

'Ready?' he said.

'I think so,' Cara said, and hoped the butterflies in her stomach would go away.

'Good,' he said. 'Now take it nice and slow. You just step back. Hold them ropes like I showed you and do exactly what I do.' He smiled again. 'Move to the edge.'

Jaws clamped grimly shut, Cara did just that. Her breathing came shallow and jerky.

'Now, lean back.'

Cara snatched at a deep breath then, as Cody had shown her, fed through the rope with her left hand and released her right hand slightly, so that the twin lengths of rope slid through. She jerked back, tightened her hand and came to halt at an angle to the rock.

'Tad more,' said Cody.

Again, Cara did as she was told, nervous but trusting. She looked across at Cody as she eased herself backwards, and tightened her grip on the rope when the position of her body mirrored his. Overhead, manderwyrmes swooped and soared, blurs of orange and brown as they screeched their agitation.

'Right, now kick off, loose the ropes, then grip them again when your feet touch back on the rock. Like this . . .'

He straightened his braced legs and swung back into the air, dropping as he did so. Then, legs splayed and boots raised, he landed flat against the rock some way lower down.

Cara did the same, copying his every movement. And for a moment, as she was coming down in the air, she felt weightless and free and so exhilarated she laughed out loud.

'It's like flying!' she cried out.

Above her, she saw Micah looking down at her. The

concern on his face switched to something else at her words, and Cara had the feeling that Thrace must have crossed his mind once more; Thrace, who, on the back of her whitewyrme could truly fly, not merely jump down a cliffside at the end of a piece of rope.

'And again,' Cody called across to her.

Little by little, feet pressed flat against the rock, Cara bounced down the rockface, jump after flying jump. As her confidence grew, each one seemed easier and more wonderful than the one before. At about ten yards down, the hatchery began, the smooth rockface becoming deep-pitted with roost-holes that the manderwyrmes had dug into the sandstone. The air filled with the sound of their indignant chitters and whooping cries.

'Reckon we can gather us some eggs, Cara,' Cody said and smiled across at her. 'What do you think?'

Cara looked at the claw-scratched hollows in the cliff face. 'Reckon so,' she said, smiling back.

Reaching forward, she plunged her hand into the dark opening in front of her and felt around in the soft felt-like nest of grass and moss. There were three smooth ovals, warm to the touch. Her fingers closed round one and she withdrew a single pale yellow egg and slipped it inside the opened pack at her front. She reached into another opening and counted four eggs, and carefully removed one before moving on again. Beside her, Cody pulled a bundle of moss and grass roughly from a roost-hole and tipped all five eggs into his rucksack.

Cara pretended not to notice and hoped that Micah, above, had not either.

'You all right down there?' Micah's voice sounded from the lip of the canyon.

'Nearly done,' Cody called up, and smiled across at Cara.

'How many you reckon?' he asked.

'Dozen each?'

He nodded. 'Should be enough.'

Cara reached into another of the roost-holes and felt around. Instead of smooth ovals, her hand touched jagged shards of shell and scaly bodies that wriggled and squirmed beneath her fingers. With a gasp, she drew her hand back – and her feet slipped beneath her. Instinctively, she grasped at the rock, letting go of the rope as she did so.

Suddenly, she was falling, tumbling backwards till she was upside down. The eggs rolled out of her pack, dropped through the air and smashed on the ground far below. The rope went taut and she snapped back, whiplashed, banging the side of her head against the rockface.

Far above her, Micah was shouting. 'Cara! Cara! Are you all right?'

Cara was dangling like a hooked maggot on the end of a fisherman's line. The blood hammered in her head as she desperately struggled to right herself.

'Stay still,' came a voice close by, and Cara turned to see that Cody had lowered himself and was suspended in the air where she hung. His face betrayed no emotion; his words were soft and measured. 'Take a hold of my arm,' he said. 'Get your feet into that roost-hole there – that's the way. Now, push forward, and step out and down.'

With Cody's reassuring grip keeping her steady, Cara braced her legs, found a purchase on the cliff-face and righted herself.

'Don't think I ever dug a well quite this deep,' said Cody, and winked at her. 'I think it's time we climbed back up.'

Cara nodded miserably. 'I dropped all my eggs.'

'I know,' said Cody, and grinned. 'Lucky I got us a few extra.'

Going up was harder than coming down, Cara soon learned. But by using the roost-holes as footholds, slowly but surely, and despite her body shaking, she managed to climb. And when the wyrmeholes gave out, with Cody's arm around her, supporting her weight and taking the strain, she pulled herself up the rope, hand over hand. Micah was there at the top to help her over the edge of the cliff.

'You all right?' he said, his voice urgent and low. Cara could tell his concern was already turning to anger at her recklessness.

She nodded, and felt gingerly at the bump on her head. 'I'm fine,' she said, avoiding his eyes, which were staring unblinking into her own.

Beside them, Cody scrambled over the canyon edge onto his knees, then climbed to his feet.

'You were mighty brave,' Cody said to Cara, his eyes flashing, as if daring Micah to say different.

'Thank you,' Cara whispered back, and as she spoke tears welled up in her eyes. She *had* been reckless, she realized – but only because she'd been desperate for Micah to pay her some attention. And now he was angry with her.

Cody must have sensed what she was feeling, for he reached out and took her hand in his, and held it, his green eyes deep and still and mysterious, staring into hers in the late twilight glow. Cara looked back, and would have held his gaze for longer had Micah not suggested – his voice quiet and uncertain – that they ought to be heading back.

Thirty-Nine

With long powerful wingbeats, Aseel rose higher into the fading light, the shimmering, rock-stored heat of the day buoying him up. On the whitewyrme's back, Thrace tightened her grip with her legs and switched her black kinlance from one hand to the other. Far below, their movements were captured in an elongated shadow that rippled over the grasslands.

Aseel dipped his wings and wheeled round in a broad arc. Thrace arched her back and lifted her head, relishing the feel of the wind in her face.

She was unfettered. Free. Invincible.

She leaned forward and wrapped her arms round Aseel's neck. Below them, the grasslands were now giving way to peaks and ridges, the ravines between them dark and shadow-filled. It was a harsh terrain, arduous and dangerous to traverse on foot. Thrace had experienced such dangers travelling with the crag-climber . . .

And the kithboy.

Unbidden, and unwelcome, the memory of him returned, tangible and fully-formed.

Thrace flinched. Beneath her fingertips, she felt Aseel tremble, his great neck seeming almost to chill to the touch. He craned his neck round and stared back at her, his barbels quivering and eyes darkening from pale yellow to a deep amber. Thrace looked back, aware that the whitewyrme had sensed this sudden change in her mood – and she, in turn, sensed Aseel's guilt that the reason for this flight, wondrous and exhilarating as it was, was to search for the wyve that had resulted from his coupling with Aylsa.

He turned away, gauged the purple-blue of the sky ahead and realigned his course. A thin trail of aromatic white smoke coiled from his nostrils and blew back over his kin. And, comforted, Thrace rested the side of her head against his scaly neck, which flexed and contracted as they flew on into the deepening dusk.

Two or three early evening stars were just twinkling into existence in the velvet sky when the first of the highstacks came into view. They were tall and angled and black-silhouetted against the sky, their tops red-glowed with the molten rock that swirled and bubbled in the earth beneath them. Wisps of smoke coiled up from the vents and drifted northwards, stained crimson by the remnants of the fresh-set sun.

From time immemorial, the highstacks had been the whitewyrmes' hatchery. The females would lay their fertilized wyves beside the hot glowing vents, and the males would tend them till they hatched; turning them over, warning off would-be predators. Sometimes it took no more than a couple of months for the wyves to hatch; sometimes a hundred years. Sometimes longer.

When the taint of the marauding kith had grown too strong, the whitewyrmes had abandoned the highstacks, trusting that wyrmekin – though shunned by the colony – would protect the wyves. And Aseel and Thrace had done just that. But later, when the kith penetrated further into the weald and the colony abandoned the wyrme galleries as well, Alsasse their leader had sent back a contingent of wyrmes to gather up the wyves, and the whitewyrme host had taken them with them.

After the tribulations Aseel and Thrace had endured the previous year, which had taken them both away from the highstacks, they had finally returned, only to find the hatchery empty. With no wyves to protect, and fullwinter fast approaching, they had been unsure what to do. In the end, they had left the valley country and flown to the abandoned wyrme galleries to see out the winter; to decide what they should do next . . .

'*I went there by darkness, the night before the colony was due to depart for the west*,' Aylsa had told Aseel down in the underground nursery. '*I thought you would be able to protect it*,' she said.

'So that was where I laid it. At the top of a highstack, my wyve . . .' She had hesitated. 'Our *wyve, Aseel.*'

Now, as they approached the stacks that peppered the eastern valley country like a thousand carved obelisks, searching for that single wyve, Aseel's heart raced. With his wings shallow-beating in bursts, then held rigid and gliding, Aseel circled round highstack after highstack, his and Thrace's eyes searching the top of each successive smoking vent.

But there was no sign of the wyve.

The moon rose, full and milk-silver. Aylsa had told Aseel that, as she recalled, the stack she had chosen in her haste and turmoil, was striped – though that didn't narrow it down much.

Then they discovered the kith.

It was the taint that alerted Aseel to them. Rancid oil and rank sweat. The stench of death.

There were four of them. They were hunkered down in a circle at the top of a tall lopsided stack that was banded from bottom to top with thick strata of rock, alternating light and dark. They wore thick leather overjackets and broad-brim hats that gleamed in the stark moonlight. They had removed their packs, which lay off to one side of the flat stacktop, along with ropes, rockspikes and harpoons, and two sidewinders. A couple of spitbolts were slung over the backs of two of the hunched kith. And as Aseel came down lower in the sky, Thrace noted the red kerchiefs knotted around their necks – that, and an acrid smell of burning.

Aseel soared back into the air on widespread wings, taking care not to cross the moon and throw shadows that would alert the men to their presence. They circled the highstack warily.

One of the kith seemed to be in charge. With the end of a long club, he was hammering at a knee-high dome of baked clay that they had constructed over the highstack's glowing vent. As the clay cracked, wisps of smoke coiled up into the air, and the acrid smell intensified. The kith turned the club round in his hand and started poking and prodding at the dome, chipping off shard after shard of the baked mud that had formed a carapace around a layer of charred wood and blackened straw. And as Aseel and Thrace watched, the kith cleared away the smoking embers to reveal . . .

A wyve.

Thrace felt Aseel's body tense beneath her. These kith were trying to force-hatch a wyve. Aseel's wyve.

An overwhelming fury surged through Thrace's body. She gripped the kinlance in one hand and raised her hood with the other. Aseel turned to her. His eyes were glowing a deep blood-red. Far below, the kith with the club leaned forward.

'Easy does it,' he said as he rolled the wyve from the ashes and began tapping it with the club.

All at once, the wyve broke open. There came a muted cry and the wyrmeling inside flopped out onto the rock, mewling and twitching. Its head was large; disproportionately so in contrast to its scrawny scale-free body and twig-like legs. One wing rose, papery and angular; the other was no more than a nubbed stump. Its eyes were huge but rheumy blind. Its muzzle had not yet formed. Instead, there was a hole where a snout should be, white-spiked with irregular fangs.

'Damn thing's half-formed,' one of the kith opined.

'That's just too bad,' said the kith with the club, 'since this is the only wyve we've found in these roosting stacks – and since none of us here has fifty years to spare to see it cooked proper . . .'

Snatching the sack from the kith beside him, he seized the wyrmeling and was about to thrust it inside when he froze, his eyes wide and uncomprehending as the shaft of Thrace's lance pierced his chest. At the same moment, Aseel's blast of white-hot fire engulfed the kith beside him.

As the whitewyrme and rider soared back into the night sky, the blazing kith stumbled from the highstack, illuminating its striped layers as he fell. Aseel turned and dived back down at the two remaining kith. One of them had slipped the spitbolt from his back; the other had seized a sidewinder. Both of them were taking aim.

Thrace levelled her lance at the taller of the two and let out a high-pitched screech. The sharp point of her kinlance penetrated the man's skull smooth and clean, like a hot spike through an ice crust. He dropped to his knees, then slumped forward, his body thrown into spasm as his sidewinder skudded harmlessly across the surface of the rock and disappeared over the edge.

The remaining kith raised his spitbolt and fired as they swooped past. The bolt struck Thrace at the shoulder, glancing harmlessly off the soulskin but knocking her off balance. With a cry, she fell from Aseel's back and tumbled across the flat rock of the highstack before coming to rest beside the glowing vent, kinlance clutched in her hands.

Overhead, the whitewyrme faltered in the air, tipping to one side and arcing round to dive again. Thrace leaped to her feet.

The kith was reloading.

He was heftily built, with broad shoulders, beard, beetlebrow, bad skin. His eyes were filled with panic and loathing, and his fingers trembled as he wound back the bow of the spitbolt. Thrace ran at him, her kinlance raised above her head. The kith lowered his weapon, bringing it down level with her chest. Thrace struck out with a raking kick and took the kith's legs from under him. He went down hard, dropping his spitbolt and sprawling on the ground. With the kinlance gripped in both hands, Thrace brought it down hard. The needlesharp point tore through the knotted kerchief, missing his bull neck by a fraction, and pinned him to the ground.

'Let me up,' he squealed, squirming, kicking out, reaching up and fumbling at the knots of the kerchief. 'You filthy little—'

Thrace kicked him hard between the legs. He bucked and howled and grasped at himself.

'Lie still,' she told him. She hadn't spoken in anything but wyrmetongue for so long that the words sounded strange and guttural to her.

The kith whimpered softly, but stopped struggling.

Behind her, Aseel had landed noiselessly, his eyes still glowing a fiery red and smoke twisting up from his nostrils. He folded his wings and moved swiftly to the glowing vent beside which the kith with the club lay. He was dead, the half-formed wyrmeling clutched in one outstretched hand. Aseel crouched down, prised the man's clenched fingers apart and tenderly picked up the wyrmeling. It too was dead.

Cradling the small lifeless wyrmeling to his breast, Aseel nuzzled it gently, his eyes amber-yellow and half-closed. He then carefully held the tiny corpse out over the glowing vent and, with a wind-rustle sigh, let it drop into the depths.

When he looked back at Thrace and the kith, his eyes were glowing blood-red once more.

Thrace tugged her kinlance from the ground releasing the kerchief and the kith, who remained motionless on the ground, staring back up at her. She levelled the point at his chest.

'*Wait*,' said Aseel, his voice soft and measured and full of sorrow. '*First, I would have you question him . . .*'

He inclined his neck and looked at the dead kith at his feet, then over at the other dead kith sprawled near the edge of highstack. Below, flickering in the darkness, the third kith still burned.

'I want to know where they have come from,' Aseel said softly, and Thrace could sense the cold fury in his voice. *'So I can go there and put an end to this.'*

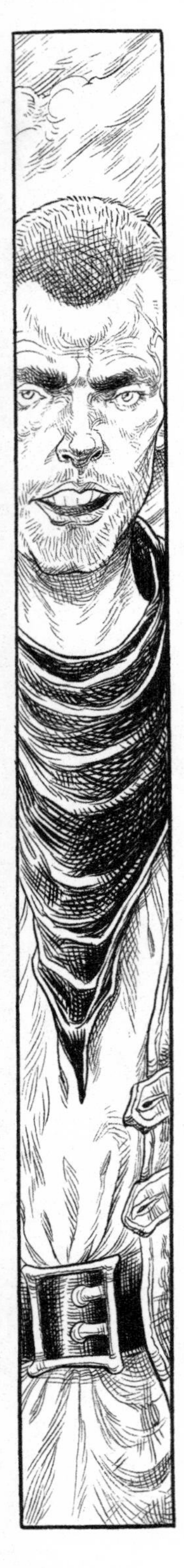

Forty

The silver coin flashed as it spun. Josiah snatched it from the air and thrust it into the front pocket of his breeches.

Solomon Tallow smiled. 'So the talk round the campfires is of rebellion?' he said, and tousled the boy's mess of tangled blond hair.

Josiah nodded. 'And the young merchant encourages it,' he confirmed. 'Says you're too harsh on the sick folks . . .'

'And you're sure about that leg of his?'

The boy nodded again. 'Seen it with my own eyes,' he said.

Tallow tossed him another coin. 'Well, keep up the good work, y'hear?'

'I shall, Mr Tallow, sir,' Josiah promised earnestly.

Tallow stood up from his campfire and stretched expansively, then patted his stomach. 'Be sure to thank that mother of yours for the stew,' he told the boy, who was gathering up the iron pot and ladle at the gang-master's feet.

Josiah looked up and smiled. 'I sure will, Mr Tallow, sir,' he said. 'And you can trust me with that other business too,' he added before slipping away into the dark.

In front of Tallow, the settlers' campfires twinkled in the blackness like stars. They illuminated the settlers' haggard faces, which were creased with worry and hollowed out by exhaustion. The mood was quiet, sombre; so different from the high spirits of ten days earlier when they'd set forth from the new stockade. Back then there had been laughter and excited chatter. And songs. Call and response, and rousing choruses, with fiddle players and tin-whistle pipers accompanying their swooping harmonies.

This mood had lasted for most of the first day and into the second. But by the third day of trekking through the scorch-hot bone-dry badlands, the songs and chatter had fallen silent. And on that third day, the first of the settlers fell sick.

He was a strapping young farmer, tall and heftily built, and the last person anyone would have thought might have succumbed to illness. Yet succumb he did. Blinding headaches and numbing weariness, followed by nosebleeds that would not let up. His wife had pleaded with Solomon Tallow to wait up a while, said that she couldn't cope on her own with the four kids. But Solomon Tallow had held firm.

'We must press on or our water'll run out,' he said, and the woman's tears did nothing to weaken his resolve.

The man died the following day and was hastily buried in a shallow grave, a wooden post with the name Jed carved into the wood marking the spot. On that same day, half a dozen more of the settlers went down with the same sickness. And the day after that, forty or so more. Same symptoms. Same outcome. A line of posts was left in the wake of the column of greywyrmes that picked their way across the badlands towards the shimmering blue outline of the high country peaks.

The posts were not the only sign of the harshness of the trail through the badlands. It had been travelled by others. Their skeletons littered the cracked rock, the bones stripped clean by carrionwyrmes and bleached white by the elements. The remnants of oxen and mules; men, women and children, and babies, their small toothless skulls gurning and gruesome. The bone trail. There were upturned wagons and broken carts. Backpacks and empty watergourds. And sometimes, ordered piles of belongings; trunks and crates all roped together, that families must have left to lighten their load, intending to return and collect them – but failing to do so.

Thomas Hughes & Family

Harlan Bridges

FALLOWFOOT

The letters that had been painted so neatly and clearly were cracked and peeling.

Each time the settlers passed such forlorn remains, they clustered closer to the flanks of the great greywyrmes that trudged indomitably on through the heat. Those who had gone before them, the settlers knew, had died when their beasts of burden had perished. At least *they* had these huge creatures to haul their ever more precious gourds of water, no matter how sick and weak the settlers themselves became. If only the gangmaster would slacken the pace a bit . . .

Fear and discontentment began to smoulder. And once it had caught a hold, it spread through the convoy like a bush-fire. The settlers wanted to have time at least to bury their dead with dignity and due respect. And they wanted answers for this strange and malevolent sickness that was striking so many of them down. And on this, the tenth evening, when the column had come to a halt for the night – the hobbled greywyrmes creating an outer ring and the settlers inside the circle; setting up camp, making fires and setting stewpots upon them – the talk of some kind of rebellion was rife.

Josiah had listened attentively, like he always did, in the shadows, out of the light of the campfires, and reported what he'd heard back to the gangmaster.

Solomon Tallow strode over to the nearest campfire and stopped in front of Nathaniel Lint the Younger, who was sitting picking miserably at a flame-charred side of squab-wyrme. The young merchant's right leg was bandaged, a cloud of flies buzzing round it. The binding was stained dark, and a putrid stench hung in the air.

Nathaniel spat out a lump of gristle and tossed aside the stripped bone he'd been gnawing. He looked up at Tallow, his eyes beseeching.

'I dressed the wound like you said,' he began, a tearful whine colouring his voice, 'but it's begun to fester, Solomon. Don't reckon I can make it much further . . .' The merchant stuck out his chin, attempting to look resolute and brave. 'Best thing is if I take me a gourd or two, and a greywyrme, and head back to the stockade – get me some medicine and rest it up . . .'

Tallow looked down at him contemptuously. 'Happen we're going to have to amputate,' he pronounced solemnly, pulling his broadblade gutting knife from his belt. He reached down and ran the back of the knife along the merchant's leg, some way north of the knee; tutted sympathetically. 'But it'll have to be chopped off high enough to ensure all the infection is removed.'

He reversed the knife and cut through the soiled bandage. The binding fell away to reveal the rotting slab of wyrmemeat that Nathaniel had concealed beneath, to give the impression of putrefaction. Tallow skewered it and tossed it into the fire.

'Looks like you just made a miracle recovery,' he said, fixing Lint with a dead-eyed stare.

The merchant recoiled and sat staring miserably into the firelight as Solomon climbed to his feet. The gangmaster looked round at the settlers' faces staring back at him from the other campfires, hope-filled and longing to be reassured. He wiped his hands on his breeches, then raised them as he addressed the camp.

'I'm sore aware of the sickness that has come among you,'

he announced, his voice deep and bluff. 'It is unfortunate,' he added, and pretended not to notice the outraged muttering that greeted the inadequacy of his description, 'but it ain't catching. Wealdsickness. That's what it's called. It's caused by the thin air up here. Course, it affects ox and mules and such, as y'all know. But it can also afflict folks. Some worse than others. There ain't no rhyme nor reason to it.' He paused. 'Nor no cure.'

The settlers exchanged glances, aghast, wondering afresh what they had let themselves in for.

'However,' Solomon went on, 'the good news is that we're about to enter the high country, so if you ain't yet fallen sick already, you're unlikely to do so.' He rubbed a hand over his stubbled scalp. 'And by journey's end tomorrow, we hit the first of the lakes. Clean fresh water and a full day to rest up and recover.'

For the first time in days, a buzz of excited conversation spread through the camp.

Solomon turned to the young merchant huddled by the campfire. The gangmaster's dark eyes were hard and humourless.

'Fetch the pitcher,' he said gruffly. 'That's if you've finished with your malingering.'

Nathaniel flinched, but got to his feet and threaded his way through the constellation of yellow flickering campfires to Tallow's greywyrme. It was standing tethered to the others, its head lowered, eyes half-shut and great grey flanks rising and falling like a pair of immense bellows.

Reaching up, Nathaniel tugged on the creature's reins,

bringing its neck lower, and he clambered up into the saddle. Then, leaning back, he closed his fingers round the stoppered vessel strapped securely in place behind the broad saddle. He fumbled at the buckles as he untied the leather straps, and lifted the brass pitcher by the handle on its side.

The pitcher was half-full, judging by its weight and the way the precious flameoil it contained sloshed around when Nathaniel tilted it. Maker alone knew how much such a quantity of flameoil would fetch back on the plains, he thought. With this pitcher, together with the others locked securely away in Tallow's quarters back at the new stockade, he'd be able to pay his father back a hundred times over and still be a wealthy man. Assuming, that is, he did not have to share the proceeds with anyone else.

Nathaniel sighed unhappily. How *was* he to escape from Solomon Tallow?

Twice he'd tried. Twice he'd failed.

On the first day of the journey, he'd attempted to slip away in the hustle and bustle and high spirits, but although Solomon had appeared not to notice the young merchant hanging back at the rear of the column, and Nathaniel had turned away and begun heading towards the new stockade, he hadn't got far. Tallow had sent his henchmen after him and dragged Nathaniel back to the head of the wyrmetrain, amid much laughter and amusement from the settlers.

Now, for four days, he'd faked a leg injury, hoping the gangmaster would let him leave. But all to no avail. Nathaniel was beginning to consider himself jinxed. Either that, or Tallow was some kind of mindreader.

He could hear him now. His bunch of wyrmehandlers had gathered round the gangmaster's campfire, each holding small bottles containing flameoil tapped from the greywyrmes in their charge. Tallow was laughing and joshing with them, keeping spirits up in that easy way he had, his voice hearty and bluff, yet with an undertone of menace.

Nathaniel trembled. Maybe, just maybe, he thought, it would be third time lucky.

Climbing down and setting the sloshing pitcher beside the recumbent greywyrme, Nathaniel slung a watergourd over one shoulder and a pack of supplies he'd gathered for his escape over the other. It grieved him to leave the flameoil, but it was heavy and the likelihood of his completing the ten-day hike with it were slim. Besides, there was flameoil enough back at the stockade. He snatched a last look round the encampment of settlers, grateful that he wasn't one of them, then slipped between two of the resting greywyrmes and out into the darkness beyond.

Far to the east, the first creamy blush of moonrise was lightening the sky. Nathaniel Lint set off towards it at a brisk pace. He hadn't noticed the tousle-headed boy watching his every move.

'You did like I asked?' Tallow said, and smiled as the boy, Josiah, handed him the heavy brass pitcher.

'I soured his watergourd with rock salt,' Josiah affirmed, 'and replaced his dried provisions with half-rotten wyrmemeat – wrapped up in rockthyme to hide the smell,' he added proudly.

'Good lad,' the gangmaster replied, unstoppering the pitcher and watching closely as the wyrmehandlers emptied the contents of their bottles into it, one by one.

He looked back at the boy, and when he spoke, his voice loud and sonorous, it was for the benefit of his wyrmehandlers as much as for Josiah.

'You see, lad, I couldn't allow a pampered whelp like Nathaniel Lint to stay behind and spread discord at the settlement. I thought he was going to be useful up here,' he said, and shrugged. 'But I was wrong, and I soon saw his little game – aiming to recruit a gang himself and challenge my authority.'

His dark eyes raked the faces of the wyrmehandlers lined up before him.

'Times are changing,' he announced. 'We don't need rich merchants from the plains pulling our strings. No. It's weald-hardened kith such as us will determine the future of the high country.'

Tallow's voice rose, so that the camp at large could benefit from his wisdom.

'A future where good honest folk can stake out a place for themselves and benefit from the protection of them kith that guided 'em there.'

He turned back to the boy.

'You see, Josiah,' he said, his voice suddenly low and confidential.

The last wyrmehandler emptied the two fingers of flameoil his greywyrme had produced in the last day or so into the pitcher and stepped away to respect the gangmaster's privacy.

'I ain't a brutal man,' Tallow said. 'I could have slit the whelp's throat and had done with him when he first started acting up. But such bloodshed would only have upset the good folks around us. No, it's better this way . . . Nice and quiet. And no fuss.'

Tallow smiled as he reached into his waistcoat. He drew out a silver coin and tossed it to the boy.

'Now, I don't suppose that mother of yours has got any more of that delicious stew?' he said.

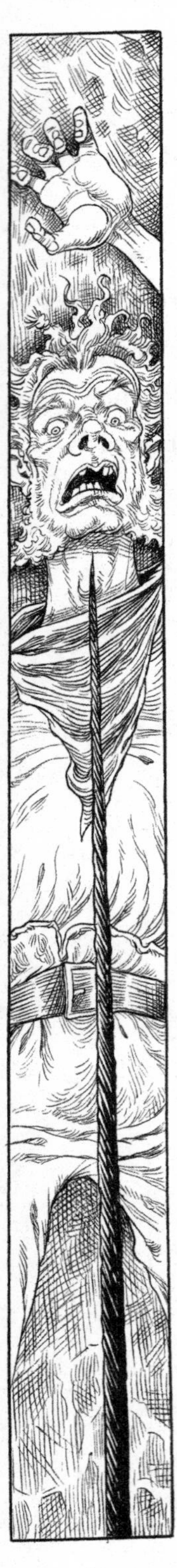

Forty-One

'Where have you come from?' Thrace demanded, the point of her kinlance levelled at the man's heart.

He was a tough-looking one, this kith. Scowl-faced and stocky, with small, frightened-looking dark eyes and bunched fists. Even though he was lying on his back, he looked like a fighter who didn't know he was beat.

'You move and you die,' Thrace said, and she twitched her kinlance to emphasize the point. 'Where have you come from?'

The guttural human words seemed to choke in her throat, and beside her she noticed Aseel flinch at the sound of them. He braced his shoulders, flexed his neck, and his blood-red gaze hardened as curdled smoke trickled from his flared nostrils.

The kith stared up at the wyrmekin girl standing over him. She was the first of her kind he'd encountered. Dark-eyed, clear-skinned; lithe in the suit of white she wore, that clung to her body like a second skin. She was beautiful, he had to admit, just about the most beautiful creature he'd ever laid eyes on, but terrifying for all that, with her harsh expression and black lance and that great whitewyrme of hers by her side, hissing and steaming like some liquor still about to blow.

'From the ridge country to the west of here,' the kith said slowly, beads of sweat collecting on his broad forehead and trickling down the sides of his face. 'Been rounding up them greywyrmes that pass through there . . .'

Thrace's lance quivered, and the kith flinched nervously.

'Not to kill, you understand,' he said shakily, attempting to smile. 'No, but to harness like. To send 'em back to the badlands.'

The kith glanced across at the whitewyrme, whose eyes, blood-red and furious-looking, unnerved him even more than the kingirl's lance.

'We don't treat 'em rough,' he said, a boyish sincerity to the words. 'Real gentle we are with the great brutes. Have to be, else Solomon Tallow don't pay us when we get 'em to that stockade of his . . .'

He was babbling now, in a frantic attempt to keep the lance from skewering him or the whitewyrme from turning him into a flaming torch, like it had done to poor Israel.

'Wyrmes are wonderful creatures, their ways strange and wondrous to behold, and I for one don't hold with hurting them, not one bit . . .'

'Tallow?' Thrace said. She knew that name. He was the leader of the gang that had seized the wyrmeling Asa, sold him to the keld . . .

'Solomon Tallow,' the kith repeated, nodding furiously. 'He has this plan to use the greywyrmes. Harvest their precious flameoil. Use them as pack animals to take folks from the plains up to the high country, in a way their mules and ox cannot on account of the wealdsickness . . . Gathered hundreds of folk at the new stockade, he has, and thousands more will follow them, I reckon . . .'

He stopped suddenly, aware that he'd gone too far; said too much.

'You kith,' said the kingirl, her voice soft as a sigh to the man's ears, yet fearful. 'You spread your taint, destroying everything you touch. Wyrmes. Wyrmelings . . .'

She leaned forward, and as the lance slid smoothly into the man's chest, she brought her face close to his, her beautiful dark eyes staring into his startled, disbelieving ones. She twisted the lance.

'Wyves,' she whispered.

Thrace stepped back. She was breathing hard, her heart hammering in her chest, and the cold fury that came upon her whenever she encountered the murderous kith made her body quiver and muscles flex with a life of their own.

'*What did he say?*' Aseel's voice, soft and rustling like wind through half-summered trees, calmed her, soothed her.

She slumped to her knees, suddenly exhausted.

'*The kith said there are more coming*,' she said in comforting, sonorous wyrmetongue – though the words themselves made her want to sob. She could see the fire in Aseel's eyes flare once more. '*Thousands of them are gathering in the badlands at a place he called the new stockade.*'

Aseel dipped his great head, his eyes half-closed and nostrils flared. When he spoke, his voice was quiet, little more than a whisper. Weary. Full of sorrow.

'*The new stockade*,' he repeated.

Forty-Two

Cara teased the last tangle from her wet hair and placed the fine-toothed scrimshaw comb on the rock beside her. She was aware that Cody was watching her with those green eyes of his. He'd been watching her for some time now – ever since she'd stepped out from behind the wedge-shaped rock bluff, with the spring water pouring down into the clear pool at its base.

When they had stumbled across it, Eli had seen at once how Cara's face had lit up at the prospect the spring and pool afforded for bathing and washing out clothes. Cody had noticed too, though Micah, as usual, had not. Instead, he'd wandered further along the trail with that sad haunted look he'd had since the three of them had returned from gathering the manderwyrme eggs.

Eli had crossed to the rope-like waterfall, cupped his hands in the twist of water and drunk long and deep, then wiped his dripping hands over his forehead, down the back of his neck. Arms raised, he'd sniffed tentatively at his underarms and grinned.

'Happen I've had just about enough of stinking like a polecat,' he'd said. 'What do you say we stop here and indulge in some ablutions?'

He'd looked across at Cara, who had laughed delightedly and agreed at once.

'Now, we menfolk'll step back a ways,' he'd continued, glancing at Ethan and Cody, 'while you take yourself over there, Cara, and bathe.'

Ethan had giggled, and Cody had blushed furiously, but both of them followed the cragclimber back round to the other side of the bluffs, out of sight. And Cara had wasted no time.

From her backpack, she had retrieved one of the pale-green cakes of soap she'd purchased back at the scrimshaw den, and soon the pool frothed and the air was perfumed by the sweet fragrance of myrtle. She had washed herself, then her clothes, and finally, luxuriously, her long auburn hair, the grime and dust of days out on the trail dissolving away in the clear cool springwater. Then she'd slipped on the white linen shift that she'd been saving since the last wash at the falls, so long ago, and stepped round the corner of the rockbluff to begin combing her hair.

Ethan and Eli were off gathering brushwood some distance away, and there was no sign of Micah. But Cody was there. He was sitting on a rock, pretending to sort through his pack – but watching her all the while.

Not for the first time, Cody was struck by the kithgirl's beauty. She had finished combing her hair. Now it framed her face, emphasizing the soft golden tan of her skin, the fullness of her lips and the delicate band of freckles that crossed the bridge of her nose and crinkled up when she smiled. And those eyes; bright and gleaming, like shards of polished turquoise . . .

They were looking at him now, with a mixture of amusement and tenderness that set Cody's heart thumping. Cody looked down, overcome with shyness. He found himself staring at the scrimshaw medallion of the dragon, nestling against the gentle heave of her breasts.

His medallion. The one that he, Cody, had given her. Not Micah's. Micah's one was lost. She was wearing *his* one. His, his, his . . .

'Where do you think Micah's got to?' Cara asked.

The small question had come seemingly out of nowhere. It jangled inside Cody's head. Micah was always there on her mind. Even now.

'Daydreaming as usual, I reckon,' he said wryly. He laughed, to show that he meant no disrespect by the words, even though he did, and was relieved when Cara laughed back.

'Or checking the horizon for wyrmes and their riders,' she said, and if she felt she was betraying Micah it did not show.

She got up and walked over to where Cody was sitting, the contents of his pack spread out at his feet. Her white shift, Cody noticed, clung to her body, still wet from the pool. He tried not to notice how the linen contoured her breasts, her hips; how the hem reached only a little below the top of her legs. Instead, he looked up into her eyes as she sat down beside him. And this time, he did not look away.

'Got any other trinkets to give to me?' said Cara, smiling mischievously as she fingered the medallion round her neck.

Cody's expression was serious, his eyes fixed on Cara's. 'Don't have nothing to give,' he said quietly. 'No wealth. No possessions. No great learning, nor fancy words . . . All I've got is myself.' He paused and his eyes glistened as he spoke. 'But I would gladly give myself to you, Cara, body and soul, if you ever asked or wanted me to.'

Cara swallowed. She looked at him closely, this hard tough young man, whose rages frightened her but whose sensitivity and passion warmed and agitated her like she was a pot of water set upon a fire to boil. She reached out, stroked his cropped hair, her hand resting at the back his head, which she pulled gently towards her. She bent forward and placed her lips upon his forehead. Kissed him once. Then again.

Cody looked up. A smile flickered. He wrapped his arms around her shoulders, brought her closer.

Their lips pressed together; parted. Their tongues touched . . .

At that moment, Micah emerged from round the side of the cliff, and stopped dead. He stood for a moment, unnoticed and unmoving, then turned away and disappeared back the way he'd come.

Forty-Three

The sky was full of whitewyrmes and their riders. The girl, Zar, and her young wyrme, Asa, hesitated on the rockslab ledge of an upper gallery and looked out into the bright dew-soaked morning.

High above them, the two kingirls from the jagged ridges, their eyes sparkling brightly from behind the masks of black sootgrease that crossed their faces, were engaged in some kind of rolling manoeuvre in the air. The young male whitewyrmes they rode pitched and rolled in somersaults and figures of eight, the daubed black markings that encircled their necks seeming almost to flash as they did so.

To the east, over the rolling grasslands, the three kin from the black pinnacles, their thin plaits writhing like snakes, were in the middle of an aerial mock-battle with three kin from the western salt-flats. The black pinnacles' wyrmes were young and agile. They swooped and dived with great skill and ease, but the ancient battle-scarred wyrmes from the salt-flats were stronger and had guile born of long experience. As Zar and Asa watched, they outstripped the black pinnacles' wyrmes in straight flight with strong measured wingbeats, then turned and blocked them with the swishing curves of their great tails.

To the west, meanwhile, the kin from the yellow peaks were skimming over the blue-grey mountains, their jagged saw-edge peaks seeming to stretch away into the distance for ever. Since the incident with the cragclimber and his group in the grasslands, when Kesh had wanted to torture the kithyouth, Zar and Asa had got to know the yellow peaks' kin well.

Kesh had not returned, and Ramilles and his wyrme, Aluris, were the leaders now. The others, Timon, Baal and Finn and their wyrmes Aakhen, Amir and Avaar looked up to them and followed their lead. Now, as the dawn sun glinted on their white scales, they rose and fell on the distant thermals in an undulating formation, with Aluris and Ramilles out in front.

Zar smiled. She liked the big brawny kin with his curly black hair and piercing blue eyes. Like an older brother, he'd been kind to her, and Aluris had been kind to Asa, teaching him how to manoeuvre in the sky, taking advantage of updraughts and anticipating air currents, and how to fly through ravines and canyons no wider than a wingspan.

To the north and south, more whitewyrmes and their riders were on the wing. Everyone, it seemed to Zar, had left the galleries to patrol the skies. Eighty, ninety wyrmekin, Zar wasn't sure. But what she did know was that she and Asa were the youngest, with the most to learn and the least time to do so. She wished Thrace and Aseel were here, but they had been gone for two days now, and hadn't told her where they were going . . .

Next to her, Asa gave a low growl, his eyes darkening to a rich amber. Blinking into the sunlight, Zar followed his gaze. High over the smoke-hazed mountaintops to the west, there was something twisting and writhing in the sky like a storm-cloud on the horizon. As the dark cloud came closer, growing larger, the sun picked out shades of burnished black and blue as it flexed and bowed – and revealed itself to be a vast flock of wyrmes.

They spread out across the sky, the sound of their wing-beats growing loud and insistent. Their blunt-muzzle heads and vast wings stood out stark against the pale-blue sky. They were huge and brutal-looking, and Zar had never seen wyrmes like them before.

Behind them she saw that there was a second flock of smaller wyrmes. They were white and silver in the morning light, whitewyrmes like Asa, flying in a rigid formation and seeming almost to hang back. As the great host of blue-blackwyrmes approached, Zar's stomach lurched when she realized that Ramilles and the yellow peaks kin were directly in their path.

* * *

All at once, a blueblackwyrme broke formation and dived down at Ramilles and Aluris, a jet of yellow flame flaring from its parted jaws. Ramilles ducked down and pulled up his hood as the searing heat scorched the air.

This wyrme seemed intent on killing him. But why?

Quick and nimble, Aluris beat her wings and soared up over the shoulder of the oncoming wyrme. Ramilles twisted round and lunged with his kinlance as they passed overhead. It scored a line down the neck of the massive blueblackwyrme, then tore through its wing, leaving it gaping and ragged.

The wyrme went into a tailspin and, as Ramilles and Aluris swerved back round in the air, they saw the fatally wounded creature crash into the ground far below with a splintering thud and a puff of smoke and dust.

Ramilles trembled. He hated to kill a wyrme. But it had given him no choice . . .

Just then, an agonized scream split the sulphur-taint air, and Ramilles turned to see that a dozen more blueblackwyrmes had descended and were in pursuit of Timon and Aakhen. They opened their jaws and the whitewyrme and her kin were engulfed in flame. As Aluris and Ramilles watched, horrified, the wyrme and rider turned about and flew back into the attacking throng. As Timon screeched, his blazing kinlance took out one, then another of the blueblacks. Then a third. Their bodies tumbled down out of the sky – along with the kin and his wyrme, spent now, as they arched down to earth like a blazing comet.

'*Why?*' Ramilles cried out in wyrmetongue. '*Why are you doing this?*'

'*The taint!*' roared the blueblackwyrme spiralling towards him, his voice harsh and guttural. '*You bear the taint!*'

Behind him, forty more took up the cry. '*The taint! The taint!*'

All around Ramilles and Aluris, the sky was full of the monstrous wyrmes, huge and ungainly in flight but immensely strong and with flaming breath that had an awesome reach. Aluris flew into the midst of the throng, dodging slashing claws and heavy clubbing tails, the blueblacks unable to breathe fire at such close quarters for fear of incinerating each other.

There were hundreds of them, and Ramilles cut a swathe through the great dark shapes with his kinlance, allowing his whitewyrme to soar upwards into the thin clear air high above. He looked back down and struggled to make sense of the unfolding horror. The blueblack flock were passing below. They swept up Baal and Amir and tore them bloodily limb from limb. Finn and Avaar turned and tried to outrun the host, only to be consumed by jets of flame.

Aluris flew higher. Ramilles' heart was pounding; his stomach churned. The lance in his hand felt cold and clammy, and sweat ran into his eyes, making them sting. He looked around desperately for the rest of the kin – from the black pinnacles, the jagged ridges, the saltflats . . . Instead, his gaze fell upon the host of wyrmes hovering over the peaks some distance to the west.

Whitewyrmes.

He thought they had abandoned the galleries for ever. Yet here they were, back again, and with a horde of savage wyrmes, unknown in the valley country, to do their fighting for them. He didn't understand. Whitewyrmes might have shunned kin but they had never sought to kill them – until now.

Ramilles tore his gaze away from the host and looked back over his shoulder. Beneath him, he felt Aluris shudder.

The blueblackwyrmes were nearing the sandstone bluffs of the wyrme galleries, their guttural cries echoing through the colonnaded caverns. There they were, the wyrmekin, strung out in a thin line of glittering white. Their faces were shadowed beneath raised hoods and their black lances were levelled as they braced themselves to receive this sudden onslaught. The eyes of the whitewyrmes they rode blazed blood-red as they hovered in the air on steadily beating wings.

Ramilles tore off his hood, eyes stinging and a lump in his throat.

As he watched, helpless, the blueblack host thundered into the thin streak of white. The line of wyrmekin quivered, bent back, but for a moment refused to break. The whitewyrmes and their kin were holding their own, their black lances stabbing out in front of them, wreaking havoc. Wyrme after wyrme tumbled and crashed into the canyon beneath the cliffs. But the blueblackwyrmes kept attacking with relentless ferocity. Abruptly the line broke, and with a low moaning sigh, the whitewyrmes and their riders scattered – only to be picked off individually, or in two and threes, by the pitiless horde. The barkshod kin from the saltflats, the masked kingirls from the jagged ridges; Mara and Keel, from the southern grasslands . . .

Ramilles could watch no more. Nor could Aluris. She arced round sharply and sped down into a jagged ravine to the south.

Looking back, Ramilles saw the hovering host of whitewyrmes pull back their wings and glide slowly down towards the wyrme galleries. Victory was theirs. Yet even at this great distance, he thought he saw sorrow in the stoop of their sinuous necks and the pale yellow of their eyes.

'*We must leave this place*,' Zar said breathlessly.

The sounds of the battle far above reverberated down through the tunnels and echoed round the clawscritch walls of the nursery chamber.

'*Leave?*' Aylsa looked up from the infant boy curled up fast asleep in the folds of her coiled body. 'To go where?'

'*To the east*,' said Asa, '*to find Thrace and Aseel. They'll know what to do*.'

Zar looked into Aylsa's eyes. '*Monstrous blueblack wyrmes*,' she said tearfully. '*A vast flock from out of the west are attacking all the kin and their wyrmes without mercy*.'

The whitewyrme dipped her head and nuzzled the infant awake. '*So they've come east*,' she said, and when she looked up, her yellow eyes glowed pale with fear and sorrow. '*It is the taint*,' she said, climbing to her feet, the boy cradled in her claws. '*They will kill all they find . . .*'

She walked across the chamber and out into the tunnel beyond. Zar and Asa followed, comforted momentarily to be with the older wyrme, who seemed to understand something of this new and unexpected terror.

'*Hush, little one,*' Aylsa purred to the infant in her arms, breathing out sweet aromatic smoke as she spoke. '*It'll be all right,*' she said reassuringly, even though, deep down inside, she knew that it would not.

'*Did you need to kill so many?*' said Alsasse, and he was aware of how thin and feeble his voice must sound to the leader of the blueblackwyrmes.

'*There is no turning back now, snowwyrme,*' Beveesh-gar snarled. '*The taint must be eradicated.*' His eyes narrowed. '*Along with any wyrme that bears it.*'

Behind him, his son, Hasheev-gul growled throatily. '*They fought hard, these kin,*' he said, and shook his head solemnly. '*We lost many of the host . . .*'

His blue eyes stared into Alsasse's yellow ones. Alsasse looked away, unable to bear the penetrating gaze of the blue-blackwyrme a moment longer.

The three of them were standing at the top of the galleries, the lowering sun casting their shadows long over the sand-stone rock that was cracked and uneven beneath their claws. Far below them, the canyon beneath the galleries bore grim testament to the truth of Hasheev-gul's words.

The ground was littered with corpses. Scores of corpses.

Blueblackwyrmes. Whitewyrmes, and the kin who had ridden them. Their bodies lay broken or burned, inert – but given the gruesome semblance of life by the rockwyrmes and carrion-wyrmes that picked greedily over their flesh and bones.

Beveesh-gar cleared his throat. '*They fought well indeed*,' he acknowledged. '*For whitewyrmes*,' he added. '*It seems these kin of theirs taught them something useful after all. How to fight. How to defend themselves . . .*' He nodded his head sagely. '*Something that we blueblackwyrmes have tried to teach you, snowwyrme.*'

'*But . . . but it is not our way*,' Alsasse protested, trying hard to meet the blueblackwyrme's accusing look.

'*Your way*,' said Beveesh-gar, and his gruff voice was loaded with contempt. '*We have already heard far too much about your way, snowwyrme. Your way led you far from here to a place where you could not survive . . .*' He paused, coughed, the sound deep down in his throat like molten lava bubbling. He breathed in wheezily, his eyes watering, before collecting himself. '*Our way has led you back here and restored you to the home of your ancestors . . .*'

'*Our way is the only way*,' broke in Hasheev-gul.

His father nodded, his eyes still watering as he struggled not to start coughing again.

Hasheev-gul looked at him with concern. '*And though we find this a cold and inhospitable part of the weald, we shall go further to the east, to eradicate the taint of the two-hides*,' he continued softly. His cold blue eyes fixed on the whitewyrme. '*As you should have done.*'

* * *

As darkness fell, two whitewyrmes slipped out of the shadows of the lowest tier of the galleries and took silently to the air, gliding on outstretched wings over the bodies strewn across the canyon depths. The larger of the wyrmes clutched a bundle in its foreclaws while the smaller, a young wyrme, carried a hooded rider with a kinlance on its back.

It was this that alerted the blueblack sentinel high above on the lip of the highest gallery. With a guttural cry, the massive creature launched itself clumsily into the air as the whitewyrmes below beat their wings and soared off to the east.

Aylsa turned her neck to see the black shape closing in from behind them.

'*Faster*,' she cried out desperately, as much to herself as to Asa, who was flying beside her.

But it was no good. The blueblackwyrme was too fast. Already Aylsa could smell his sulphurous odour and, as his jaws parted, the blast of fire seemed almost to bite into her swaying tail. Asa was directly in front of her now. She wanted to slow her pace, to protect him and Zar from the intense heat of the fire, but she knew well enough that if she did that, then they would all perish.

Craning her neck, she looked back at the blueblackwyrme. His eyes were narrowed; his thick neck extended and pulsing. He was readying himself for another blast of fire that, this time, would surely envelop them all. She was about to turn back and endure the fire as best she could, when she saw something out of the corner of her eye.

It was a flash of white, swooping down out of the sky as fast as a bolt of lightning.

The blueblackwyrme must have seen it too, for he turned his head – just as the kinlance penetrated his thick skull directly between his eyes. He was dead in an instant, and tumbled down out of the sky, wings collapsing and neck and tail limp. He disappeared, noiseless, into the darkness below, and it was seconds later when the sound of his body crashing down onto the floor of the canyon echoed up through the air.

Aylsa drew level with Asa, and the pair of them slowed down as they looked round to see who had come to their aid.

'*Ramilles!*' Zar exclaimed. '*I thought you were dead . . . .*'

Ramilles raised his kinlance in greeting, and as the clouds opened up and the moon shone down, Zar saw blood dripping from its point. '*I thought the same of you,*' he said grimly.

'*Where are you heading?*' his wyrme, Aluris, asked, her wing-beats matching Asa's and Aylsa's.

'*To the east,*' said Aylsa, her eyes fixed steadily on the horizon. '*In search of Aseel.*'

Forty-Four

'There's kith to the east of us,' said Eli. 'A whole load of them, I reckon.'

'We spotted their campfires from the top of that ridge yonder,' said Ethan, his gaze flitting restlessly about. 'Didn't we, Eli? We didn't stop to count them exact like, but there must have been fifty or more flickering in the dusk, weren't there?'

''S right, lad,' the cragclimber confirmed. He sat himself down in the tall grass and began loosening the ties of his boots. 'Happen we ought to get a few hours shut-eye, then set off before dawn. And we should head south – skirt the fringes of these here grasslands, keep close to the ridges.'

Cara nodded, then patted the blanket she was sitting on. 'Sit yourself down, Ethan,' she said, smiling up at the youth. 'I've saved you some of last night's broth and corncakes . . .'

'Is that the way it's gonna be?' Cody's voice came

from a little way off in the gathering dusk. 'Always moving. Never stopping anywhere for more than a day or two? Hitting the trail every time we sight another human soul?'

He sounded miserable, Cara noted, out of sorts. It was the old brooding Cody from before their kiss at the waterfall.

'That's the way of the wyrmeweald,' said Eli slowly, pulling off one boot and then the other. 'Leastways, it is if you're fixing to survive more than a season or two.'

He looked out across the rolling grasslands. Cody was sitting on a low boulder, his bulky outline just visible against the glowing horizon.

'Kith in such numbers are best avoided,' the cragclimber went on. 'My guess is these are the ones been trapping greywyrmes, rounding them up, harnessing them. I smelled the greywyrme musk on the wind,' he said and nodded, as though to himself. 'They must've bagged themselves a mighty herd.'

Cara handed Ethan a bowl of the broth and a couple of corncakes, then dished out more of the broth from her canteen and gave it to Eli. The meal was cold on account of Eli forbidding a fire, but the pair of them ate hungrily. Cara got up from the blanket and walked towards Cody's silhouette.

As she approached, he reached forward and scooped up a handful of loamy earth in his big calloused hands. It was dark and frangible. He sniffed it, rubbed some between a finger and thumb, then let the whole lot drop to the ground.

'This is good soil,' he said appreciatively.

Brushing the last of it from his palms, Cody climbed to his

feet and surveyed the vast expanse of the grasslands around him, the grass flexing and bending as a gentle breeze ruffled its yellowing blades and seedheads. He plucked one of the plump clusters of seeds, rubbed it between his palms, then blew away the winnowed husks before turning to Cara. In the half-light, she could make out the questioning look in his eyes.

'Is this the life you want, Cara?' he asked. 'This endless travel, with only a hole in the ground each fullwinter to call home?'

Cara coloured. Life on the trail was hard compared with Deephome. She'd grown up never having to concern herself with where the next meal was coming from; never having to worry about finding somewhere warm and dry to spend the night. But then that old life of hers had been built on a lie – a lie that Micah had saved her from.

'We have no choice,' Cara said. 'Eli's right about that. You've seen how kith can be.' She frowned. 'You remember what happened at the scrimshaw den, don't you?'

Cara saw Cody flinch, then turn away. He looked back out across the rolling grasslands. They stretched off to the west as far as the eye could see, the last glow of sunset bathing them in golden light.

'It's a pitiful shame is what it is,' Cody said, 'that such a bountiful land should be the sole preserve of thieves and murderers.' His voice was tight, constricted. 'Without such folk, we could settle here, Cara. You and me. And farm . . . I reckon anything'd grow up here. Wheat. Corn. Tatoes.' His green eyes sparkled with excitement. 'Pumpkins and apples . . . Happen there's neither vegetable nor fruit that would not thrive in soil as rich as this.'

For a moment, the image of a farmstead, with lush fields and well-stocked outhouses, hovered before her like a mirage, tantalizing yet frail. Then it faded abruptly.

'And when kith came?' she said. 'Or . . .' Cara shuddered. 'Keld? What then, Cody? What would we do out here in the open?'

Cody's shoulders hunched and his head slumped forward, but Cara could see his powerful hands were bunched into fists.

'It's a pitiful shame,' he muttered through clenched teeth. 'A pitiful shame . . .'

Cara was about to put her arms around him, to soothe away the anger and frustration of the old Cody, the way she knew she could; and to bring out the new Cody – the Cody who thrilled and excited her with the intensity of his feelings. But then she saw Micah.

He was standing a little way off, looking distracted; a dark figure against the horizon glow. He was wearing his hat, had a full pack on his shoulders and a walking staff gripped in one hand. Seeing him there, Cara was reminded of the first time she'd laid eyes on him.

How rough and ready Micah had seemed back then; the seasoned weald traveller with his trailworn boots and hacke-ton, and the bold swagger to his walk. Her heart had leaped at the sight of him. Now, instead, it seemed to tighten in her chest as she felt a familiar pang of guilt.

She left Cody standing hunched and immobile, his back to her, lost in his thoughts, and waded through the long grass towards Micah. As she approached, she saw his face was white and mask-like. It was the same blank expression he'd worn for days now – almost as though he had seen inside her, had read her thoughts and knew of her feelings for Cody.

But then, how could he? Cara asked herself. She'd been so careful, trying not to show favour, avoiding Cody's glances, turning her attention instead to Ethan and Eli. And yet . . .

'You're leaving?' Cara stopped in front of Micah, her eyes searching his impassive face for clues. 'Just like that? Slipping away into the dusk without saying a word? Why?'

'I've squared it with Eli,' Micah said in a low voice, looking away from her to the far distance. 'I . . . I need some time on my own is all.'

Cara followed his gaze. He was looking out across the grasslands towards the west where, beyond the horizon, there lay the wyrme galleries. And the kin. The guilt she'd been feeling dissipated, to be replaced by hurt. Betrayal. Of course, *that* was why he was going.

Because of the kingirl. The one he couldn't forget. Cara had imagined that she and Micah would love one another for ever and ever. It seemed she had been mistaken.

'I hope you find what you're looking for,' she said evenly.

Micah turned his head to look at her. His dark-rimmed eyes were glistening and his face, no longer a mask, had a haunted stricken look. He glanced at Cody, then back at

Cara, and when he spoke his voice was raw with emotion and pierced Cara's heart.

'I hope you do too, Cara.'

Forty-Five

Thrace and Aseel stood at the top of a jagged ridge looking westwards, the kingirl's hair and her white-wyrme's barbels set in motion by the warm breeze from the east. Before them, the grasslands were spread out, flat and rolling and gold-leafed in the low sun. Neither of them spoke.

Finally Thrace broke the silence, her gaze still fixed on the far horizon. '*Yes, you were right. I think I see them now*,' she said. '*A kin patrol from the galleries coming this way*.' She stole a glance at the wyrme. '*They must have picked up the taint from the wyrmetrain on the wind*.'

'*The taint*,' Aseel sighed, the words hissing from his mouth like floodwater gushing through a broken riverbank. His eyes pulsed from amber to red.

'*We can stop these two-hides and their wyrmetrain*,' Thrace told him. She raised her kinlance. '*The wyrme-kin acting as one can kill them all . . .*'

'*And then?*' said Aseel. '*You heard the words of the*

two-hides trapper. More are coming. They are gathering in the place of dust and heat to the east, where they drain the wyrmes of their oil and enslave them. Unless the settlement there is destroyed, the taint will grow and grow until it covers the whole of the weald . . .' He inclined his long neck towards Thrace. *'But if the flameoil is set alight, it will turn that settlement of theirs into an inferno . . .'* He paused, his eyes glowing dark red. *'Along with whoever gets close enough to ignite it . . .'*

Thrace held Aseel's gaze for a moment, then nodded grimly. *'Yes,'* she said, *'if that's what it takes to stop the two-hides once and for all, then that is what we must do.'* She smiled, tears welling up. *'We shall die together.'*

Aseel's eyes paled with sorrow. *'No, Thrace,'* he told her. *'I must do this alone.'*

'Alone?' she breathed. *'Without me? But why, Aseel?'*

'The two-hides murdered my wyve. I have nothing left to lose . . .' Aseel lowered his eyes. *'But you have.'*

'I . . . I don't understand,' Thrace whispered, her voice as cracked as splintering wood.

The whitewyrme sighed, then, without speaking, inclined his neck. He rested the side of his head against Thrace's belly, his eyes half-closed and barbels twitching.

'There are two hearts beating within you,' he said at length, and straightened up.

Thrace gasped. *'You mean . . . ?'*

Staring down, she placed the palms of her hands flat on her belly and tried to sense the life growing inside her.

A baby. Micah's baby . . .

Those nights in the winter den, when she had lain in Micah's arms, half-crazy with loss and longing for her life with Aseel, a life that had seemed over . . .

Micah had soothed her, had eased her sorrow. Had made her love him . . .

But then Aseel had returned once more, the great whitewyrme who had rescued her as an infant, who had raised her, taught her to love and defend the weald. And she had been prepared to go with Aseel to the new stockade, even if it meant death for them both.

Aseel.

Micah.

How could she ever have decided between them? She pressed her hands more firmly against her belly. But now the decision had been made for her.

'*I have lost my offspring, Thrace,*' said Aseel, his voice gentle yet firm. '*You must not do anything to endanger yours. Go back to the galleries and take good care of the wyve inside you,*' he told her. '*And send the kin to deal with these two-hides in the wyrmetrain when they leave the ridges and come out into the open spaces of the grasslands.*'

Thrace stared into Aseel's eyes. Then she stepped towards him, her arms outstretched. Aseel dipped his head, his jaws parted and, as Thrace embraced him, her ear pressed against the black zigzag scar, she was enfolded in warm white aromatic smoke.

After a few moments, Aseel pulled away, raising his head, his wings. Reluctantly Thrace had to let go and step back. Her soulskin shone brilliant white in the failing light. Aseel raised his wings and, flexing his hindlegs, launched himself off the top of the ridge. He circled above Thrace once, twice, his yellow eyes staring down at her with a mixture of love and sorrow. Then, with a flick of his tail, he soared off to the east, the rhythmic wingbeats fading as he disappeared into the night.

Standing alone, Thrace stared after him into the darkness, weeping silently, tears coursing down her face. The distant upland was speckled with the glow of kith campfires. She lowered her head, a curtain of ash-gold hair hiding her grief as she did so.

A short while later, she heard the sound of wingbeats behind her, and the quiet *scritch-scratch* of talons on rock as the kin patrol landed on the ridge top. She hurriedly wiped her face with the back of her hand, and turned to see Aseel's mate, Aylsa, standing there, along with little Zar and Asa, and the kin, Ramilles, with his wyrme, Aluris.

Thrace's sorrow turned to a sudden burning anger that rose up inside her, implacable and merciless. She gripped her kinlance and pointed at the campfires in the distance.

'*The kin must gather*,' she told them, '*to meet the two-hides in the grasslands and kill them. Kill them all.*'

Ramilles climbed slowly down from Aluris's back. Aylsa inclined her neck, her pale eyes searching the ridge top for

Aseel, and Thrace saw that she was cradling her kinchild in her foreclaws. Zar's face was streaked with tears, and Asa would not meet Thrace's gaze.

'*What is it?*' Thrace asked.

'*The rest of the kin . . .*' Zar began.

'*They're dead*,' said Ramilles, his voice choked and bitter. '*All of them*.'

Forty-Six

The day broke sultry and oppressive. Drab pink stained the eastern sky and tipped the serrated ridges and jagged peaks. Mist hovered low above the ground in the dips and hollows.

Poking out of it, like islands set in the swirling white, were the tops of tents and benders, and the great arched backs of resting greywyrmes. Embers glowed through the mist, red and purple, blurred like ink on wet paper. High above, in the lightening sky, sharp-eyed carrionwyrmes wheeled round and round, watching closely as the first of the settlers stirred, eager to land and pick over whatever scraps the camp might leave behind.

As the carrionwyrmes cawed and screeched impatiently overhead, men and women emerged from their shelters, raised their eyes to the heavens, stretched, or scratched, or stamped life into their feet. Children appeared and began at once to scamper

about. The greywyrmes ringing the camp snorted as they were prodded to wakefulness by their bleary-eyed handlers. Breathing out smoke, the huge creatures pulled themselves up from their sleeping positions – front legs kneeling, rear legs sprawled out behind them on either side of their massive tails, and long necks twisted round and resting on their backs – and looked about for their feedsacks.

One of the wyrmehandlers came striding into the camp, his legs bowed and shoulders rolling. The tether of the lumbering greywyrme that towered beside him was wrapped round his hand. His leather longcoat glinted in the sun, along with the knives at his belt and the sidewinder slung across his shoulder – and the smooth skin of the scar at his jaw. He surveyed the settlers, his dark eyebrows arched in something hovering between bemusement and contempt, and when he spoke his voice was gruff, dismissive.

'Get yourselves packed up,' he told them. 'Mr Tallow wants a specially early start.'

Like wildfire taking hold, pockets of activity spread out until the entire encampment was a hurry-scurry of sound and movement, with each settler family completing its own tasks and then coming together to help fellow travellers; the old, the infirm, the unfortunate. Eating and packing away. That was the order of the day, as it was every day – as it had been since that morning, nigh on nine weeks earlier, when the wyrmetrain had set forth from the badlands.

Those first mornings had been difficult. Inexperience had

led to confusion. Mistakes had been made. Now, everything ran like greased cogs, and the air thrummed with purpose.

'Ain't they the spit-image of a colony of ants,' Solomon Tallow observed drily. 'All busy, busy, busy.'

He was standing on a rockspur at the edge of the broad hollow looking back over the makeshift encampment. Beside him, his chief wyrmehandler chuckled.

'And just as easy to crush underfoot,' he said lightly.

'Now, now, Enoch,' Solomon chided. 'That ain't no way to talk about our precious charges here.'

The man shrugged, his disfigured face squirming with distaste. He stroked his stringy blond moustache thoughtfully, his eyes narrowed.

'I sure won't be sad to see the back of them,' he said, and spat on the ground.

'Patience, Enoch,' said Solomon cheerfully. 'These here folk are farmers. They plough and plant, then reap a harvest. And when they do, we'll be back to take a share of their bounty.' He chuckled. 'In return for our continued protection.' He raised his hands and cupped them to his mouth. 'Stand by your wyrmes!' he bellowed, and smiled to himself as his words caused the hectic activity to grow more frenzied still.

'Mr Tallow. Mr Tallow, sir. Can I ride up front with you again?'

Solomon turned to see the boy, Josiah, hurrying towards him, a bundle wrapped in greasepaper and tied up with string clutched in his hands. He smiled wolfishly.

'More of Molly's fine home cooking?' he said.

'Mary, sir,' said Josiah, correcting the brawny gangmaster without thinking. He blushed. 'M . . . Ma's name is Mary.'

'Mary. I knew that,' said Solomon, unflustered. He nodded at the parcel. 'So what exactly you got there?'

'Cornmeal pasties,' Josiah replied eagerly. 'Flatstone-baked this very morning and still warm. Ma sends them with her . . . her . . .' His face crumpled, confused-looking, as he struggled to remember her exact words. 'Sincere regards,' he said at last.

'Sincere regards,' Solomon repeated and chuckled to himself at the formality of the words. Mary or Molly – or whatever her name might be – was clearly at pains to conceal from her son the closeness that she and Tallow had shared along the trail.

'Can I then, sir?' Josiah persisted. 'Can I ride up front?'

Amused by the boy's eager face and earnest entreaties, Solomon leaned forward and tousled his hair. 'Happen you can, Josiah, lad. And we can share us them fine pasties.'

'Yes, sir,' said Josiah happily. 'Thank you, sir.'

Solomon turned away and took the tether from Enoch, who had been holding the gangmaster's greywyrme in check. He tugged down hard, bringing the massive creature's broad neck low to the ground. The greywyrme chirred throatily and smoke coiled from its nostrils, but it did not resist. It had learned not to. Tallow checked that its flameoil drain was in place, then took a hold of the strap on the side of the neck-saddle and hauled himself up. Reaching down a hand, he gripped Josiah's wrist and pulled the boy up next to him in the saddle. Then he turned and looked back over his shoulder.

'Move on out!' he called.

The wyrmetrain lurched into motion, starting at the front and rippling back down the line, one wyrme after the other, till the entire column was trudging forwards. The gangmaster's greywyrme picked its way stolidly up the snaking dusttrail that led out of the mist-laced hollow and up over the ridge beyond. The others followed. The hulking greywyrmes trudged, ungainly but sure-footed, their drivers urging them on with sticks and whips, and with the settlers endeavouring not to slip on the loose scree or turn their ankles in the cracks and crevices in the rock as they struggled to keep up. Solomon leaned back in the saddle and rubbed the back of his shaven scalp.

'Memory serves, Josiah,' he said, 'we have no more than one or two such ridges still to climb before we reach our final destination.'

'The grasslands,' Josiah breathed.

'The grasslands,' Solomon Tallow confirmed. He patted his stomach expansively. 'Time to sample them delicious pasties, I reckon,' he said.

Josiah nodded. 'Sure thing, sir,' he said. 'And if you like 'em, Ma said she can rustle up some more when we set up camp this evening.'

Solomon turned to the boy, one hand gripping the reins, the other scratching lightly at the side of his nose. 'There ain't going to be no camp this evening,' he said, his voice measured. 'We arrive at the grasslands. We unload. Then me and the boys return to the stockade with the wyrmes.' He smiled at the boy. 'And you begin your new life as a farmer.'

Solomon reached over and patted the boy reassuringly on the shoulder. 'Enterprising young pup like yourself,' he said. 'You're going to be just fine.'

He paused and glanced back over his shoulder at the great wyrmetrain once more. They'd all be fine, Solomon thought. Probably. And if they were not, well, that was none of his concern. He'd be back to collect either way. After all, it was what the great lords down on the plains did. Well, he, Solomon Tallow, aimed to be lord of these here high plains, and he and his men would take their due.

''Sides, I'll be back soon enough,' he told the boy. 'With a fresh bunch of settlers. Happen you and your ma'll have established yourselves by then.'

Josiah nodded, but made no reply. His gaze was fixed on the wall-like incline ahead as, lurching from side to side, the greywyrme slowly but steadily climbed higher.

As the wyrme drew closer to the crest, Josiah sat forward in the saddle, back straight and neck craned. It was midday and the sun was directly overhead, throbbing hot and casting little shadow. A small wyrme, the size of a jackrabbit, sat at the top of the rise observing the oncoming greywyrme, its tasselled beard trembling – then, discretion winning over curiosity, it skittered down the rock and disappeared into a jagged crevice.

Josiah held his breath.

The next moment, as the great lumbering greywyrme beneath him finally reached the top of the ridge, the land abruptly opened up and Josiah found himself staring out across an empty plain of tall swaying yellow-green grass that was so vast it seemed to stretch on for ever. His eyes widened and he snatched a sharp intake of breath, his brain struggling to take in the sheer magnitude and grandeur of this great high-country wilderness.

'Well, boy?' said Solomon Tallow, his voice breaking into Josiah's awestruck thoughts. 'How d'ya like the look of your new home?'

Josiah raised a hand. He shielded his eyes from the high sun, though there was nothing he could do to cut out the glare of the grasslands themselves, that were glowing so bright it was like they were on fire.

He shook his head, for once at a loss for words.

From behind came whoops and cheers and cries of triumph as others reached the top of the ridge and were afforded the same view. Family members fell upon one another, hugging and kissing. Friends congratulated each other with backslapping and arms round shoulders. Children who had been on their last legs minutes earlier jumped up and down, caught up in the excitement of their elders, and ran on ahead, suddenly full of boundless energy. An old woman with a straw bonnet fell to her knees at the top of the ridge and offered a silent prayer of thanks . . .

'Well, Josiah?' Solomon persisted, as they continued down the far side of the ridge and the jagged rocks gave way to some low nubbed hills. 'What *do* you think?'

Josiah pushed back his shock of blond hair. He nodded. 'It's big,' he said.

'Big,' said Solomon, and laughed. 'I like that.' He slapped the boy on his shoulder. 'That's a good answer, Josiah,' he said. 'Big.'

As they crossed the border between foothill and plain, and the blistering east wind picked up, the sound of the parched grass hissing and sighing rose up around them. Josiah looked about him. There were scrubby bushes and stunted shrubs in among the long grass, he saw, their leaves dried and curled, and those fruits and nuts that had not already been foraged, shrivelled on the branch. And as they trudged on, he noticed sump-pools and dewponds shining like mirrored glass, their water low, but the footprints in the surrounding mud offering proof that the grasslands were not as devoid of wildlife as he had first thought.

Beside Josiah, Solomon Tallow turned in the saddle and looked back. The last of the greywyrmes had already left the final gravelled slopes of the ridge country and were trampling down the grass. He turned back and scanned the flat horizon.

Up ahead, a dust-devil spun, blurred and conical, the needle-like point at its base touching down on the ground time and again, like a bee probing flowers for nectar, stirring the dying grass and raising the dust beneath. Solomon squinted into the clogged air for a moment, then half climbing to his feet in the saddle, raised a hand.

'Make a halt!' he bellowed. 'And get them wyrmes unpacked! This is as far as we go!'

He tugged hard on the reins and pulled the great greywyrme beneath him to a standstill. Behind him, the other wyrmehandlers did the same.

Solomon turned and, face set solemn, extended a hand to Josiah, who looked at it for a moment before taking hold. His own small bony hand was all but lost in the gangmaster's great meaty paw, and he felt the hard callouses graze his knuckles.

'It's been an honour knowing you, boy,' said Solomon, grinning broadly and pumping the boy's hand up and down. 'You been my ears and eyes on this trip and I appreciate it. I shall not forget.'

He climbed to his feet and jumped down from the necksaddle. Josiah was about to follow him, when something caught his attention. He paused.

'Looks like there's a storm approaching,' he said, and pointed off towards the horizon far to the west.

Solomon turned and looked, his eyes squinting against the brightness of the plains. Far above his head, the sky was still clear, and the sun beat down, searing and relentless. But the boy was right. There *was* something there. He frowned. It looked like a great dark stormcloud all right, but it was advancing across the grasslands towards them – which was impossible, since the wind was coming from behind.

'Whatever that is,' Solomon Tallow pronounced, 'it sure ain't no storm.'

Forty-Seven

The settlers stopped what they were doing and looked up into the sky. The belongings that were being untethered from the backs of the greywyrmes were momentarily abandoned; barrows of seedsacks, bundles of timber, tools and farm implements, carefully wrapped in oiled wyrmeskin, were left dangling from ropes or stacked in small piles in the tall grass. All eyes were on the approaching stormcloud spreading across the sky.

Young and old clustered together, talking in awestruck voices. The children were transfixed. Some were frozen to the spot, trembling, their mouths open. Some ran this way and that from one group of adults to another, seeking reassurance. Others were hoisted up onto their parents' shoulders for a better look. None of them could take their eyes off the dark cloud on the horizon.

'What d'ya think it is, Cain?' asked one of the

ploughhands, looking up at his friend, who was standing on the back of their greywyrme.

'It sure as hell ain't no weather,' Cain shouted down. 'Looks more like a flock of critters. Thousands of 'em . . .'

His words broke off as the greywyrme beneath him abruptly reared up, its eyes rolling and smoke snorting from its flared nostrils. Cain made a grab for a rope, but missed and keeled over backwards and landed heavily on the ground, cussing as he did so.

'What are they, Pa?' asked a boy, his voice shrill. He was perched on his father's shoulders, holding his ears and kicking excitedly against his chest with the back of his heels.

'A wonder of our new home, Gideon Junior, that's what it is,' came the reply. The man shook his head – as much as his son's grip would allow. 'I ain't seen nothing like them back on the plains.'

'But what *are* they?' the boy persisted.

Sitting astride his greywyrme, Solomon Tallow was asking himself that self-same question. With sixteen years in the high country under his belt, he thought he'd seen it all. Skitterwyrmes and rockwyrmes on the scree-covered slopes of the high plateaus; pitchwyrmes and snatterjabs fishing the falls of the valley country; cliff colonies of bluewings, spikebacks and manderwyrmes in the eastern canyons. And in the ridges, ferocious redwings, plump squabwyrmes, stormwyrmes . . . And greywyrmes, of course. Even in the highstacks, where, on rare occasions, he had caught distant glimpses of the great whitewyrmes.

But he had never seen wyrmes like these.

He lowered his spyglass and snapped it shut. These wyrmes were gigantic, twice the size of the lumbering greywyrme he was sitting on, yet judging by the speed of their approach, as fast as any redwing. Their blueblack scales looked like fire-scorched metal. Their claws were like sabres. Their wings seemed almost to flash as they beat up and down. And, as they drew closer, Solomon could hear their guttural chittering and chirring. They seemed to be calling to one another, the way the great whitewyrmes were said to do.

On the ground below him, Enoch, his chief wyrme-handler, was getting uneasy.

'I don't like the look of them,' he muttered as he struggled to keep a tight rein on the gangmaster's fretting greywyrme.

Solomon grinned, putting on a show of bravado for settler and wyrmehandler alike. 'They're just migrating wyrmes,' he told him. 'Probably off to roost some place. They won't bother with us if we don't bother with them.'

The wyrmehandler shrugged, then stumbled forward as the greywyrme lurched to one side. 'Maybe so,' he said, 'but they sure are spooking this here wyrme.'

The other greywyrmes were becoming just as agitated. All of them. With their hindlegs still hobbled by ropes, they stamped round in circles, trampling down the long grass – as well as some of the settlers' possessions; boxes and barrels and precious farm tools which had already been unloaded. They bucked and bellowed, their necks extended and tails swishing wildly from side to side and, for all the whipping and beating they were doling out, Tallow's wyrmehandlers were facing a losing battle in their attempts to hold them in check.

What was more, the greywyrmes' growing agitation was beginning to prove contagious. The settlers themselves were becoming uneasy, for as the dark cloud grew closer, it was becoming all too clear to the naked eye that it was in fact a flock of gargantuan wyrmes.

'I don't like them,' a small boy whimpered, tears filling his eyes as he clung onto to his father's leg. 'Make them go away, Pa.'

'It's all right, Zeb,' his father told him. He eyed the swirling mass of blueblack creatures in the distance warily. 'They don't mean us no harm.'

'Y'sure?' the boy said and looked up, his big brown eyes pleading for reassurance when his father did not reply.

'*Are* you sure, Silas?' asked his wife quietly. She sounded frightened.

Silas shook his head. 'There ain't no point in scaring the boy, is there?' he whispered.

But Zeb must have heard him. 'They're fixing to eat us, ain't they?' he said, his voice oddly matter-of-fact. 'Ain't they, Pa? That's what such critters do up here in the weald. They're gonna gobble us all up . . .'

'Of course they're not,' his father snapped, his own misgivings flipping the words from comforting to angered, and the boy burst into tears.

A little way off, the rangy old farmer with the rabbit-skin hat, Amos Greenwood, and his wife Ida, clutched at one another anxiously. Close by, a mother swept her little girl up in her arms and hugged her tightly to her chest. 'Bekkah, Bekkah, Bekkah,' she hushed over and over in her ear. Two thick-set brothers, eager to keep their possessions safe from the increasingly agitated greywyrmes, tottered past, red-faced and sweating, a huge wood and leather chest swaying between them. Alarmed by the approaching flock, an extended family, some three dozen in number, clustered together, the womenfolk at the centre – from a hunched bewhiskered great-grandmother to twin baby girls in arms – and the men, armed with knives and hoes and pitchforks, around them, keeping guard.

'Just in case,' the head of the family, a broad-shouldered father of six youths, kept telling them. 'Nothing to worry about. But just in case . . .'

The pretty young widow, Mary, was scanning the groups of settlers for any sign of her son.

'Josiah!' she called. 'Josiah, where are you?'

She couldn't see him. She couldn't see him anywhere.

Up ahead was Solomon, his shaven head gleaming in the sun, but for once Josiah did not seem to be with him. And as Mary watched the gangmaster load the great sidewinder mounted on a metal brace to his greywyrme's neck-saddle and aim it at the sky, her heart missed a beat. Something was not right. Below him, holding the greywyrme's tether, his chief wyrmehandler – Enoch, she thought his name was – pushed two fingers into his mouth and blew hard, and the air rang out with a strident whistle.

At his signal, the other wyrmehandlers released the greywyrme tethers they had been clinging to and swung the spitbolts and sidewinders from their backs. Then, gripping them in their hands, they dropped to their knees and pointed them skywards.

Finding themselves free, the terrified greywyrmes pawed the ground, then reared up and roared, their eyes rolling back in their skulls. One of them managed to slip the ropes that hobbled its rear legs, and it stampeded off across the grasslands, bellowing raucously at the top of its lungs. Two more went with it, screeching with fear. Ropes came loose upon their backs, tarpaulins flapped, and sacks and crates tumbled to the ground as they stumbled on . . .

All at once, from high above, an earsplitting screech drowned out their pitiful cries. The flock of huge blueblackwyrmes was almost overhead, and one of them broke formation, folded back its wings and swooped down suddenly out of the sky.

The unhobbled greywyrme glanced up, white-eyed, and lumbered on as fast as it could. The two others, their rear legs still bound together, stumbled and lurched; awkward, ungainly. And as the horrified settlers watched, the blueblackwyrme opened its massive jaws and released a bolt of white-hot flame that engulfed both greywyrmes in a vast fireball, before swooping down on the third.

Gideon clamped a hand over Gideon Junior's eyes. Bekkah's mother hugged her daughter even tighter and turned away. From the settlers all round them, a low despairing moan went up.

Screaming with pain, the blazing greywyrmes staggered on, like huge bonfires on legs, flaming fragments of rope and wyrmeskin fluttering to the ground in their wake and starting small fires in the parched grass. Meanwhile, half a dozen blueblackwyrmes had joined the first, and were tearing the third greywyrme limb from limb, the contents of the various loads on its back being thrown high in the air with each slashing blow of their talons.

The settlers had seen enough. They abandoned their greywyrmes, their possessions; they tore the heavy packs from their shoulders and tossed them aside, and they scattered in all directions, dashing off into the shoulder-high grass. Crouched down, the wyrmehandlers watched them go. They primed their spitbolts. They waited . . .

Moments later, a dark shadow engulfed them as the blueblack flock blotted out the morning sunlight.

'Fire!' Solomon Tallow roared, pulling the trigger of his sidewinder as he did so.

The heavy bolt thudded into the neck of the blueblackwyrme that was heading out of the sky straight towards him, a jet of fire roaring from its gaping mouth. For a moment, the creature seemed almost to hesitate in the air, before crashing down to the ground. Its jaw snapped shut. The flames were extinguished.

From behind the gangmaster, the wyrmehandlers fired, then swiftly reloaded and fired again. The air hissed with the sound of the flying bolts and the dull thud of metal on scale as they found their mark. A dozen or more mighty blueblackwyrmes came plummeting down to earth, some dying in an instant, others lying wounded and wheezing and gasping for breath.

Far above Solomon and his gang of wyrmehandlers, the flock of blueblackwyrmes began to circle, spiralling down to attack in waves, their open jaws spitting jets of fire. Six more greywyrmes were incinerated where they stood. The handlers crouching down beside them jumped back to escape the inferno – only to be seized by huge curved talons and lifted, wriggling and squirming, high into the air, then dropped.

'Enoch! Tam! To me!' Solomon bellowed. He swung his mounted sidewinder to the left and fired another bolt. 'Isaac! Shadrak! And you, Lev! Over here!'

Below him, the greywyrme bucked and struggled.

'Get rid of the load!' the gangmaster ordered the wyrmehandlers as they ran up towards him. 'Then climb aboard!'

He tilted the sidewinder back and sent a bolt thudding into the side of a swooping blueblackwyrme. It fell heavily a short distance away, wheezing and gasping, white froth bubbling from its nostrils, its eyes encrusted in green mucus.

Having cut the load from Solomon's wyrme, the five wyrmehandlers clambered onto its back, the spitbolts in their hands primed and ready to fire. They looked about them, hunkered down. Around them, the rest of the gang and the greywyrmes were faring less well.

Pockets of grassland were ablaze where the torched greywyrmes had collapsed and lay bellowing and flailing around as they burned. Their handlers scattered and fought in ones and twos before being set upon by diving blueblackwyrmes. Only the gangmaster's great sidewinder was keeping him and his wyrme from the same fate. As he fired bolt after bolt at the wyrmes attacking him, Solomon Tallow began to notice that most of them appeared to be sick.

They coughed. They wheezed. Thick phlegm rattled around inside their lungs. Some seemed too weak to pull out of their dives and crashed instead into the ground. All of them had the same crusted green mucus around their eyes, affecting their sight and making their attacks increasingly erratic.

'Hold on tight, boys!' Solomon shouted. 'We're going to make a run for it!'

Tugging hard on the bridle, he hauled the greywyrme's head round and dug the heels of his boots viciously into its neck. The creature bellowed and turned and began lumbering back towards the ridges to the east. From overhead there came a hoarse rasping roar, and Tallow swung round in the saddle and fired the sidewinder.

There was a gurgled cry as the bolt buried itself in the throat of the one-eyed wyrme that was bearing down on him. Behind him was another of the massive creatures. As he cranked back the sidewinder's drawstring, Solomon quickly reached for another bolt from his belt.

But not quickly enough.

He was seized in the wyrme's great hand, two curved claws piercing his shoulder. With a flap of its great wings, the blue-blackwyrme wrenched him from the saddle and soared back up into the sky, the other wyrmehandlers staring up at the hapless gangmaster, too fearful of wounding him to fire their spitbolts. Solomon dangled helplessly, the pain in his shoulder raging like fire as the great wyrme screeched and howled deafeningly in the strange language of its kind.

What was it waiting for? he wondered. Why didn't it drop him to his death?

The pain in his shoulder was agonizing. At least death would be quick . . .

Beating its wings and rising still higher in the sky, the blue-blackwyrme held the gangmaster out in front of it. Solomon stared into the wyrme's mucus-encrusted eyes in horror. It was toying with him.

With something like a casual shrug, the creature raised its free hand and drew the point of a claw slowly down Tallow's front. The outer hide split open. Flying higher still, the wyrme repeated the action, this time slicing through the inner hide. Blood erupted from the jagged red wound; plump innards bulged and spilled.

Solomon stared down at his stomach, scarcely able to take in what was happening to him. He clamped his hands to his belly, desperately trying to hold his guts in. His ears were roaring. His hands were slippery with blood.

The blueblackwyrme roared at him in its harsh guttural language. Solomon gagged at the stench that poured from its ulcerated mouth – a stench that grew more foul still as he was drawn up towards the creature's parted jaws.

'No!' he screamed.

A pair of blade-sharp fangs closed over his shaven head . . .

There was a splintering of bone; a spurt of blood. The blueblackwyrme's jaws opened and the gangmaster's lifeless body was sent tumbling back down through the smoke-laced air. It landed heavily, like a sack of seedcorn in the long grass, just missing a group of cowering settlers who looked round and gasped, or screamed, or clamped their hands over their mouths as they stared at the dead body, its belly split open and skull crushed.

'It's the gangmaster, Mae,' a stricken voice whispered. 'Solomon Tallow . . .'

The farmer, Amos, raised himself up on his elbows and peered through the long grass. The blueblackwyrmes had all but destroyed the wyrmetrain by the looks of it, and the grasslands were dotted with the flaming pyres of the heavily laden greywyrmes. Only one remained alive that he could see, far in the distance, clambering up the screeslopes, returning to the ridge country from which they'd come. Overhead, the blueblack host circled, fewer in number and low in the smoke-stained sky. And as Amos watched, the wyrmes gathered themselves and flew off across the grasslands towards the hiding groups of settlers.

'They're coming, Amos,' his wife whimpered. 'They're coming . . .'

The farmer and his wife shrank back and hugged each other, their eyes shut tight.

'Never thought it would end like this, Ida . . .'

Crouched down concealed in the long grass, other settlers did the same. Whispering reassurances and stifling cries; holding onto one another.

No one noticed the flashes of white in the eastern sky at first. And when three whitewyrmes appeared out of the smoke-clouded air, arrowing down, the settlers were at a loss to understand what they were seeing. On their backs, the three whitewyrmes carried white-clad riders, each one armed with a long black lance.

'They're kin!' Cain the ploughboy muttered to his friend.

The two of them watched as the whitewyrmes flew deep into the heart of the blueblack host, which scattered before them. Then, fanning out, the kin and their wyrmes set to hunting them down. The tips of their lances glinted in the muted dazzle as the kin stabbed repeatedly, leaving a trail of dead and dying blueblackwyrmes in their wake.

Lying in the long grass, curled up in a ball, his hands cradling his head, Josiah tried to blot it all out. He had Tallow's silver coins in his pocket. He'd wanted to work for Solomon Tallow. He'd wanted to prove himself . . .

But then, when the wyrmes had come, he had run. Run as fast as he could. Back to his mother.

He felt ashamed, and had to suppress the sobs rising in his throat.

The thing was, in all the confusion with the greywyrmes going crazy and the blueblackwyrmes attacking, he hadn't been able to find her. Nor had he managed to get back to Solomon Tallow. And now he was lost and alone, just wanting it all to stop. The shrieks. The bellowing. The sweet smell of burning wyrmeflesh . . .

He took a hand away from one ear.

It was quiet.

He opened his eyes. Through the stems of grass he could see the towering forms of the blueblackwyrmes sitting on their haunches, their heads bowed. Hundreds of them.

Josiah lay very still and fought back the desire to scream.

Standing in front of the closest blueblackwyrme was another kind of wyrme, its skin as white and dazzling as the others were firerock dark. Its snake-like whiskers were quivering and its jaws opened and shut, almost as if, Josiah thought, it was talking . . .

'*Tell your wyrmes to give up*,' Aylsa said. Her eyes narrowed as she noted the evidence of the blueblackwyrme's ill health. The misted-up eyes. The streaming nose and mouth. The hideous wheezing, as though every intake of breath might be its last. '*Our country has made you sick*,' she pronounced. '*Just as your country made us sick*.'

The long silvery barbels at the corners of Aylsa's mouth twitched.

'*You do not belong here*,' she told the blueblackwyrme. '*You must return to your homeland, or die . . .*'

Hasheev-gul turned and stared down at his dead father. Then he pulled himself up to his full height, struggling not to cough as he did so.

He stared at the whitewyrme before him, at the two-hides next to her, cradling an infant, and at the two other whitewyrmes and their two-hides, who were standing a little way off. Those black spikes of theirs had wrought terrible damage to his host – but this low flat country they called home threatened to do worse.

'*You don't deserve our help, snowwyrme*,' he growled. '*I curse the lot of you. You and these tainted wyrmes who now stand beside you*.' He turned his burning eyes away and stared back towards the west. '*But you're right. This stinking land of yours*' – he coughed violently, blood spattering on the rocky ground before him – '*is killing us . . .*'

He beat his wings and, with great effort, took to the air. The remnants of the once mighty blueblack host rose with him and fell into formation as best they could, their wingbeats slow and laboured.

Thrace, Aylsa and her kinchild watched them go. Silent and

unmoving behind them, Zar and Asa, Ramilles and Aluris also watched. When at last they turned away, they saw the small settler child standing a little way offin the long grass, his pale face soot-stained and his clothes claggy with rich dark soil.

He raised a hand and scratched at his thick tousled hair, then swept his arm round in a broad arc. 'What about us?' he said.

Forty-Eight

Dozens of small fires flickered like gemstones in the swaying grass; a skein of black smoke hovered above. The air was still.

Eli made his way through the long yellow-green grass, his spitbolt wound and loaded in his hands. Ethan walked beside him, his jag-blade knife drawn, while Cara and Cody followed close behind, both of them holding loaded spitbolts of their own.

They came to a burning mound, pink and blue flames flickering over the charred remnants of a greywyrme that had been loaded up with what looked like someone's worldly possessions. The dead wyrme's skin was blistered and charred. Beneath the blackened tarpaulin and half-burnt ropes, fire still smouldered.

Eli moved past the carcass and stopped beside another corpse, that of a monstrous blueblackwyrme. He examined it for a moment, his eyes narrowing, before slipping his pack from his shoulders. Beside him, Ethan stopped and whistled.

'I ain't never seen a more fearsome wyrme,' he said. 'Have you, Eli?'

'Not exactly,' said Eli, taking a huge claw from his rucksack and comparing it with the claws on the blueblackwyrme. 'Been wondering what manner of creature this belonged to for a while now,' he said. 'Looks like I finally have my answer.'

He stooped down and observed the green mucus crusting the creature's eyes, and sores pockmarking its muzzle.

'Fearsome, maybe, but it was sick before it died,' he observed.

Behind them, Cody pulled back the tarpaulin on the greywyrme's back, dislodging a small wooden box that fell to the ground with a metallic crash. The lid fell open and silver knives, forks and spoons tumbled out onto the scorched grass.

Cara stared at the polished cutlery. 'How . . . how sad,' she whispered huskily, her eyes filling with tears.

'Whoever owned them,' Cody said, 'they had brought everything they needed for settling here.' He raised his spitbolt and pointed at some of the other objects strewn in the grass around them. 'See there. Sacks of seedgrain. Timber. Farm-tools. A loom . . .'

He looked deep into Cara's eyes.

'They could have built themselves a farmstead with all this – furnished it, sown crops . . .'

'Built a new life,' Cara said softly, holding his gaze. 'A good life.'

'A good life,' Cody agreed. 'Right here in the grasslands.' He reached out and drew Cara to him. 'Well, what do you say, Cara?' His eyes sparkled. 'Shall we do likewise? You and me?'

Cara looked up to see the cragclimber and Cody's brother looking back at her.

'You know me, Cara,' said Eli with a rueful smile. 'I don't hold with settling down. But it seems to me you two are old enough to make your own minds up on the matter . . .'

'I don't hold with settling down neither,' broke in Ethan hotly, his face flushed an angry red. 'And I'll take my chances with my good friend Eli here.'

There were tears in Cody's eyes as he stepped forward and embraced his little brother. 'Guess this is a parting of the ways,' he said.

'Guess it is.' Ethan's voice was muffled in his brother's shoulder, but Cody could feel the sobs racking his body.

Cara hugged the cragclimber. 'Thank you, Eli,' she whispered. 'Thank you for everything.'

When she stepped back she noticed that the four of them were not alone. Heads were appearing in the long grass as settlers rose to their feet and looked around. And as the breeze picked up and the pall of smoke began to clear, she could see that in the distance, more were gathering around the smoking hulks of the greywyrmes that littered the grasslands and were busy salvaging anything they could find that had not been destroyed by the flames.

Solomon Tallow was dead, along with most of his wyrmehandlers. The surviving few had fled. But the settlers, watchful and cautious, had hidden at the first sign of trouble and most, if not all, had survived unscathed.

Cara pointed. 'Eli, look!' she exclaimed, but the crag-climber had seen them already.

Great whitewyrmes, standing on their haunches, facing each other; three on one side, two on the other. And standing a little way off, black lances planted in the loamy soil, three wyrmekin.

Eli motioned for Cara and the others to follow him, and set out towards them, his heavy boots trampling down the grass. As they drew near, Cara saw that the wyrmes' barbels were quivering and their jaws were parted as they talked to each other in those strange wind-and-rain words of theirs. Eli stopped, holding back a ways. He watched and listened, and the others did likewise.

The two whitewyrmes' necks were bowed low in supplication and their eyes glowed the palest yellow, while the eyes of the three whitewyrmes facing them were flushed an angry red. A small settler boy stood between the opposing wyrmes, looking first one way, then the other.

Cara felt a tremor course through her body as she saw that one of the wyrmekin who stood observing was the beautiful kingirl, Thrace. On either side of her were two others. A younger girl, eight or nine years old, and a tall well-built youth with red cheeks and dark curly hair.

'What are they saying?' Ethan whispered to Eli.

'The pale-eyed wyrmes are from the wyrme galleries,' Eli said slowly. 'They are telling the kinned wyrmes . . .'

He paused, listening intently, his eyes half-closed in concentration.

'How sorry they are that they . . . that they brought the blueblackwyrmes to this place . . .'

He listened some more.

'They are offering the wyrmes, and their kin, a home with them in the wyrme galleries . . .' Eli went on. 'They say they want an end to the slaughter . . .'

The older of the two wyrmes bowed his head lower still and nuzzled the small settler child standing before him, wreathing him in smoke.

Eli nodded thoughtfully.

'What is it?' Ethan prompted him.

The cragclimber looked up. 'He says these two-hides seem different. They do not look or act like hunters . . .'

As the smoke cleared, the boy raised his head and spoke in a loud clear voice. 'We don't mean you no harm. My ma and me and the rest of these folks; we just want to settle, live in peace and grow our crops.' He glanced around. 'You whitewyrmes saved us. And we are in your debt.'

The wyrmekin interpreted, and the older of the whitewyrmes looked down at the child before him and then across at the settlers, who were slowly gathering at a safe distance. He raised his neck and spoke in a soft windblown sigh.

The cragclimber smiled as he translated the wyrme's

words. 'He says there has been too much killing,' he told the others. 'If the colony and these kith can learn to live together, they can share the grasslands and its bounty . . .'

At this, Cara noted, one of the three wyrmes, who was cradling an infant in its white-scaled arms, stepped forward and spoke.

'A new beginning,' Eli interpreted.

Two of the kin – the dark-haired youth and the young girl – nodded. But Thrace, the beautiful kingirl, turned abruptly away and strode towards them. Cara's heart thumped in her chest and Cody took a hold of her hand.

'Micah?' Thrace said to Eli, her voice harsh and croaky. 'Where is Micah?'

Eli's pale-blue eyes searched the kingirl's face, then turned to Cara. Cara swallowed nervously and was reassured to feel Cody's hand squeezing her own.

'Micah left us,' she said, trembling as the kingirl turned her ferocious gaze on her. 'He went east, into the ridges. He . . . We . . .'

But the kingirl was no longer listening. Instead, kinlance in hand, she brushed past Cara and set off through the long grass towards the ridge country.

She did not look back.

Forty-Nine

Nathaniel Lint the Younger leaned on his walking staff, a crooked rough-hewn length of dogwood, and permitted himself a smile, regretful and self-mocking.

He was barely recognizable as the pampered young merchant who had left the new stockade with the wyrmetrain all those weeks ago. He was gaunt now, hollow-cheeked. Dirt-filled lines scored his forehead. His fine clothes, with their fur-trim and fussy lace adornments, had long since been reduced to rags; his expensive tooled leather boots had fallen to bits and the fashionable broadbrim hat he wore was now battered and shapeless, stained white at the crown with sweat.

What a sight he must look, Nathaniel realized, with the flapping soles of his boots tied into place with strips of sun-cured wyrmehide and the ragged pelt of a greywyrme draped around his shoulders. He'd tailored it himself, spending half a day hacking it off a carcass with his knife.

His beloved knife. With its curved blade and bone handle. It had meant the difference between life and death on the trail. He'd fought off carrionwyrmes with it, killed and gutted flitterwyrmes and plump squabwyrmes, and used it to fashion both the walking staff and the rudimentary cloak that protected him from the sun during the searing days and kept him warm at night.

Nathaniel had left the wyrmetrain with two gourds of salt-spoiled water and a pack of ruined wyrmemeat that he'd abandoned on the first night. Now, here he was, three weeks later, looking across the sun-parched badlands at the lookout tower and bunkhouses of the new stockade, that shimmered in the heat haze. He had become a hardened weald traveller, or at least, with his calloused hands and brown weathered skin and the broad keen-edged knife for killing anything he needed, he sure looked like one. And how surprised Solomon Tallow would be when he found that the young merchant had survived . . .

Nathaniel smiled to himself. When the gangmaster arrived back at the new stockade, he would be ready and waiting for him.

He took a swig from the lighter of the two watergourds, fresh-filled three days earlier, and was about to set off again when a shadow fell across him. Nathaniel looked up, shielding his eyes from the sun, to see a whitewyrme flying low overhead.

He threw himself down in the dust instinctively, and his hand reached for his knife. He heard steady rhythmic wing-beats and looked up to see the great whitewyrme fly on towards the new stockade. Its eyes glowed a deep blood red, and its long serpentine neck craned forward, a black zigzag scar stark against the white scales.

It did not seem to see him.

As he watched, the creature tilted its wings and arced down over the corrals and courtyard of the stockade which, Nathaniel now saw, was crowded with the wagons and tents of new settlers from the plains. With single-minded ferocity, the whitewyrme demolished the lookout tower with a blow from its tail, then set a hay barn ablaze with a jet of flame from its gaping jaws.

Screams and cries floated back to Nathaniel on the hot breeze as the settlers began streaming from the tents and bunkhouses and out across the badlands. The great whitewyrme hovered over the new stockade, systematically tearing the roofs off the buildings with its curved talons, and filling the interiors with flame. In seconds, the bunkhouses were ablaze, along with the rest of the hay barns and the great hexagonal silo.

Nathaniel's heart thumped in his chest. Everything he had struggled to achieve was being destroyed in front of his eyes by this crazed creature.

It was above the tavern now, its claws ripping at the roofbeams. The gang members Tallow had left behind had spilled out into the dusty courtyard and were firing spit-bolts up at the whitewyrme. But the creature ignored the wounds they were inflicting, its sinuous neck curving down and its nostrils flared as it clawed more timber from the tavern roof.

It was searching for something, Nathaniel realized . . .

Aseel's nostrils quivered as they caught the deep sweet musk of flameoil. This was what he had come for.

He clawed away wooden floorboards to reveal a small chamber at the heart of the building. It was packed with earthenware pitchers, each one stoppered with wax. Several had toppled over and smashed, and their contents had spread out across the floor, releasing a pungent odour.

The thorns of the two-hides bit into Aseel's neck and flanks, tore his wings and stung his tail, but he ignored them. With the last of his strength he reached down and smashed the rest of the pitchers with a sweep of a claw.

This was it.

From deep within his chest, a tumult of emotion erupted – pain and sorrow and anger and hurt. Aylsa's voice, rainflecked with false hope for their wyve. The dead wyrmeling limp in his arms. The grief in Thrace's eyes at their parting. The stench of death that had clung to the two-hides trapper – a stench that was spreading to the whole of the weald.

It had to be stopped . . .

* * *

Nathaniel saw the whitewyrme's eyes blaze a deep visceral shade of red that matched the blood streaming down from the spitbolt wounds pockmarking its body. With a violent shudder, the wyrme opened its jaws wide and sent a long shimmering blade of flame roaring deep into the heart of Solomon Tallow's quarters.

There was a blinding flash of light as a massive fireball lit up the sky over the new stockade, and Nathaniel had to close his eyes to protect them from its dazzling glare. The sound of a colossal explosion followed moments later, rumbling across the badlands like thunder.

When Nathaniel opened his eyes, there was no sign of the great whitewyrme.

Or the new stockade. All that remained was a pile of charred and burning timber strewn across a blackened crater.

A stream of settlers picked their way across the badlands, dazed, confused, and heading east, back towards the safety of the low plains. Nathaniel Lint watched them for a moment. Then, gathering up his walking staff and watergourds, he climbed to his feet, turned and set off in the opposite direction.

Fifty

He would die slowly, this youth she'd been hunting for so long. Sitting there, gazing into the embers of his campfire as the sun rose over the ridges, he had no idea that this would be the last dawn he'd see.

The keld mistress's bone-white fingers tightened round the handle of her knife, with its blade of polished obsidian, black and weighted and fangsharp.

She had continued the hunt, even after the massacre on the clifftop, when she had lost her slaves and her dear, dear friends. They hadn't stood a chance out there in the open against the kin and the wyrme. Such fighting was not the way of the keld. Crevices, caverns, the dark dank places into which enemies could be lured and dealt with at one's leisure; that was the keld way.

Slow. Thorough. Deadly.

The youth prodded the dying fire with a stick, stretched, then looked up at the dawn sky.

The keld mistress had waited for this moment through the long dark night, and all the nights before – the nights on the trail, tracking the five kith by the light of their campfires, or on the frequent occasions they went without fire, creeping close enough to listen to their whispered conversations, the sound of their breathing; quiet coughs, gentle snoring. And by day, in her tattered cloak of dust and filth, silent and stealthy as a shadow, she had followed in their footsteps, unseen and unsuspected, even by the cautious old cragclimber.

All the while, she'd fought the urge to snatch at her revenge, to hurry the reckoning with a swift blow or an impetuous attack. No, she would do this slowly. The keld way.

When the youth had left the others in the grasslands and returned to the ridges, she had been exultant. The wide open spaces had filled her with dread – the vaulted sky with its threat of kin; the flat undulating grass with sightlines to the horizon. She'd had to watch them from too great a distance and it had been hard. But then he'd come back to her. To the crevices and ravines; the twisting gulleys and shadow-filled ridges.

And here he was now, the dawn light playing on his handsome face. She would remove it in due course.

First, she would move within knife range. Approach from behind, slash the tendons behind the knee as he rose to his feet. Once down, a blow to the temple, to stun. Then, the binding. Hands, feet. Arms bent back at that excruciating angle; thumbs dislocated and connected to ankles by looped wyrmegut. She would drag him to the cave in the ravine. It was shallow, little more than an overhang, but it was dark and hidden and would suit her purpose.

And then she would begin . . .

The keld mistress licked her lips as she rose silently to her feet and crept towards the youth. There was a soft sighing noise, moist-sounding, and the keld mistress felt a sudden intense pain. The sharp metallic taste of blood – her blood – filled her mouth as she looked down.

The shaft of a black kinlance was sticking out of her chest, its tip wet and glistening. The polished obsidian knife clattered to the ground.

So, this is how I die, the keld mother thought, her lips twisting into a rictus smile. Quickly.

Fifty-One

'Thrace,' Micah murmured, his voice trembling and weak.

A wizened, white-haired hag lay face down on the rock between them, blood seeping out from beneath her ragged cloak and pooling at Thrace's feet. A polished stone knife reflected back the glow of the dying campfire, the embers flashing orange then black, and the last pale yellow flames dancing on the nubs of the charcoaled sticks.

'This keld was about to kill you,' Thrace said. The words felt blunt and strange in her mouth, so different from the soft murmurings of wyrmetongue. 'I followed your trail from the grasslands, and when I found you, I found her . . .'

Micah looked down at the body, then back at Thrace. Her corn-silver hair hung down, gleaming, straight, casting her face in shadow. The suit of soulskin clung to her body, pale and opalescent in the dawn light, while gripped in her hands the kinlance was black as night, its tip wet with keld blood.

The keld.

They had dogged Micah's footsteps throughout his time in the weald - Red Myrtle the cavern hag, the monstrous winter caller, the hideous gang that had infected the sanctuary of Deephome. And the keld raiding party which Kesh and Azura had massacred at the top of the rocky outcrop.

Micah rolled the corpse over with the toe of his boot. He stared down at the white face.

This was the keld who had thrown the grenade that killed Kesh. But it was Eli and him she'd been after. Must have been. Why else would she have tracked him here, her stone knife poised over him as he sat alone and unsuspecting staring into the embers of the fire?

Micah stepped over the body and stood in front of Thrace. By rights, he should be dead now – would be dead if it hadn't been for this kingirl.

He loved her, body and soul, and had done since the first moment he had set eyes on her as she lay, helpless and injured, at the foot of the highstack back in the valley country. But he knew his love for her was hopeless. After all, she was kin – savage, strange, unknowable; at one with the great whitewyrme she rode. Aseel would always come first.

Even during Thrace and Micah's time together in the winter den, Micah had known she wasn't truly his. And when

Aseel had returned, Thrace had left with him, just as Micah had feared she would.

And so he had tried to forget her. Maker knew, he'd tried! And he thought he'd succeeded, with Cara. Sweet trusting Cara, who had loved him with all her heart – until she realized that he couldn't forget Thrace. The kingirl had haunted his dreams and invaded his waking thoughts, and always would.

But it was still hopeless. Micah knew that. And yet, as he looked at Thrace now, standing before him, he could do nothing to prevent the old familiar ache from stirring in his chest.

'You followed my trail from the grasslands?' he said. 'But why?'

Thrace lowered her head, her hair falling over her face like a veil.

'Aseel left me,' she said. 'And he will not return.'

Micah saw a shudder pass through her body. She lowered the bloodied kinlance and leaned on it for support.

'He told me he was going to destroy the settlement in the badlands, whatever the cost. He no longer cared about his own life.'

She looked up, the ash-gold hair parting to reveal her stricken face.

'He would not take me, even though I would willingly have died with him – and I understood the reason . . .'

Micah stared back at her, trying to read the look in her eyes, a mixture of pain and sorrow, and a strange exaltation.

'*That's* why I followed your trail from the grasslands,' she said. 'Why I had to find you, Micah. Why we have to be together, you and I . . .'

'Why?' Micah asked.

Thrace reached out and drew Micah to her. She smiled and her face softened, her eyes wistful and bright. She took Micah's hand and placed it on the gentle swell of her belly.

'Because of this,' she said.

'A child,' Micah breathed.

Thrace nodded. 'Our child.'

WHITEWYRME

LAKEWYRME

MANDERWYRME

Carrionwyrme

REDWING WYRME

STUNTED WYRME

EXODUS

About the Authors

Paul Stewart is a highly acclaimed author of books for young readers. Chris Riddell is a renowned political cartoonist and illustrator of children's books. Together, Stewart and Riddell have formed an award-winning partnership and created the bestselling Edge Chronicles series, which has sold more than two million copies and is now available in more than thirty languages.

Visit the authors at www.stewartandriddell.co.uk and www.openroadmedia.com/stewart-and-riddell.

CPSIA information can be obtained at www.ICGtesting.com
Printed in the USA
BVOW08s1620091016

464567BV00001B/66/P